THE VOICE OF LOVE COMPANY

Daniel Klapheke

Cover photo courtesy of the USMC

NOTE TO THE READER

The following pages contain the stories of real men—my grandfather being one of them—and their experiences. A handful of characters, based on real people, were added to illustrate the brotherly bond created in combat and show how these kids viewed the horrors of war.

While this is a work of fiction, the dates, times, locations, weather, battle conditions, military tactics, Japanese fanaticism, casualty numbers, and visceral experiences of the Marines are all very real. Exactly what happened between May 13 and June 23, 1945, will never be known, but the story captures the essence of my Grandfather's experience with little embellishment.

For Papa
I hope I told your story well.

CHAPTER ONE
CORPSE FEET

DRUNK WITH EXHAUSTION, I COLLAPSED like a wet sack of laundry beside the yawning entrance of a tomb. I figured while I had a minute, I'd get some essential nutrients in me. Under my poncho, I fumbled with the pocket button on my blouse for a good twenty-seconds before I was able to access the waterproof bag that served as sanctuary for my Lucky Strikes. The rain continued to pummel me and course through every aperture in my poncho. I'd sooner have shot myself in the head than expose my precious smokes to the deluge, so I turned toward my only option.

I leaned my rifle against the short courtyard wall behind me and reluctantly started crawling across the slippery stone of the tomb's terrace to its opening. The enormous spool of communication wire on my back banged against the frame of the door with a clang, forcing me to slither like some kind of damn amphibian. Halfway inside, I propped myself on my elbows in a patch of dry, crypt dirt and went to work lighting a cigarette. Getting one lit was a bigger pain in the ass than it should've been. My hands wouldn't hold still for even a second. I eventually triumphed.

Lying like a cadaver in the tomb, I took a couple of drags and listened to the droplets of water rolling off my helmet and smacking the powdery dirt. The rain outside sounded muffled and distant. The smell of burnt flesh in the enclosure became too much to stomach and I had to get miles away from that damn vault. I lit a second cigarette, removed my helmet to use it as an umbrella for the cigs and back-crawled to my former position next to my rifle.

My hands continued to fail me as I attempted to remove my canteen. After three tries, I gave up and turned my open mouth skyward to catch some rain. An image flashed through my mind of the dead Jap's agape mouth collecting water back on the hillside. I nearly choked and decided to resume the canteen removal campaign. It took me damn near forever, but I finally unclipped it from my belt. A simple clasp was never so complicated. I watched my hand, as if it wasn't mine, tremble under the canteen's weight as I raised it to my mouth. The water tasted like Okinawa mud with a hint of rotting flesh and dysentery. A real treat, let me tell ya.

The rest of my unit caught up with me. Sergeant Angier crumpled beside me and snatched the cigarette I proffered.

Miraculously, the rain fizzled to a stop. For fifteen minutes, we sat relatively undisturbed save for the occasional crack of a rifle and the rumble of battle echoing from the East where the 1st Marines were giving the Japs hell. They were pursuing Ushijima and his 32nd Army down the center of the island to the South. My leg ached like hell, and my feet felt like they were boiling.

Lieutenant Pope found us and sat on the low wall beside Angier. He leaned toward Angier and made him light his cigar under a cupped hand. I sat up with a nervous stomach. *Please God, don't send me out again right now. Let me stay here with the rest of the fellas. I can't string comm wires today.*

"Okay, boys, here's the dope." He paused to catch his breath. "We're going to hold here until further orders. You all get some rest. You have until 1700." With a bit of effort, he stood and walked away puffing on his cigar.

"Did he just give us the day off?" Capone said.

"Shit yeah!" Folgers said like a teenager with permission to cuss for the first time in front of his dad.

A reprieve from the rain *and* a few hours off! I melted with warm relief. I freed myself from the weight of the communication gear and we all went to work on our boondockers to get the sonsofbitches off our feet. Mine were so caked with mud I had to cut the laces with my K-bar knife. With my feet swollen as hell, it seemed like my boots were two sizes too small. Like a shaky, drunk surgeon, I cut back the tongue, careful not to rupture the delicate balloons inside.

After a painful and epic struggle, I prevailed. My socks were a mushy mess. They fell apart as I peeled them from my feet. Chunks of skin came off with them. My feet were a nightmare. They resembled large, white prunes with smears of blood. Blisters ruled the landscape. Some the size of a half dollar. Pink flaps of skin were artifacts of untreated blisters from the past. The nails on my little toes had liquefied and become part of the goo that filled my socks. The rest of my nails looked like they belonged on a corpse. Hemingway didn't have enough adjectives to string together an accurate description of the smell.

Stanley Wright, one of our company corpsmen, told me to wash my feet with water from my canteen. He gave me a foot powder to coat them with when I was done.

I did as he said, then sat there, leaning back on my hands and staring at the corpse feet at the end of my legs. Will my dear Hody still love these feet? Will my monster hooves scare my little girls?

"Any one of you happen to be a podiatrist?" I asked. "Manicurist, perhaps? I could really use a pedicure."

"Go get some new boondockers." A guy sitting a couple of yards from me pointed at a pile of dead Marines. "They ain't usin' 'em no more."

I looked at the pile of bodies then back at him.

"Your feet are busted up bad. Those damn things you're wearin' only gonna make 'em worse. Go get you a goddamn pair of new boots."

I didn't know what was more horrifying—the idea of "borrowing" boots from a dead kid, or that the idea actually wasn't all that bad. I stared a little longer at my ghastly tootsies as I considered crawling over to do some macabre window shopping at the local dead man pile.

"What's the date?" I asked the group without looking up.

"I don't know," Capone said, "but I know it's around the middle of 1945. Weren't we supposed to be 'home alive in '45'? Goddamn war."

"Looks like it's 'out of the sticks in '46' for us," Folgers said.

Hut lay on his back, tugging like a sonofabitch on one of his boots. "I'm pretty sure it's June 1."

"Holy hell," I said more to myself than anyone else. I was hospitalized a year ago to the day for an infection in my foot and ankle at boot camp. Apparently, my poor damn feet just weren't meant for the life of a Marine. I could still feel that fathead doctor at the Naval Hospital dicing up my foot like a goddamn jack-o-lantern.

CHAPTER TWO
JUNE 1, 1944—A YEAR EARLIER

I ALMOST CALLED THE HORSE'S ass of a doctor everything from soap to nuts. Instead, I said, "You got any bourbon, Doc?" He didn't answer me. He just carried on jabbing a needle in my ankle. He drew back on the plunger, sucking puss into the syringe.

"It'd make this a lot easier for me," I said as I winced and turned my face toward the ceiling. He looked at me like I was an idiot.

"Is it rheumatic fever?" I asked.

"We'll know in a minute."

The asshole took out a scalpel and stabbed my ankle. "Holy fu....." I bit my tongue and took a deep breath of the sterile air of the treatment room. I wanted to unleash my full lexicon of oaths on him but there was a cute nurse standing behind him holding a tray of gauze and what-not. She wore an unusually clean, white shirt with big buttons and wide lapels. Her chestnut hair was loosely pulled back and pinned under a nurse's hat. She reminded me of my wife who I'd promised I'd behave myself in front of the ladies.

My swearing would make the most vulgar sailors proud if you really want to know the truth. I admit, I could clean up my act. The problem is, the military didn't exactly provide an environment that nurtured such an endeavor. My wife had said my choice of words made me sound uncouth, but I preferred to think I was a wordsmith of colorful language. Forever an apprentice in the art of profanity.

"Harry, you're doing well," the doc said with a smug look on his face. "Just keep still a little longer." Easy for that bastard to say. It didn't bother him a damn bit.

I fiercely gripped the sides of the treatment table and gnashed my teeth as he cut out a neat square just below my ankle bone. Somehow I refrained from hollering out. Believe me, the last thing you wanted to do is piss off a doctor who was in the middle of some kind of mining project on your flesh. Apparently it wasn't draining fast enough for him, so he squeezed my foot like an orange to get more pus out.

It hurt like a sonofabitch, but it was sort of a relief too. My ankle had been swollen for several days. What happened was, on Saturday, the 27th of May, I woke up with severe pain in my left ankle after a hard day of training the day before. I thought maybe I had slept on it wrong, so I carried on with my exercises.

Before noon, I could no longer walk on it. My drill instructor let me take a rest, but by that evening, my foot and ankle had swelled up like a grapefruit. I could no longer stand on it. My pal, Walter Hansen—we called him "Handsome Hansen" because, so help me God, he looked like Cary Grant—helped me limp to sick bay where the doc told me I had rheumatic fever and sent me to the base hospital for treatment.

The docs at the hospital couldn't say for sure that it was rheumatic fever, but they couldn't say for sure what the hell was wrong with me either. On June 1—three days later—I was transferred here, to the U.S. Naval Hospital in San Diego.

After chopping up my ankle for fifteen minutes, the cute nurse handed him a pile of gauze and some of the what-not I'd mentioned earlier.

After doing some tests—or whatever the hell they do, the doc determined it wasn't rheumatic fever, thank the good Lord above.

Eventually the swelling went down, and they started a regimen of cramming sulfa pills in my mouth every four hours. They made me sleepy. So what I did was sleep, a lot. When I wasn't snoozing, I kept myself busy working jigsaw puzzles and reading the newspaper. The Allies stormed the beaches at Normandy on June 6, so I wanted to keep up with the reports coming in on that development.

Anyway, getting back into shape proved tough at first. I had gotten lazy in the hospital. I was part of Platoon 721. For the most part, the guys there were okay. Aside from razzing me for being old (I was only twenty-six, but a lot of them were teenagers), or for being from Kentucky, I seemed to get along with just about everyone.

The guys somehow figured since I was from Kentucky, I wasn't accustomed to wearing shoes and that's why my foot swelled up. Now, how they came up with that, I didn't know. If they thought I was a hillbilly, they didn't know their geography. Louisville was hundreds of miles from the East Kentucky hills.

They didn't let it go about my age and my home state. It didn't help that one of my favorite libations was Old Kentucky Bourbon. So, you guessed it, they proceeded to call me "Old Kentucky." That was all it took to acquire a new name in the military. Everyone, it seemed, had a nick name. It was almost a badge of honor. Unless, of course, you got stuck with something like "Peaches," "Betty," or "Asshole." I'd take Old Kentucky, thank you.

Thomas Brandt, a young guy from North Carolina, called me "Whistler." It didn't stick with the other guys, they liked Old Kentucky better. Tom called me Whistler because I wouldn't cut it out with the whistling. I enjoyed it. It calmed me. I usually did it when I was in a good mood. I would often offer my renditions of Glenn Miller, Benny Goodman, or Bing Crosby. A lot of Miller. If I was in a frisky mood, I'd end up whistling *In the Mood.* When I felt like dancing with my wife, I'd usually whistle *Moonlight Serenade* or Benny Goodman's *Moonglow.*

Sometimes someone would ask what I was whistling or they

would join in before I realized I was even doing it. When I was home, my youngest daughter, she was only a baby, but she'd perk up when she'd hear my whistling. She knew Daddy was home. If I was whistling, I was happy. That was all there was to it.

And, boy, they had a field day with my last name, of course. My family name was Klapheke. That was pronounced, *Kluh-peak.* So I constantly got "Hey, Klap-key!" Or "how's it hangin' Klafeeky?" And "Klupeeky" was always an option. Even those who didn't give me a hard time tripped up when trying to say it right. It often came out as "Kuh-pleak." Lord have mercy, it never ended. If someone didn't know my name, I became "Mac," "Bub," "New Guy," or "You."

Everyone picked on each other for something. We were always exhausted from training and a little on edge and snippy. Catch us on a bender during liberties and we were all good chums again. Many of us knew each other better than our family members. That's the hardest part of war. You learned to love these guys, you really did, and then you got separated from them. Handsome Hansen shipped out with the 5th Marines in July. Whether we'd cross paths again, I had no idea.

My training carried on and orders came down in December that my unit was set to depart for the Pacific theatre. My lovely wife, Rosemary, made the trip from Louisville to see me before my departure. She was my life, that Rosemary. Her close friends and family called her Hody. When she was a youngster, her parents called her Rosie. She had a hell of a time saying that and it always came out "Hoe-dee." It stuck. So everyone called her Hody.

We were able to squeeze in some time together here and there between my training. She'd catch me up on how my baby girls were doing, we'd take walks, and we'd engage in activities I am not at liberty to discuss, if you know what I mean.

I don't know how the hell it happened, but before shipping out, I got special permission to take Hody out on the town. We had a swell evening together. That is, of course, until I got run over by an automobile.

CHAPTER THREE
THE ACCIDENT

ALL THE SUDDEN I WAS lying in the middle of a street with a broken leg and Hody was cradling my head. To beat all, the damn MP that arrived on the scene accused me of stepping out in front of the car. Right in front of my wife, that sonofabitch called me a coward who didn't want to serve his country. I was a lot of things, but I wasn't a coward—not by a long shot.

The names he called me and the language he used in front of my bride really got to me. If I hadn't been lying on the pavement in excruciating pain, I might have given the horse's ass a lesson in manners. To make matters worse, the driver of the car was a Marine sergeant. He insisted it wasn't his fault. Outranking me, I didn't have much of a dog in the fight.

As much as those young bastards got under my skin, I can't say I completely blamed them for thinking I had purposefully been hit by a car to avoid being shipped out. Many fellas went to great lengths to avoid deployment. It was common for draftees to shoot themselves in the foot or swallow cotton balls to feign ulcers. The MP didn't know me. If he had, he'd have known it wasn't my style to take the easy way out. That is, if you considered jumping in front of an oncoming vehicle the easy way out.

The way I saw it, if anyone had more reason to get out of service, it was me. I was comparatively old, married, had a career, and two young daughters. Having two kids, I was eligible for exemption from the draft. Only the Lord knows why I was still drafted. Kathleen, or Kay, was four years old at the time of the accident, and Patricia, or Patsy, turned one on December 17. Lots of guys had to leave their families, but leaving Hody caused her greater difficulty than most wives.

Our darling Patsy was an invalid who required considerable care and attention. Without me, caring for Patsy and raising Kay was a great hardship for Hody. We awaited the opinion of the doctors about Patsy's exact diagnosis and what we could do to provide the care she needed.

And we couldn't afford it. The Corps paid me $117 a month because I had a wife and two kids. But Uncle Sam imposed "mandatory options" of purchasing a $10,000 life insurance policy for $6.40 per month and another $12.65 per month for a war bond. All said, I got about $98 a month—not quite my salary at Mengel Company, where I had worked. I was very eager to know how Hody and my parents would handle the finances when I was gone.

A lot of boys volunteered for the Marine Corps right when war broke out, but as much as I loved my country, I hadn't rushed out to join. Many of these kids, who I thought were better men than myself, didn't have the responsibilities I had. Don't get me wrong; I was glad to serve and die for my country. America was the greatest damn country in the world, hands down. I just wasn't in a hurry to leave my wife and daughters when I knew there we[illegible]illions of fine, young men lining up in front of me.

After th[illegible]off the street, they took me to the U.S. Naval Ho[illegible]de, where they told me my left leg was broken thr[illegible] the knee. Again at the Naval Hospital, and again, [illegible]n leg. That leg can't catch a break—pardon my [illegible]

Believe it or not, my platoon didn't wait around for me. They shipped out across the Pacific Ocean while I lay around in California and got soft.

It was December of 1944 and they were headed for hell. Where exactly they were going was unknown to me. Even if I knew their destination, I never would have heard of it before. Most likely they were off to a pile of volcanic rock in the middle of God's vast ocean. Probably had some tongue-twisting Asian name unheard of by any red-blooded American.

That's how it was in America. No one had heard of these

places in the Pacific. Germany, France, and Britain were household names, but Kwajalein or Peleliu? Who the hell ever heard of those places? Most Americans descended from Europeans and were familiar with Europe. Plus, the memory of the First World War was still fresh in many minds. A lot of our fathers had served in Europe. And because Hitler seemed to be the bigger threat, America and England had decided to focus more on the war over there. The Pacific, in my opinion, should've had more press than it did.

It seemed to take damn near forever for my leg to heal. My knee started giving me problems and they thought I had some cartilage damage. The doc put on a new cast that came up to my crotch. It was uncomfortable as hell and hard to move around in. I thought that cast would never come off and the damn thing made me miserable.

Turns out, that broken leg may have saved my life. More on that later.

CHAPTER FOUR
HODY

I DIDN'T WANT TO LET him go. I pressed my face into Harry's chest one more time and felt him almost lose his balance. His crutches clanged together as he crossed his arms behind me, squeezing the breath from my lungs. One more kiss. And then another. I couldn't help but wonder if it would be our last.

Fighting tears, I forced myself into the taxi. Harry shut the door and hobbled a little before securing himself with the crutches. As the taxi pulled away, I looked out the back window, waving to him. The growing distance made him shrink. When the taxi made a right turn and a building obstructed my view, I clung to the image of him blowing kisses. I buried my face in my palms and wept.

The Oceanside Train Station was more alive with commotion than I had expected on a Tuesday morning. Wives, girlfriends, parents, and siblings of Marines were hoping to make it home for Christmas.

With money Harry's father had sent, I paid the fare and sat on a nearby bench where I lit a cigarette. Passing GIs felt compelled to engage me in conversation. They must have thought it their duty to keep a lonely little lady like myself company.

A pair of young fellows stopped in front of me.

"Hey sugar!" the taller of the two said. "Are you rationed?"

Despite myself, my cheeks flushed. The temerity of this fellow. I was both offended and flattered. Before I could respond, the shorter one asked, "Where ya headed?"

"Kentucky," I said.

"Kentucky girl, huh?" the taller one said. "I didn't know a pretty girl like yourself could come from such a state."

I blew out a cloud of smoke. "A *married* Kentucky girl."

My comment didn't phase them in the least. The expressions on their face remained unchanged. I crossed my legs and bounced my dangling shoe up and down. "Notice my wedding ring?" I said sardonically.

"That don't always mean nuthin'," the short one said.

I pressed my palms into the bench and lifted my shoe. "Here's your proof I have a husband."

"How's that?"

I struggled to keep a straight face. "Only a *married* woman from Kentucky wears shoes."

The taller one's mouth fell open and the other fellow just blinked stupidly. Wordless, they spun and walked away, glancing back over their shoulders as they headed toward the train. They filed into a line of men entering a train car near the front. The boarding call prompted me from the bench and I headed toward the women and children gathering a few cars back from the GIs.

A woman peered out of the window nearest me, two kids pulling at her hat. In the next car up, five GIs flocked around a lady about my age. From the looks of it, the train was divided into cars of women with children and cars of everyone else. My Lord, I didn't want to think what could happen on a rail car full of men for five days.

No way I was getting stuck with the men just because I didn't have children with me. I spun around, sweat trickling down my neck. Beside the benches near the depot, three blond little boys ran circles around a woman with a suitcase for each. As quickly as my high heels would allow, I headed in their direction.

I touched the mother's sleeve. "Can I help you with these? I'll need a favor in return if you're up for it."

She handed me a case. "Anything." She blew an errant curl off her face. I explained the situation and she pushed one of the boys my way. "Have at it."

Posing as a mother of a chubby toddler boy, I boarded the train with little Donald in tow. With a sigh of relief, I crashed onto my seat where I started thinking of Harry again. Boy did I hate leaving him. He had insisted that I go. It was only six days until Christmas and we both agreed I should be home with Kay and Patsy. Besides, he said he wasn't going to have any more base liberties again before year end.

With the exception of Harry's accident, my time with him in San Diego had been pleasant. I would have enjoyed more, but I had to take what I could get. I was only able to see him for three hours a day because of his training and then because of hospital visitation restrictions. I had been serving as his personal nurse and actually enjoyed pampering that big baby.

I couldn't help but think it was my fault he was hit by the car. After all, if I hadn't come to see him, he wouldn't have been out on the town that day. At the same time, I could very well have saved him from something much worse. He'd probably be on the high seas by now if I hadn't caused his mishap.

Thinking of my Harry on the battlefield made my heart race and often led to my hyperventilating. The only thing worse than anticipating your husband's deployment into battle was knowing your husband would be deployed with a lame leg. *Lord, heal that leg.*

Although it only caused me more torment, I picked up newspapers and tuned in to radio announcements for war updates. Of course news from the South Pacific was of particular interest since Harry was headed that way. The U.S. Marines had suffered massive casualties on islands like Saipan and Peleliu. I feared the numbers would only get worse.

For almost five full days, I rode the rails across the country. I actually enjoyed all of the children on the car. They were loud, but they served as a distraction from thoughts of Harry and my own girls at home. The train pulled into the station in Louisville on Saturday, December 23, 1944. Through a smudgy window, I could see Kay and Patsy standing beside Harry's parents. I said goodbye to my traveling companions and hurried off the train where Kay tackled me in a warm embrace. I had made it home for Christmas.

CHAPTER FIVE
CHRISTMAS BLUES

IT SURE WAS NICE HAVING my Hody around and I hated to see her go. It'd been over half a year since I had seen her last. It'd be another year or so before I saw her again. That depressed the hell out of me. Being away from home was new to me.

I spent Christmas in the hospital two thousand miles from home. It was damn lonesome, but the hospital staff did their best to keep my spirits up. They were nice enough, I suppose. The nurses would flirt with me a little and ask if I needed anything.

"Bourbon," I'd say.

"Sorry, Harry. No bourbon."

"Bullshit hospital."

Christmas tunes often crackled through the speakers around the hospital to cheer us up. I'm not sure it worked, but the sentiment was nice. It was simultaneously difficult and enjoyable thinking of home. Regardless, I was grateful I wasn't yet on the other side of the world fighting Japs or Krauts like a lot of fellas.

Crosby's *White Christmas* and *I'll Be Home For Christmas* had a way to really get you down. They were the WWII gyrenes (GI-Marines) Christmas songs. We wouldn't see a white Christmas for a while. And only in our dreams would we be home for Christmas. Some would never experience the holiday with loved ones again. Christmas was a wonderful time of the year to get depressed.

The newspapers and radio kept us informed on the developments in the European Theater of War, or ETO. The Germans were pushing through the Ardennes Forest in and around Luxembourg and Bastogne, and were breaking through the Allies' lines, creating a salient. The media was calling it the "Battle of the Bulge."

All six of my sisters sent me cards wishing me a Merry Christmas and quick recovery. A Christmas note from my brother Charlie understandably made it to me a little late. He was in a boat somewhere in the Pacific.

The holiday season got lousier when news about Glenn Miller's disappearance came around. As I mentioned before, I loved his music. In '42, Miller gave up his musical career to do his part in the war effort. He started a marching band in the Army Air Force so he could provide much-needed morale to the troops in the form of music. He worked his way up the ranks and was eventually promoted to major.

Anyway, Major Miller was apparently flying from England to

Paris in a single-engine plane when he crashed somewhere over the English Channel. It was a damn shame, I tell you. That man was a musical genius. Heaven was lucky to have him.

Mother sent me some cakes and a puzzle that kept me busy for a while. Her baking was to die for. She was a culinary master, I tell you. Anything that came out of her oven made my mouth water before I even opened the shipping package.

My sister, Mary Agnes, who was a Catholic nun and took the name Sister Mary Antonia, sent me a rosary she made herself. She said it was blessed by a priest and I should hang on to it for protection. I felt terrible that I had nothing to send my family in return. I could only show them appreciation by saying some extra prayers on their behalf.

I received a letter from Hody in January letting me know she made it home safely and that she had to borrow someone's child in order to board the train. I'm telling you, she was a resourceful girl. She really was.

She said she'd enjoyed the hell out of the train ride in the car filled with children. It was noisy as hell, but she loved it just the same. I could only imagine what her journey would have been like if she got stuck in a car with a bunch of men.

I'd taken the train here. The railroad system impressed me. How they shipped millions of GIs and thousands of tons of war materiel all over the country boggled my mind. The logistics involved must have been staggering.

The engineering behind the massive steam engines and cars

fascinated me. The power the engines had to pull such loads for such distances was astounding. Everything about the railroad industry appealed to me. From the way it helped build our country, to the indispensable role it played in mobilizing America for war. As soon as I stepped onto the train, I became a lifelong fan of the railroad.

My dad also wrote to inform me Hody made it home safely with no major problems. He said for a Christmas present, he paid for a repair job that was needed on my car so Hody would have transportation. He also sent me $175. That was a big hunk of change. A lot of booze and cigarettes. My dad was a swell guy. He really was.

After several weeks, the doc cut the cast down to below my knee. It felt good to move the old joint again, but it still gave me trouble. The docs decided they needed to cut and repair the cartilage. After surgery, I had yet another cast for a while.

A hundred years, and about fifteen jigsaw puzzles later, I got it off. It was very weak and needed some tending to from the staff. I was soon able to limp around and harass the nurses a bit. I eventually graduated to a walking stick and quickly got moving. I felt so soft and weak. I had lost eighteen pounds of muscle since the accident and was eager to get back to the hard-as-nails physique I had achieved in boot camp.

I was granted liberty and decided to go up to Los Angeles. I didn't do much there, but it was nice getting out of the hospital for a while. I'd been to L.A. and Hollywood a few times on past liberties. Hollywood was a swell town. There was always something to see or do. The only trouble was that it cost a lot of dough.

The broadcasts were the only exceptions. They were free. I'd seen and heard the live broadcasts from the big NBC and CBS studios. They were really something. I'd even seen some movie actors and actresses such as Eddie Cantor, Ginger Rogers, Johnny Mercer, Dick Haynes, George Burns, and Gracie Allen. Boy, that Ginger Rogers was a real looker!

Limping around Hollywood became a pain in the ass and I decided to cut my visit short and head back.

A few weeks later, I started exercising again. It was like starting all over again. With my old unit gone, I had to get to know a new group of guys. It's hard switching platoons—believe me, I know.

I swear I didn't know how my family was able to keep up with all my ever-changing addresses. In just seven months, my address changed five times.

First, there was Platoon 721 Recruit Deposit Marine Corps Base (RDMCB) in San Diego. Then there was the U.S. Naval Hospital, Bldg. 222, Ward 2 in Balboa Park, San Diego. Back to RDMCB. And then I moved to…blah, blah, blah—who gives a damn? Anyway, I moved a lot and knew there would be more addresses to come. And unfortunately, they would be foreign.

My family continued to complain about my lack of correspondence. Everyone from Hody, my siblings, my dad, and even my brother-in-law gave me hell about how little I wrote. What could I say? I was not big on composing letters. Part of it, I think, was all the moving around I did. Every time I'd have to figure out the new damn address and who to give it to for it to ship out.

Part of it had to do with not having much to say. Laying around in different hospital wards wasn't exactly an epic adventure worth penning. During boot camp training, I was too exhausted at the end of the day to craft any meaningful letters.

When I did write home, I usually cut to the chase. I would let them know I was fine and dandy and inquire about the health of everyone back home. Then I'd usually tell Dad to say hi to everyone for me and ask Mother to send me some more puzzles and cakes or cookies. My writings weren't exactly Shakespeare, but I doubt if anyone really minded.

Regrettably, correspondence increasingly became focused on Patsy and her condition and what was to be done about it. My dad had been an enormous help in aiding Hody and keeping me abreast of the situation.

They were worried about me and I should've made more of an effort to write. In my defense, I did stay very busy when I wasn't convalescing in a hospital. I promised I'd write more.

CHAPTER SIX
RIFLEMAN 745

WHEN THEY RELEASED ME FROM the God-forsaken hospital, I sent my loved ones another postcard stating my new address. Now I was with Company B, 57th Replacement Draft. I didn't miss the hospital, but I had to admit I missed the nurses a little.

Back at Pendleton, I was recommended for "Wire School" where I learned to be a Company Wireman. I was told my gravelly voice and Kentucky upbringing qualified me for the position. What the hell they meant by that, I didn't know.

They taught us everything about running communication wires from post to post. How to unspool them, cut them, splice them, repair them, you name it. We were trained how to maintain the lines for the telephone, facsimiles, digital data messages, and teletype. They taught us about installing telephones and switchboards, finding reliable paths of transmissions, locating wire system faults and operating switchboards.

They even made us climb poles and install wires at the top of those bastards. We spent an entire week on pole climbing. We climbed God knows how high up those poles with a leather strap around our backs and the pole. The sonsofbitches made us lean all the way back until we could see the ground over our heads. Why we had to do this, I don't know, but we did. The instructors reminded us that wiremen were the foundation of communications in the Marine Corps and I guess experiencing vertigo was an important aspect of that foundation.

After the accident, the easiest friend to get reacquainted with was my M1 rifle. The M1 Garand was every Marine's favorite weapon. My rifle and I got along just fine. The Rifleman's Creed we had to memorize said, "My rifle is my best friend. It is my life...Without my rifle, I am useless...My rifle is human, even as I, because it is my life." and so on. That was how I felt about it, I did.

We had to know our rifle inside and out. They expected us to pick out our rifle from a pile without looking at the serial number. We could take the thing apart and put it back together in the dark with our eyes closed.

I knew everything about my M1 Garand. Without the bayonet, my rifle was 43.6 inches long and weighed 9.5 pounds. The bayonet added another pound or so. The en bloc clip held eight 30-06 (pronounced thirty-aught, six) rounds. The Garand's effective range was 440 yards.

I was officially designated a Rifleman. Rifleman 745, to be exact. In the Marine Corps, you were always a rifleman first, no matter your specialty training. Riflemen, like myself, whose primary job was to fire on the enemy from the front line, used the M1 Garand because it had more stopping power. This was the rifle that General George Patton himself said was the greatest battle implement ever devised. He was right. It was a thing of beauty. Before the run-in with the Ford bumper, I was getting really good with it. I was scoring at a "Sharpshooter" level during range tests. I was a few points shy of scoring "Expert," which would have increased my pay by 10%.

Getting back into the swing of PT was tough at first. My leg was stiff and weak. But before I knew it, I was able to keep up with the marches and the beach landing drills. With our full packs on, we would sometimes hump three miles in twenty-five minutes. Now, that's traveling. Making it more of a challenge, the hills in and around San Diego County were tall, steep, and rugged.

They would take us down to the beach and train us in amphibious landings, which involved jumping out of the landing crafts into waist-deep water, running to shore, and slithering on our bellies through the sand. The whole time we were instructed to keep our rifles out of the water and sand. Easier said than done.

Then we had to field strip our rifles and clean them up in a hurry. That was one of the beauties of the M1. The cleaning kit was stored in the butt and the whole rifle could be taken apart and cleaned without using any tools. Even if you did get mud, sand, or water on it, it proved to remain a reliable weapon.

We'd drill going up and down the confounded cargo nets with our heavy gear on because this was how we'd get from the transport ships to the landing boats. My knee made its disagreement with this exercise known with sharp pains and stiffness.

Then we'd hit the firing range and test our skills. There, I had some difficulty on account of my leg. Certain positions like the "Sitting Position" were hard for me. You had to sit on the deck with your feet almost straight out in front of you. You then had to throw yourself forward and try to get your elbows down almost to your ankles. From there you'd have to fire your weapon. This was hard enough without having to work out the stiffness in my leg.

One of the most demanding aspects of the training was the bivouacs. This was where we would go into the hills for several days, train, eat out of cans, and sleep under the stars without a change of clothes or the ability to wash or shave. I guessed this was what it was supposed to be like being in the field on a Japanese island in the Pacific.

In boot camp, the drill instructors were very strict about cleanliness. We were to follow the Marine Guidebook to the tee. That damn book taught us a very particular way to wash our bodies to avoid disease: we should wash our hands after using the head; inspect ourselves for lice and venereal disease; how often and how much water to drink; sharing cups or cigarettes was forbidden; it even recommended getting your bowels in a pattern of regular movement. You believe that? The Marine Corps had a say in how I went to the bathroom. Uncle Sam owned us.

The Corps taught us to brush our teeth twice a day. Before that, most Americans didn't pay that much attention to dental hygiene. The idea of brushing that often became common practice for Americans after the war. We can thank the U.S. Military for our pearly whites.

We even had to learn a whole new language—Marine Corps language. For example: My duffel bag was actually a "sea bag." My individual field equipment was "782 Gear." Cleaning our barracks was called a "field day," and candy was "Pogey Bait." There were about a thousand more terms we had to know.

The acronyms were just as plentiful. FUBAR, excuse my French, stands for Fucked Up Beyond All Recognition. SNAFU means Situation Normal, All Fucked Up. PX was Post Exchange. I was disappointed when I learned that a BLT was a Battalion Landing Team and not bacon, lettuce, and tomato. There were tons more we had to know. We even had our own alphabet. Able, Baker, Charlie, Dog, Easy, etc.

We also had an entire language of hand signals. Knowing them could be a matter of life and death. The Corps made damn sure we knew all these languages. It was drilled into us.

There was only one thing the Marine Corps was more serious about than discipline—killing the Japanese enemy and training us to be damn good at it. The drill instructors constantly reminded us that the "Japs" or "Nips" were not the goofy, slant-eyed characters the funny papers made them out to be. They were well-trained, fierce warriors who would do anything they could to kill you. They were fanatics who didn't fear death. They were animals that would eat you. That's what they said. They'd eat you.

A lot of Americans, especially the boys in their mid to late teens or early twenties, had grown to hate the Japanese and were eager to kill some Japs. And they wanted to get up close and personal to do it. I understood the sentiment. I remembered Pearl Harbor. I remembered the Raping of Nanking, the Bataan Death March, and all the other atrocities they committed since then. I hated them already for taking me away from my girls. But a desire to see action was not something I shared with these guys.

As I said, I had a family to think about. That was why I initially tried to get in with the Navy like my little brother Charles Jr.. A lot of guys did. I wanted to do my part, but I did not want to take the most dangerous route in order to do it. I'm not saying the Navy wasn't dangerous, because it was. I just didn't want to be in the trenches surrounded by cannibalistic Japanese warriors.

So, with every intention of joining the Navy, I headed to the nearest recruiting center when I got the draft notice.

The line at the center was long, and while I waited, a recruiter from the Marine Corps talked me into switching to their shorter line. I guess it was a dirty trick, but now that I was a part of the Corps, I really appreciated what they stood for. I enjoyed knowing that I was part of an elite group. It was almost comforting to know that if you were going into battle, you were doing it with the best soldiers America had to offer.

The Pacific Theater of Operation was tailor-made for the Marine Corps. Unlike Europe, the Pacific was nothing but amphibious landings. Each island needed the Navy to blast the hell out of it and then send in an assault force that was designed to spearhead the beaches and overwhelm enemy targets with rapid and shocking power.

The Corps did a swell job getting us ready. The Marines so far had taken heavy casualties across the Pacific, but in every case they kicked the Japanese's asses. In most battles, the Japanese lost ten times as many soldiers as we did. In February and March of '45, that ratio did not remain true.

My buddy Handsome Hansen and the 5th Marines landed on Iwo Jima on February 19. The invasion beach was a slaughter house. By the middle of March, the fierce fighting had caused heavy casualties. They told us 6,821 U.S. Marines were killed and 19,000 were wounded. The brass said the battle for that stupid damn island was the bloodiest of all in the Pacific so far.

News came in that the hero "Manila" John Basilone only lasted a couple of hours on Iwo. He had received the Medal of Honor for killing something like a hundred Japs on Guadalcanal back in '42. He toured the U.S. selling war bonds for a while after that, but volunteered to return to battle. He trained Charlie Company at Pendleton the summer I was there.

It was a hard day when reports came into Pendleton that Manila John had died. He was supposed to be invincible. Harder for me was the realization that Walter Hansen was on that beach too. A number of guys I knew were there. If I hadn't been hospitalized because of my foot problems, I'd probably be lying on the beach of Iwo Jima. The war became more real to me then.

I took solace from the fact that when the smoke cleared, the eight square mile piece-of-shit-island was littered with the bodies of 21,000 of the 22,000 Japs who defended the island.

The Corps promised recruits they would see some action and engage the Japs eye-to-eye. It wouldn't be like the Army, where they fought long distance wars, or the Navy, who "just floated around in their boats." Marines would get up close and personal. Kill the enemy with their own hands. That's what Handsome Hansen and Manila John did. They'd engaged them eye-to-eye. What a waste of life.

What happened on Iwo filled me with fear. It also pissed me off. The Marine Corps had made me hard as nails and I felt like I could take on anything. Like many around me, I was filled with piss and vinegar. I was ready to kill some Japs. I was unstoppable. That is, until word came down that we were shipping out. I was scared again.

CHAPTER SEVEN
HODY

HARRY'S PARENTS, CHARLES SR. AND Carrie cared for my darling girls while I was in San Diego, cooking them hearty meals and reading to them every night. Charles had made it his personal mission to search for answers regarding Patsy. He must've known how tough it surely was for Harry to be so far from his girls and ignorant of Patsy's future. He tapped all of his business and political resources to help with Patsy. He had accumulated many connections over the years.

He had been the general manager of OK Stove and Range Company in Louisville. The "O" was for Ouerbacker and the "K" was for Klapheke. Harry's grandfather, Henry, and Mr. Ouerbacker co-owned it. It was the largest coal stove manufacturer in the South. When Grandfather Henry died, it was up to Charles and his two brothers to run it. When some friction arose, he bought them out. He was doing well, you might say. Harry even had a black chauffeur take take him to private school as a kid.

Unfortunately in the 20s, the industry changed to gas stoves and Charles didn't make the change quick enough. The company went belly up. After that, he managed the Madrid Garage. Then he became a City Buyer. What all that entailed, I had no idea, but he seemed to do it well.

Charles had already acquired the opinion of several well-respected doctors regarding Patsy's condition and how to proceed in the future. In January, one concluded she had Microcephaly and "cannot develop into a normal child."

In February, the doctor who delivered Patsy, agreed with the diagnosis and stated "the child is helpless...the chances for improvement of this condition are very poor." Two days later, a third specialist confirmed the diagnosis.

Charles wanted to hear the opinion of our family's usual doctor, but he was called to war. Not settling for the opinions of the previous doctors, he invited Colonel Braden over for dinner in early April. Braden was a noted specialist who did all the brain and nerve operations at Nichols General Hospital in Shively, Kentucky.

At dinner, Carrie and I listened as Charles and Colonel Braden discussed politics and how FDR was handling the war. During the meal, little more than generalities were mentioned about Patsy, who lay fussing in a crib on the far side of the room.

Carrie blinked at me. "Well, Rosemary, you hardly touched

your plate."

I laid my napkin over the remaining chicken and potatoes. "My apologies. I guess I'm anxious about the examination."

I only picked at one of Carrie's famous desserts. At the end of the table, Colonel Braden ate the last of his meal. He wiped the corners of his mouth with a starched napkin and suggested retiring to a bedroom to examine Patsy.

I wiped my sweaty palms on my skirt and pushed back my chair to stand, willing my knees to keep me upright.

Carrie recruited Kay to help her clear the table and wash the dishes. I lifted the baby from the crib, unfortunately working her into a crying frenzy. In the bedroom, I sat on the edge of the bed and gently bounced Patsy.

Colonel Braden sat in an overstuffed chair at the corner of the bed and gave me a patient smile. Charles filled him in on who had examined her in the past, nearly shouting to be heard over Patsy's sobs. The Colonel stopped him and insisted that he go no further. He didn't want his conclusions to be influenced by the opinions of others.

Colonel Braden reached his hands toward the baby. "Rosemary, give me a few details about her development that might help me."

"What would you like to know?" I handed Patsy to him.

"I want to know what *you* have observed. Any peculiarities you've noticed from her birth forward."

I straightened my skirt and did my best to tell him everything about Patsy I could think of.

Patsy's crying lessened enough for Braden to physically examine her. He maintained a friendly, professional banter, as if nothing were wrong.

When he'd looked her over, he handed Patsy back. My outstretched arms shook and my voice cracked as I asked the terrible question "What do you think?"

Braden bowed his head for a moment, then turned to Charles. "Just how far shall I go?"

Charles sniffed and rubbed his nose. "All the way, and let's have it cold and frank."

Colonel Braden looked into my eyes.

"Here it is, and it's not very encouraging. The soft spot on Patsy's head closed prematurely and the bone structure of the skull has solidified to a point where it will not permit expansion with the development of the brain."

My lips quivered. "What does that mean?"

"I am afraid that irreparable damage to the brain has already been caused to a point where there is no relief. Her brain will not improve. Her body will continue to grow and she may be able to sit up in four or five years, but she will never be able to walk."

Though it wasn't a surprise, my stomach rolled.

Colonel Braden stood quietly as I took one breath, and another. "There is question as to whether she will ever talk. If she does, it will be rather incoherent and there is a possibility of her living a normal life of sixty to sixty-five years. Of course she will be more susceptible to children's diseases than the normal child and is more apt to pass on under these circumstances."

I fought off tears and sat on the bed with all the courage I could muster. “I fell,” I choked. “I fell before she was born. Did that cause this?”

“No.” Braden touched my hand. “The fall would have nothing to do with this condition.”

The news was devastating, but somewhat encouraging, too. Colonel Braden agreed with the other doctors in all but one account. An important one. He said she could live a long life. Unfortunately, he was not finished delivering the news.

He suggested Patsy be kept apart from Kay because of the “child psychology.” He said that Kay would imitate the baby and pick up bad habits.

“I recommend she be placed in an institution where professionals can look after her.”

I grappled with the moisture burning behind my eyelids.

“It’s what’s best for her,” Braden said in a reassuring tone.

“And Rosemary,” Charles piped up, “it would take the burden off you. Patsy would get the care she needs and you can give Kay more attention.”

I sat, trying not to let my facial expression betray the emotional turmoil inside. Satisfied with the conference, Charles showed Colonel Braden to the door and thanked him. The two men exchanged whispers as I gathered my baby to my chest and bawled.

CHAPTER EIGHT
SHIPPING OUT

OUR ORDERS CAME DOWN AND it was time to ship out. Sea bags in hand, we gathered at the dock on April 13 and were corralled into a never-ending line. We climbed about 5,000 stairs to the deck. If I were to wager a guess, I'd say the transport ship could carry eight or nine hundred of us with plenty of room to spare. The only problem was over a thousand of us were piling into it. It was the largest sardine can on earth.

I can remember the date, because the day before we got some bad news. On the afternoon of the 12th, we gathered around a radio to hear the latest broadcast. In a solemn tone, the announcer said that President Roosevelt was dead. We later learned he died in the company of his mistress, Lucy Mercer, in Warm Springs, Georgia. He was having his portrait made when he keeled over.

Many of us took this pretty hard. FDR had been our president for twelve years. Almost half my life. It was tough news to swallow, and we worried what Harry Truman would do with the war effort.

After FDR's death, Truman asked Eleanor if there was anything he could do for her. She said *he* was the one in trouble and asked what *she* could do for him. She was right. He had gigantic shoes to fill. And during a scary time for our country. For many of us, the anxiety of heading to war diverted our attention.

The Navy made sure we understood who was in charge on *their* boat. They constantly reminded us we were "guests"—not very welcome guests, either. The Navy and the Marines had always butted heads.

Since the Corps' inception in 1775, sailors didn't understand why a new-fangled breed of soldiers needed to accompany them. At the time of the Continental Marines, a new fighting force was necessary for amphibious landings, boarding enemy ships and keeping enemies from boarding American ships. The Marines also maintained discipline on the ships. Basically, they served as cops. Naturally, the Navy hated them.

They were quick to order us around. The Marines had to step aside and clear the way for Navy work parties. The bosun's mate made announcements over the intercom: "Now hear this! Now hear this! All Marines clear the deck and make room for Navy personnel." The announcements were a constant annoyance. We had to comply, too. We didn't have a choice. Several times a day, we had to "lay below" until we heard the "all is clear" announcement.

We learned to hate the men of the Navy. You put a bunch of macho men, trained to kill, on a boat for several weeks with guys who order you around all the time, you're going to have problems. Add to that an immense amount of boredom and cramped living conditions. The place was ripe for fighting.

I was fortunate enough to have a top bunk. Prime real-estate. Sleeping quarters were tight. Bunks were stacked five high and were so close you could hardly turn over without hitting your shoulder on the bunk above. Twenty-four inches separated your butt from the nose of the occupant below. To make matters worse, all of your gear had to be stowed on the bunk with you. Calling it cramped was an understatement. On the top, though, I had a little more room to move.

Leopold Walden stayed in the bunk below me. A youngster from Kansas City, he was only eighteen years old. His top teeth stuck out too far, accentuating the constant smile on his face.

I was trying to rest my eyes when I felt him climbing into his bunk under me. "Wow, your ass is only a few inches from my face. I hope you don't eat a lot of beans."

I leaned over the bunk and saw that he was laying the opposite direction as me.

"Why don't you try turning around," I said.

I heard him rustling around, the whole stack of bunks shook.

"Huh, that's better. Thanks." He popped his head out and

said, "You're a gentleman and a scholar, Kentucky."

You didn't have to be a private dick to know this kid was a few peas short of a casserole. Poor kid was about as smart as bait, but he had a heart of gold. He and I got along real swell. I met him at communications school at Pendleton after my accident and we hit it off pretty well despite our age difference.

He was quite disgruntled when he learned the coffee we were issued was mostly Nescafe Instant. He made a big stink about it not being Folgers brand. Though a teenager, he was already addicted to coffee. He was a grumpy sonofabitch (for him) until he got his hands on some. With a name like Leopold, he was an easy target for nicknames, but we called him "Folgers."

On a liberty, he bought some Folger's coffee grounds and snuck a small bag into the barracks. Sergeant Jackson found it in his foot locker and questioned Leo about it. When Leo made it known that the Corps provided inferior coffee, Jackson didn't take too kindly to it and made him eat the coffee grounds. It was rough watching him try to force it down his throat. After choking down a couple of tablespoons, a storm of vomit ensued. That's when he acquired his nick name.

As a "boot" in the Marine Corps, you have to learn to tolerate a lot. They beat you down until you kinda get accustomed to all the new rituals and torturously particular ways of doing things. Like all aspects of the Marine Corps, Folgers eventually adjusted to Nescafe. I never heard him complain again.

It wasn't too long before he was drinking an abnormal amount of coffee again. He'd drink it all day if you let him. The whacky kid preferred it over water during training. My mother would've told him it stunted his growth. It wouldn't have fazed him.

After securing my bunk, I headed topside to watch our disembarkation from the deck. Filled with a little nervous energy and looking for a good view, I whistled Duke Ellington's *Sophisticated Lady* as I ran my hand along the top rung of the railing. Folgers tagged along.

No crowds gathered to bid us farewell. No dames crying and waving their handkerchiefs. As the ship pushed away from the harbor, I thought about Hody, Kay, and Patsy. I hadn't heard anything from home in a while and was eager to know the latest developments on Patsy.

Folgers jolted me out of my reverie when he swatted me on the shoulder. "What's buzzin' cousin? Look at the size of this damn ship." He panned his pointed finger the length of the deck.

"Crazy, ain't it." I suddenly wasn't in a talkative mood.

"How far down do you think that water... holy hell, is that a dolphin?"

Together, we watched as the American mainland grew smaller and smaller and eventually disappeared beyond the horizon.

Being on the high seas made me think about my kid brother, Charles Jr., who we called Charlie. He was a Lieutenant Junior Grade in the Navy in charge of some damn ship somewhere. He had written me a letter telling me all about it. He'd gotten excited as hell over it too. He said he was in charge of a Landing Craft Control boat for the 7th Amphibious Force, the LCC

25479, or some damn thing.

According to his letters, Charlie and his crew were known to be in the waters around Leyte Gulf and the Philippine Islands in the fall of 1944. The Americans fought to liberate the Philippines after having lost them in early 1942.

During the Battle of Leyte Gulf on October 15, 1944, the Japanese launched their first suicide bomber attacks. Charlie's involvement was uncertain, but he reported his boat was alongside ships the suicidal pilots attacked. In letters home, he assured our parents that his boat was too small to be a target. He did mention he had a kamikaze plane in the sights of his .50-cal machine gun only to lose the shot due to an interfering flag pole on his boat.

We were told all about these goddamn Kamikazes. The Japanese considered dying in a kamikaze attack the most honorable fate. The nation celebrated suicidal bomber's sacrifices and their families revered the pilot's loyalty and bravery. To Americans, the kamikaze tactic was a display of the inhuman lengths the crazy Jap warrior was willing to go. Thousands of men on the decks of American ships who were exposed to the absurdity were literally driven insane.

It was hard to imagine my little brother standing on the decks and watching the storm of incoming suicide planes and the outgoing torrent of shells from his ship and the thousands of earsplitting anti-aircraft guns surrounding him, the horror he experienced must have been crippling. I wish I could've been there with him.

Our ship zigzagged across the Pacific for three weeks. Even at that stage in the war, the Navy wasn't taking any chances. The zigzagging was meant to make it harder for Japanese submarines to pinpoint our position. The voyage was pretty uneventful. We played a lot of poker and bridge and shot craps. We did anything that occupied the mind. Gambling was always an escape. Who could disassemble and reassemble their rifle faster? Who could do the most push-ups? My favorite was the boxing matches.

I think I owed about five guys money and two or three owed me. We weren't bookkeepers, but everyone acted like they were. Each guy seemed to know exactly how much another was indebted to him. Somehow, everyone's recollection wasn't always the same. Go figure. How much did it matter anyway? Most of us would die before we could pay our debts.

We did calisthenics on gangways and anywhere else we could find room. We met for numerous briefings. We had more Spam than I cared to eat. Other meats were over-cooked and tough. The accompanying vegetables were a soggy mess. It was hard to tell what was what.

The days slowly crept by and I was always looking for something to pass the time. Unfortunately, a lot of our time was consumed waiting in lines. There was a long line for everything—for food, the head, showers. You name it, there was a damn line for it. Some Marines would say we were in line fifty percent of our time on the boat.

I'm not a big reader, but I thumbed through a few books. I actually wrote some letters. Boredom was the overwhelming feeling on the ship. Next, was apprehension. I spent a lot of time walking the decks whistling Glenn Miller tunes and sometimes even cut the rug a little when no one was looking.

Where we were headed was still unclear to us. Folgers caught wind we were going to Guam for some more training. From there, only God and Uncle Sam knew where.

Our boys landed on Okinawa a couple of weeks ago, so we assumed that's where we were headed after Guam. Topside remained cagey about the details, but we were constantly reminded we were going to catch holy hell wherever we were going and that the U.S. Marines were going to stick it to the Japs.

CHAPTER NINE
GUAM

WE ARRIVED AT GUAM ON April 30, a Monday. A city of tents and a hell of a rain greeted us. The tents weren't half bad—not swanky by any stretch of the imagination—but nicer than I had expected. I didn't know what I expected exactly, but I didn't think they'd have electric lights and wood floors. Not bad.

The chow was pretty good and they had movies every night. We got four cans of beer a week—Old Pabst Blue Ribbon. It was actually pretty good when cold. Sleeping at night was a rather swell affair because it was cool and our sacks were fairly comfortable.

Guam got an absurd amount of rain, and the stifling heat on sunny days made training all the more difficult. Another unsettling aspect of Guam was that you kinda had to look over your shoulder all the time. The brass reminded us there were Jap holdouts hiding in the jungle. They'd been there sine we won back this island in July of '44—almost a year ago. Those crazy Japs were so brainwashed, they didn't know when to cut it out and scram.

I was scraping my breakfast plate in the mess tent when I heard "mail call" hollered. A crowd of us hurried toward the voice. I hadn't had mail in weeks. I had been getting more and more anxious to learn about Patsy's condition. What was her diagnosis? Her prognosis? Would she be able to live a quality life? I was hoping for a letter with some answers.

In the middle of a small crowd, I strained to hear the company mail orderly call my name. After ten or twelve, I heard mine. I snatched the small care package from the skinny orderly's hand and sprinted full tilt to my cot. There were some goodies from mom and a letter from Hody and Dad. I read Hodie's first.

In her usual, neat handwriting, she let me know how much she and the girls missed me. She wanted to know how I was doing, if I was safe, and if I was behaving. She said the doctors were hopeful about Patsy's future and I didn't need to worry about her right now. I pressed the letter against my nose and drew in its smell then set it on the cot beside me.

Dad's letter however, was a wallop in the gut. He said I should know the cold hard facts about my daughter. He laid it all out for me. And boy, he didn't pull any punches. That was Dad's style. Just get the message across without any unnecessary blathering. He was used to business dealings and political rhetoric. All his letters to me were very written in a formal style, business like.

This one was no different.

In his usual typewriter print, he explained he had Colonel Braden over for dinner and asked that he examine Patsy. He told me of Colonel Braden's qualifications and said he considered his opinion the final word. Braden said the same as the other doctors but added that Patsy would live a long life.

It was a real kick in the head when I read that the consensus seemed to be that my darling Patsy needed to be institutionalized. Dad said he would help make arrangements as soon as I wrote back to tell him how I wanted to proceed.

The letter flattened me. That doctor had just said my little angel needed to be put away. I was devastated. Oh, how I longed to be with Hody. I couldn't imagine how she was handling this. I was powerless on the other side of the world, counting on my sweet wife to make awful decisions and endure hardships on her own. The only relief I was offered was the fact my parents were nearby to help her.

Dad also mentioned Hody was a real trooper when Colonel Braden delivered his news. Dad said she was quick to blame herself for a fall she had early in the pregnancy. Colonel Braden insisted it had nothing to do with Patsy's condition, and if he said so, that was good enough for me.

Of course, any mother would feel that way. Especially a woman who'd been through what she had. Back in January of 1943, our four month old daughter, Judith Rose, died on our fourth wedding anniversary.

Hody and I were in the middle of mass when we were ushered from our pew to the back of the church. After receiving the news, Hody collapsed. I caught her and pressed her tightly to me. We forced ourselves into the car and sped toward home. With my vision obstructed by tears and Hody's sobs filling the car, the drive home took forever.

The paramedics who were already at the house, had done their damnedest to save Judy, but they weren't able to resuscitate her. Hody and I were beside ourselves with grief. How exactly were you supposed to handle something like that?

The doctors said she died of what's called "crib death." There was nothing the nanny could have done about it. It was just her time to go. It was a horrific day. Not a day went by that I didn't think about my little angel.

As much as it hurt to read Dad's letter, I'm glad he shot straight with me. No BS. No beating around the bush. I didn't want to hear more wishy-washy translations meant to save my emotions. Dad knew that. He knew I needed it straight from the horse's mouth. He told me he'd take care of everything back home and that I should focus on staying alive.

CHAPTER TEN
PREPARE TO MOVE OUT

FOLGERS AND I WERE PART of the 6th Marine Division, also known as the "New Breed" because it was just formed on Guadalcanal six or seven months ago. We were in the 3rd Battalion which was given the nickname "Blizzard." The Battalion was split up into companies I, K, and L. In military speak, they were referred to as Item, King, and Love Company. We were assigned to Love Company. Our Sergeant was a hard-boiled veteran of Peleliu and Guadalcanal. His name was Geoffrey Angier. He was built like a fireplug and the only thing shorter than his black hair was his patience. His chin stuck out too damn far and his face had a permanent look of anger etched upon it. He was a good two or three inches shorter than me, but his confident demeanor made him seem much bigger.

He missed the landing on Okinawa, because he was wounded

on Peleliu by mortar fragments. It took him a long time to recover, and when he finally did, he caught malaria.

He was a hard-ass, but he had reason to be. He knew what we could expect and it wasn't good. Boy he hated Japs too. Between yelling at us, he'd sometimes get a bit soft and tell us some of the horror stories from his experience. Now, I don't know whether he was trying to motivate us or scare us, but I was a good bit of both.

He told us we were going to Okinawa. The rest of Love Company and the 3/22 (3rd Battalion/22 Regiment), after dominating the northern half of Okinawa, were headed south to meet the rest of the 10th Army. Never giving details, he said we'd replace them soon. The Japanese army was retreating to the southern end of the island. We'd be moving fast, so the Headquarters Company would often be near or at the front line.

We got back to training for the umpteenth time. Between drenching rains, the old sun would come out, and it got hotter than hell. We all longed for the sun to set and give back our cool sleeping conditions.

I had chow duty when Folgers and I weren't training as company wiremen with Angier as our communications sergeant. It would be our job to link the front line with artillery batteries, command posts, and headquarters. It was a way for the men on the front line to communicate to headquarters what the conditions were like, what supplies were needed, et cetera.

Very important too, was the communication we would provide to the artillery and mortar squads. Target coordinates would be delivered from the front line to the squads so they could zero in on enemy positions. The training was all pretty fascinating to me and didn't sound too perilous.

Sgt. Angier told us we would be operating a lot at night. Unfortunately, that's when the Japanese were known to do a lot of their dirty work. The bastards snuck around, killing Marines while they were in their foxholes trying to get some shut eye. Therefore, verbal signals and passwords had to be hollered out at night when you moved around so your own guys wouldn't blow your brains out.

We were told that we'd use words with "L" or "R" because the Japanese couldn't pronounce words with those letters in them. We would be told the passwords when we met up with the rest of Love Company—they changed daily.

Sergeant Angier reminded me that I'd be calling out a lot of the passwords because of my "gruff-ass voice." Lately, a terrible sore throat added even more distinction to my voice. I developed it almost as soon as we arrived on Guam. It got so bad I couldn't talk for a while. It made me nervous as hell, I tell ya. I thought I was getting malaria or something. A lot of fellas there had it. Guys all around shook violently with fever chills.

Sick bay injected me with God-knows-what and I got better, but it took damn near forever. The last thing I wanted was laryngitis on the front line while I was trying to yell code words. It hurt to smoke cigarettes too. That was maybe the worst part about the sore throat ordeal.

It wasn't long before we left for Okinawa, so I took the time to write some letters. I wrote to Hody—a "behavior report," if you will. I couldn't tell her about my whereabouts because the mail censors would have cut it out anyway. I reminded her that I would support any decision she made about Patsy.

I received a letter from my dad. He told me not to worry about anything at home. He said to focus on the party we'd have when we were all together again. He was fixing the basement up for a grand party. I smiled, imagining myself double-fisting highballs with my family.

He also told me that Charles Jr. was somewhere in the area and to keep an eye out for him. Dad knew that Charlie was in the Navy and it was unlikely that we'd ever see each other, but it was a fun thought to entertain. He realized there really was no way for any one of us to find out where the other was. Mail censors scanned everything we said so none of us knew a whole hell of a lot about anything of great import. And since Charlie was always moving, we had no idea if he was anywhere near me. Last we'd heard, he was in the Philippines.

Dad was able to inform me that my brother-in-law, Earl Whalen, was on Okinawa. I guessed he could share that information because our troops had been there for over a month. Earl was married to my second oldest sister, Lucille, and Dad treated him like another son. He was a real part of the family.

After our marriage, Hody and I lived in a small apartment above Earl's restaurant on Bardstown Road near Slaughter Avenue in Louisville. It wasn't much, but we fixed it up to suit us. When Hody got pregnant with Kay, the smell of hamburgers and whatever else they were cooking in the restaurant made her sick, and we had to move.

Earl was in the Naval Construction Battalion, or the corps of Seabees. He established floating docks, carved out roads, built bridges, and so forth. He may've had something to do with erecting the tent village on Guam where I stayed. Of course I was worried about him, but I took comfort in knowing he was where my old unit was and it wouldn't be long before I was with them. I wondered if I'd run into him. What a hoot that would be.

I ran into George Kilmeade, a buddy of mine from my old unit at Pendleton. He was limping around with a bandaged left foot. Over a couple of Pabst Blue Ribbons, he filled me in on what I'd missed since my accident in December. He told me about the different islands they had traveled to in the Pacific, and then of course, the invasion of Okinawa.

"We stormed that beach like gladiators ready to kill hundreds of Japs with our bare hands!" He put his cigarette in his mouth to free up both hands so he could pantomime strangling someone. "We hauled ass onto that beach like hell fire was raining down on us. I could swear bullets flew past my ears." He ran in place—well, limped—with an invisible rifle in his hands. He was an animated fella. Kind of corny, but I liked him.

"Nothing, Kentucky," he said. "There was nothing going on. No Japs shooting at us. No artillery shells falling around us. The beach was completely quiet. It was eerie as hell, I tell ya. We thought for sure the Japs were playing one hell of an April Fool's joke on us."

George sat down on a telephone pole lying beside the tent. You could tell he'd overdone it. He propped his bandaged foot on his knee and let out a little groan. His face contorted with agony as he looked to the sky.

"That's what they prepared us for, Kentucky. They told us to move our asses and get off the beach. The brass predicted we'd lose 80% of our men on the landing. They said because we were so close to Japan, it would be the toughest landing of the whole damn war. I was scared as hell, Kentucky. We all were. There was a lot of vomiting going on."

"I heard about that." An unusually large footprint marked the mud at my feet. "Not the vomiting, but the landing. It's a crazy thing. I'm glad you guys didn't have to go through a bunch of hell on the beach. What happened to your foot?"

"Damnedest thing," he started as he threw his hands up. "We were moving over a hill and an asshole Jap sprung out of nowhere and started shooting. We blasted the hell out of him. Goddamn if he didn't get off one more round as he was falling. Right in my damn foot. So I was carried out and they brought me here. Million Dollar Wound, Kentucky. I may be going home soon."

George told me how the 6th secured the northern half of the island and were making their way south. He was shot as they approached the Shuri line, a strong defensive position that extended from east to west across the island. He told me how the Japs used holes and tunnels, and that they were meaner than hell.

On May 8, I was laying on my cot, halfway through a letter I had started two days before, when a skinny kid named Ryan Somethingorother burst into the tent. He announced that the Germans had surrendered. He made the shape of a gun with his hand and held it to his temple as he said, "that scoundrel Hitler put a bullet in his own brain last week."

The German Army began laying down their guns until the last of the bastards did on the 7th. Hallelujah. They declared May 8 as Victory in Europe Day, VE Day. Hats off to the American boys in the ETO for kicking those Nazis' asses. Now it was the Marine Corps' turn to convince the Japs to follow suit.

Sunday the 13th was Mother's Day. Boy I wished I could've been home with Mom on her special day. At Mass that morning, I did the best a guy in my situation could do for his mom—I offered the Mass and Communion for the swellest mother a fellow could have. Of course, I always included her in my prayers and Mass every Sunday, but this day was different. Not only was it Mother's Day, but my company was scheduled to ship out the next day. All the guys offered Mass to their mothers. Our chaplain, Father Gregory, devoted much of his homily to what we had ahead of us. He spoke of the courage and strength we could find through God. He prayed God would be with us and bring us home safely.

Just as Father Gregory said Amen, a comedian two rows

behind me hollered out, "We're the goddamn 6th Marines! Amen to that!"

CHAPTER ELEVEN
HODY

KAY'S BLOND PIGTAILS HAD SOMEHOW tangled in the string on her rain gear, so I worked at the knots until the stove hissed. Water poured over the pot's sides as I pulled it off the eye. Every night was another version of this challenge. Preparing dinner had become a feat in itself. Kay's curiosity got her into trouble. Patsy couldn't keep a pacifier in and often whined and cried. Chores were a burden. I had been doing it alone for over a year.

I pulled another pot from the cabinet, careful to make as little noise as possible. A stranger slept in the next room.

Money was short. In an effort to make ends meet, and without conference with Harry, I was forced to rent out one of the bedrooms in the tiny, two bedroom house.

The family was nice enough, I suppose, but they weren't

overly considerate. Neither adult contributed to the household chores while their two rambunctious children contributed significantly to the mess. I found myself cleaning up after them as much as my own kids. Despite my best efforts, the single bathroom never seemed to be cleaned, making it all the more difficult to share with strangers.

The man's name was Wille. He worked nights and slept much of the day, which was why I tried desperately to contain the noise in the kitchen. He was a grumpy man and was even worse when he didn't get his sleep or when he'd been drinking. He was a tall gorilla in a tank top. When his wife left on errands, I was uncomfortable being alone with him. Though it was my home, I found myself walking on eggshells to keep my tenants happy and paying rent.

I was not always successful at keeping the girls in order while tending to such things as dinner. Even if I got plenty of sleep and healthy food, caring for an invalid baby while catering to the needs of a hyperactive five-year-old would be taxing for anyone.

My only relief was my weekly trip to the market. Harry's parents watched the girls for an hour or two while I strolled through the grocery aisles searching for items that fit the budget.

The bare essentials were all I could afford. Not much more was available anyway. Americans were rationing so more could be sent to the boys fighting overseas. A few staple products remained on the shelves, but many had become inaccessible luxuries. Aromatic bath soaps, make up, perfume, and even Coca Cola teased me with their alluring packaging.

* * *

Forgetting it was still hot, I grabbed the pot I had removed from the stove-top and burned my hand. Before I could treat it, Patsy began to gurgle and spit up.

She had become increasingly difficult to care for. My constant fatigue from sleepless nights was not the only culprit in the difficulty. Patsy's condition appeared to be worsening. The prospect of professional care was hard to ignore.

After clearing sputum from the baby's mouth and throat, I carried her over to the sink where I could run the tap water over my burn. Outside the window, the gorilla's wife smoked a cigarette on the back step without a care in the world. *Useless.*

Wetness weighed down Patsy's cloth diaper. I took a deep breath. I was too tired to get mad. I'd changed her diaper only ten minutes ago.

After settling Kay into the bed in our shared room, I read a book to her while bouncing Patsy on my leg. I gave Kay a kiss on the forehead and promised that Daddy was thinking about her and would soon be home.

In the small front room, I turned on the radio and collapsed in an armchair with the baby on my chest. A sigh escaped my lips as I realized I hadn't brushed Kay's teeth before tucking her in. She hadn't had a bath in a few days either. *Choose your battles, right?*

The CBS World News report from Guam was already in progress. The overly-energetic announcer was speaking of what they called Kamikaze attacks.

"Thousands of airplanes and hundreds of small torpedo boats laden with explosives have been slamming into U.S. ships in the waters around Okinawa." He was interrupted by static in the speaker.

"The onslaught," he continued, "appears to be the largest and most relentless aerial attack in history. Hundreds of U.S. ships have been damaged or destroyed and thousands of casualties fall daily."

I couldn't listen anymore. I made the effort to get out of the chair, baby on my hip. As I was turning the volume down, he said something about the psychological toll the Kamikaze were taking on the American boys.

I fell into my seat, Patsy's head knocking lightly on my shoulder. In the dark, quiet room, I tried counting my blessings, but Patsy's labored breathing rasped, breaking up any calm I tried to muster. A sound I was accustomed to, but still frightened of. Every night I wondered if that breathing would cease before the sun came up.

Patsy eventually fell asleep in the armchair and I hoped I too would get some much-needed rest. I prayed for Harry's safety and return home. I desperately needed his help.

The gorilla walked heavily through the room and slammed the front door behind him as he headed to work. The racket woke Patsy into a crying fit.

CHAPTER TWELVE
LANDING

MONDAY, WE GEARED UP AND boarded the transport ship for Okinawa. We were all nervous as hell. Everyone was either quivering or talking up a big game. They were full of bull, though. They put on a good act, but they were shaking in their boots.

As the island of Okinawa materialized on the horizon, the butterflies in my stomach grew into fire-breathing dragons. Hundreds of ships were still in the surrounding waters. Battleships, carriers, destroyers, you name it. I knew this was a big operation, but seeing it for myself was overwhelming. The sheer size and numbers of what America produced and put in the water was staggering.

Pride consumed me. I was a tiny cog in something so gigantic and powerful. The Japs must've been soiling their pants. As we got closer, the island resembled a disturbed hive with planes buzzing around it like angry bees.

I couldn't believe my eyes when Japanese Zeros dove at American boats. A number of them hit the water and only a handful inflicted any damage to our ships. Shell after shell, the American guns sent a barrage of anti-aircraft flack into the air. U.S. Corsairs zipped through the air giving chase to the Jap planes.

We gathered around the deck to watch the show. "Those sons of bitches are still at it!" somebody on the deck behind me yelled. Apparently the Kamikaze attacks hadn't let up much since Love Day, or landing day.

A commanding voice came from the center of a crowd. "Boys, if you haven't done so, hurry up and write your wills, perform your last rites, or whatever it is you do."

I thought he was joking until I saw him handing out paper and pencils. We were told to write our last will and testament, take atabrine tablets to prevent Malaria, and see our chaplains for any final prayers. Guys lined up to grab Marine Corps letterheads to get to work. I followed suit.

Our ship slowed to a dawdling pace and headed toward what the brass referred to as the Green Beach landing area. Kamikazes were still slamming into and around our Navy to the south. I thought of Charlie, big time. I still didn't know if he was in the action to our right. I said a silent prayer for his safety.

As we neared the shore, I could see the pock-marked hills of the island that were disfigured by the U.S. Navy's pre-landing bombardment. They shelled the island for months before Love Day. And then for a week before the landing, they shelled the shit out of it again to further soften the defenses. Wow, what a sight. I bet it was a real kick to see that.

Just off Green Beach, a Kamikaze plane barreled toward our ship from port side. We were paralyzed as it approached. Anti-aircraft guns from our ship spewed a frenzy of rounds skyward. We all hit the deck, covered up, and kissed our asses goodbye. The good Lord spared us though. The Jap Zero missed our ship and splashed into the water a hundred yards starboard. Welcome to Okinawa!

We went over the side of the ship down cargo nets and boarded a landing craft. We made it to the beach with no further problems. The Kamikaze attacks down south of us had subsided to intermittent attacks.

From the looks of it, the Shuri defense line was creating heavy casualties. Wounded seemed to pour from the hills. They moved non-life threatening wounded to field hospitals and the more serious cases to hospital ships. Most were carried on stretchers and covered to their chin with a muddy blanket or poncho.

The war quickly became more frightening and real to me. Most people in their lifetime would never see this kind of carnage. It was appalling.

While waiting to move out, I helped carry young men whose legs or other body parts had been blown off. I helped a kid we were carrying on a stretcher move his severed arm closer to his body because it had slid down toward his leg. He wanted the useless limb to rest where it belonged. To him it was like a gruesome Teddy bear he needed next to him for security.

For me, on that first day on Okinawa, the sight of the dead was hard to digest. It just didn't seem real. The wounded men hollering and bleeding everywhere was hard to accept as real. It was awfully tragic and horrifying to witness. But seeing the dead was like a nightmare. A dream with no base in reality. The blood was too red, the skin too glassy, the cuts seemed to shout, the torn skin like horrible mouths.

The first body I helped with was a boy named Thomas. His name was on his dog tag, but I couldn't make out the surname. It was crusted over with blood. It started with an O or Q. He was missing a big chunk of his face. A guy named Gerald and me carried Thomas's body to the pile of Marine carcasses on the beach and gently laid him on top of the stack. I covered his face with a poncho to keep off the rain.

It was hard for me to take my eyes off him. As I walked away, I kept looking back at that kid's body being pummeled by rain. He couldn't do anything to protect himself from the downpour. He never would again. I thought of his parents.

The rain continued in torrents. Okinawa, I heard from Sergeant Angier, could get as much as ten inches of rain in a single day during monsoon season. The downpour had begun on May 7 and cleared up for only a few hours on the night of the

24th.

That same night there was a full moon, making conditions perfect for bombings. That's exactly what the Japs did. Seizing the brief opportunity, they initiated seven raids that destroyed a bunch of our planes and ignited 70,000 gallons of gasoline stored at the airfields. The bastards also scored hits on twelve U.S. ships off shore with Kamikaze attacks. But by the end of the 25th, our guys had shot down more than 170 Jap planes.

When we got our orders to move out on the 27th, the rain was still unrelenting. Me and the rest of the guys from the 57th Replacement Draft piled onto a truck that was headed to Naha —Okinawa's capitol. The truck was crowded with familiar faces. Among them were Ed Hoffman, James C. Griffin, Ralph Herner, and of course, Folgers and Angier. We felt like cattle on the way to the slaughterhouse. Before we could reach our destination, the truck became deeply mired in sticky mud.

We abandoned the truck and started a miserable march toward the hills. The rain had created a mud unique to Okinawa. It was both sticky and slippery. Even the tanks were bogged down in the muck. They were unable to assist in the fighting and could not move supplies into the combat zones. Airdrops had been supplying the fighting forces as best they could. Low visibility made it tough to drop them accurately. As a result, we had supply detail, which meant we had to carry a load of provisions to the front in addition to our own gear.

On his person, a Marine on Okinawa carried in the

neighborhood of fifty pounds of equipment. For me and Folgers, we had the additional weight of our comm wire spools attached to our backs. With communication repair kits and the other supplies, we probably had over a hundred pounds on us. Boot Camp certainly helped with the hard hike before us, but it did not prepare us for the confounded mud.

I could feel every pound of it on my weak leg. It was much stronger than it was a couple of months ago, but it still wasn't 100%.

Before the accident, I was a lean 170 pounds. By the time I got out of the hospital, I was down to 154. I was in the lower 160s now, so I was growing strong again, but the equipment on my back and in my hands made me feel like I was made of lead. The soaking rain, and the mud piling up on my lower legs, made it all the more miserable and difficult.

We trudged on, slipping and sliding. At times you'd step in the sticky crap and have to work your ass off just to pull your foot out. You'd almost lose your boot. It took damn near forever to walk a couple of yards.

On his back, a Marine carried the M1941 pack system consisting of a haversack, a knapsack, and belt suspenders. It contained a rolled blanket, a pair of socks, shaving kit, weapon cleaning kit, two K-ration meals, two D-ration meals, a dungaree shirt and trousers, an entrenching tool (shovel), a M1905 bayonet with scabbard, and some chocolate. My backpack was obviously modified as the Company wireman because of the damn spool.

A cartridge belt, canteen, and Ka-bar knife hung on my waist.

The almost three pound, steel M1 helmet weighed down my head, and a government-issued camouflaged poncho covered all this garb and equipment from the shoulders down.

I'd slung my M1 Garand over my shoulder. They'd recommend us wiremen carry the M1 Carbine to lighten the load. But you can't argue with the Garand's power and accuracy. The mantra of the Marine Corps is "You're a rifleman, foremost...Without my rifle, I am useless." To me, a rifleman needed the best rifle. I opted to carry my heavy "Baby Garand."

We passed columns of men coming off the front line who looked like zombies on a slow march out of hell. Their slumped posture and sluggish gait revealed their bone-wearied state. Blank stares from their vacant and forlorn faces chronicled the nightmare they had endured. They had been through the physical and psychological ringer.

"Your turn," a zombie said, looking at me with blood-shot eyes as he crept past me. I heard a kid on make-shift crutches mumble, "Good luck, you're going to need it." A chill rippled through my body. Let's just say, the sight of the battle veterans didn't do much for our morale.

We trudged on and thunder rumbled from the hills. It sounded like a 4th of July fireworks show, it really did. It was the artillery of the 1st and 4th Marines who were still fighting at Shuri, where the ancient castle was. They were probably in the mopping up stage by now. They had been fighting at the Shuri Line alongside Love Company for a couple of weeks. Love Company was moving from what they told us was called Sugar

Loaf Hill, or some damn name, and we were supposed to meet up with them in Naha.

CHAPTER THIRTEEN
HODY

PATSY SCREAMED FROM THE LIVING room, making it difficult to hear the news on the radio as I washed an endless supply of dirty dishes. There was only so much I could do for her. If I picked her up, she would only start crying when I set her down again. It was challenging, for sure, but I occasionally had to ignore her so I could get some chores done. Someone had to tidy up the place and my useless tenants sure as hell weren't going to do it.

During one of Patsy's lulls, the radio announcer mentioned something about the South Pacific and Okinawa. In his letters, Harry was not allowed to disclose where he was, but with a little deduction, it could be assumed he was on Okinawa. I ran into the living room and sat on the floor with my ear next to the speaker.

"...our war correspondent," the announcer said in a nasally voice, "reports that the U.S. Marines suffered devastating losses in a battle for a hill called Sugar Loaf in the area of Shuri, Okinawa."

My heart was in my throat.

"6th Marine Division correspondent says the fighting between May 8 and May 18 was some of the most savage fighting in the war to date—perhaps in Marine Corps History. In ten short days, the 6th Division suffered over 2,600 casualties and an additional 1,300 Marines were evacuated to due psychiatric disorders. At the end of the battle, our American boys prevailed and the town of Shuri is now in the hands of the United State Marines. In other news..."

I was in a sort of a trance. My head was numb with worry. Harry was in the 6th Marine Division—I knew that from his letterhead. Was he at this horrendous Sugar Loaf Hill? It was the first week of June, and I hadn't heard anything from him since the middle of May. He'd sent me a letter for Mother's Day. Could he have written the letter before entering the battle at Sugar Loaf? How long did it take for the mail to reach me? My mind raced. I was a mess.

The sound of the water running in the kitchen sink temporarily shook me from my reverie. I pulled myself off the floor and returned to the task of dish washing.

The front door slammed and hulking footfalls approached through the living room. It was Willie. I could smell the gin before I could see him. He leaned his backside against the counter and cleaned axle grease from under his fingernails with his pocket knife. I scrubbed another pot and rinsed it, my hands shaking.

"Heard anything from your husband?" He didn't take his eyes off his disgusting fingers.

"No."

"That's too bad. You worried about him?"

I let his asinine question hang in the air to see if he'd recognize his own stupidity. He didn't. I wished he'd go away.

"Ain't he in the Pacific? They're takin' a beatin' over there."

I used the edge of a knife to scrape an unidentifiable hunk of food from a plate.

"Where's Pearl?" I stammered, hoping to change the subject.

"Dunno."

He continued to stand there for an intolerable amount of time. I quickly finished the last dish and moved away from the sink. My fingers didn't seem to want to untie my apron.

"Here, let me get that," Willie said.

"No, it's alright, I can handle it."

"Just hold still." He grabbed my arm and the knotted strings of the apron and pulled me to him. He was close behind me. He reeked. I froze.

Having untied the strings in the back, he guided them around my sides and gathered them with the rest of the apron on my belly. I felt his nasty breath on my ear. I was scared to offend him and hoped he'd soon retreat. I held my breath and my body seized. When I felt his manhood press against my buttocks, nausea coursed through me. I tried to pull away. He tightened a bear hug around me. Our bodies surged forward and he hit his knee on the knob of a lower cabinet door. He let out a yell. I twisted around, arms flailing, and caught him with the back of my elbow on his neck. He gave me a shove and sent me sprawling to the floor.

The linoleum hit my back like a slap. All I could think to do was run. As soon as I got my feet under me, I rushed out the back door. Pearl was sitting on a rusty tricycle in the middle of the yard smoking a cigarette while her youngest played in a puddle of mud in his diaper. *She was out here all along?* A wave of revulsion roared over me.

I heard banging and slamming from inside. Patsy was screaming, Kay crying. I'd left my girls with that monster. With a reckless abandon that only a protective mother could have, I stormed back inside. Through the open front door, I could see the monster standing on the porch as if he couldn't make up his mind what to do. Patsy and Kay were unharmed but continued to wail.

He came back into the house and pointed a finger. "If you tell Pearl about this, I will kill you. Do you understand?"

With that, he turned and left.

CHAPTER FOURTEEN
WELCOME TO HELL

NAHA WAS IN RUINS. SKELETONS of buildings and houses were all that remained after the American bombing raids and Naval shellings. We found the rest of Love Company near a long building that lacked most of its roof. They were strewn about lying against rocks, logs, and burnt trees. If they were glad to see us and the supplies we bore, they didn't show it. Some grumbled a sardonic *Thank You* when we offered them more rations, but most said nothing at all to us. We didn't exactly expect a warm welcome. Replacements never got one.

The men of Love Company had to be sick of replacements. Since April 1, they had a casualty rate of over 100%. Replacements rotated in continuously. The Company started with 240 men, but fell below 100. Many of those who were left had been fighting together for nine weeks. They trusted each other with their lives and knew more about each other than their wives or mothers did. I couldn't help but feel guilty I was just now entering the fray. These guys had been going through a lot of crap while I recovered from my broken leg in a clean and cushy hospital bed.

Angier warned us that we wouldn't be received with open arms. What was the point? Statistically, most of us replacements would be dead in a day or two. So why bother getting to know another person that will, in all likelihood, die soon. I guess war was easier to deal with if you acted like replacements didn't even exist.

Some of the guys quietly smoked cigarettes, knifed at cans of rations, cleaned their rifles, or picked at their wounds. Not giving a rat's ass we were there, most of them collapsed and fell right to sleep. For the most part, they all looked dead inside. Us replacements walked around camp like we were at a high school dance with no date. We just sort of clung together.

Miraculously, the rain let up shortly after we arrived—the first time in over two weeks. Unfortunately, the clearing sky soon filled with Kamikaze. We watched the sky light up with explosions over the beach and above the sea. For the most part, it was like a lightning storm. Sporadic flashes danced across the expanse like strobe lights. Anti-aircraft fire from the Navy sent bursts of light erupting below, within, and above the retreating clouds. Explosions of downed Zeros sent up blinks from behind the dark silhouettes of the hills in front of us. The reports of each explosion were not audible for a full second after the burst of light.

Folgers, now sitting beside me against a charred log, said we were about a mile from the shoot-out with the Kamikaze.

A young man squatted in front of us. "Ya'll the new wiremen?"

"Yeah, I'm Harry, this is Leo," I said.

"I'm Corporal Jack Hutton. Everyone calls me Hut."

The freckled fella proceeded to tell us he was from Alabama. He was probably around twenty, had too many freckles, and sported a mix of dark red hair and mud on his head. He chewed gum like a cow. "Did ya'll hear about my former wiremen?"

We shook our heads.

"Thompson and Parsons," he said. "Lost them on Sugar Loaf." He paused. Not for a dramatic effect, but because he was clearly close to choking up.

He kept chomping that gum like nobody's business. Between all the gum-smacking and his southern drawl, I almost couldn't understand him.

"I don't mean to scare ya'll, but you wiremen are sniper bait. They were both picked off trying to string comm wire. Moving between the lines like you all have to is a perfect opportunity for Jap snipers to nail you. Ya'll need to be careful. Keep your head down and eyes peeled."

He stood and gave us a half-assed wave while saying, "It's nice to meet ya'll. I hope you stick around for a while." He walked away and sat next to a radio pack for a little shut eye.

* * *

In the gathering darkness, the men from Love Company looked like walking dead. Their eyes were sunken and their faces appeared stuck in a permanent expression of exhaustion and sorrow. They were battered. Some looked like they wouldn't survive the night. They were hungry and hurt.

The Kamikaze raids continued throughout the night. As tired as I was, I had a difficult time sleeping. It was like trying to sleep during an intense thunderstorm. Only this storm involved thunder that carried death with each blast. Not only did every thunderclap announce the demise of more young men, but you never knew if one would end up in your direct vicinity.

Making it worse, of course, was the reality that we were completely exposed to the bedlam as well as the elements. We were still wet from the rain and the night time temperature on Okinawa was in the sixties, making me shiver most of the night.

With each flash, I could see the faces of the men around me huddled up in fetal positions trying to get rest. The faces on the other replacements looked like I felt—frightened out of their minds.

The veterans from Love Company slept like babies.

You might think I'd take comfort in their ability to sleep, but you'd be wrong. In fact, it had the opposite effect. Their ghostly faces only showed me they had abandoned normal human emotions. The humanity had been drained from their bodies and possibly their souls. No, I didn't take comfort in watching them sleep through the cacophony. It only filled me with dread. I knew that before long, I'd be able to sleep like that. I'd be drunk with exhaustion. I'd be a soulless, despondent wreck who'd lost all of his sense of humanity. I didn't want chaos and death to become something I was accustomed to.

The God-forsaken Kamikaze raids finally petered out at around 8:30am and it would be fair to say I felt like dog crap.

"Klapheke!" Sergeant Angier screamed. "Get the phone set up!" He swiped his hand past his face, directing me toward the long building. I shook Folgers out of his sleep.

"Mom?" He said as he rubbed his eyes. He blinked a few times until he could make out my ugly mug. His face melted with disappointment.

"I hope your mom doesn't look like me. I figured you'd gotten your disagreeable looks from you daddy"

He shook his head and propped himself on his elbow.

"Come on." I said. "We've got to set up the phones."

The command post had been set up inside the dilapidated building. Love Company called it "The Factory."

At the post, field telephones, radios, switchboards, and a spaghetti factory of wires were crammed into the only corner of the building that had an intact roof. Angier presented Folgers and me to Captain Frank Haigler and Lieutenant Marcus Pope, two of the few remaining officers from the 3/22. Most of them were still lying on Sugar Loaf Hill with the wiremen. "These are our new wiremen, huh?" Pope asked Angier. Angier just nodded.

Captain Haigler resembled John Wayne, but with a smaller mouth and bigger nose. At twenty-three years old, he had a lot of war experience. He was a Marine's Marine. The son of a Navy captain who'd moved his family to various corners of the world, he had lived in Tsingtao China, the Philippines, Hawaii, as well as Chicago and New York.

Following in his father's footsteps, he wanted to make a career out of the military. He enrolled in the Manlius Military Academy in New York. From there, he joined the Navy Reserve officer Training Corps at Northwestern University. After Pearl Harbor, he fought in the Battle of Attu in the Aleutian Islands, an island chain extending off Alaska. It was a brutal, two week, battle that ended with a dramatic Japanese banzai charge. As far as I understand, it was the only engagement between the U.S. and Japanese in arctic conditions.

After Attu, he went to the opposite side of the world and landed on Utah beach at Normandy on June 6, 1944. He managed to survive the invasion and was sent back stateside for a thirty-day leave. While home, he got himself into a bit of trouble. He had a tendency to collect war souvenirs. He somehow acquired planning documents of the Normandy landing. He tried to submit the plans to the Chicago Tribune, but the Navy, understandably, put the kibosh on it.

The Navy sent him to the U.S. Marine Corps staff school. After completing the training, he was transferred to Guadalcanal, where he became part of the Headquarters Company for the 3rd Battalion, 22 Regiment.

He endured the heat and jungle rot in the battle for Guam in the summer of 1944. From there, he and the 3/22 landed on

Okinawa on April 1. During the Battle for Sugar Loaf Hill, Love Company's commander, Captain John P. Lanigan was wounded along with all of the other company commanders. They were gathered together in conference when an artillery round hit. Shards of metal and wood ripped through all of them. That was when Captain Haigler took over Love Company as the Commanding Officer (CO). Most of us grunts called him the "Skipper." It was a common practice to refer to captains as Skipper.

The night before, he interviewed the new recruits by the light of a flashlight. He tried to say my last name and decided he liked "Kentucky" better. He said he'd just stick with that. I don't think he recognized me in the daylight.

On a pile of rubble in the command post, Lt. Pope chewed on an unlit cigar as he looked over a map. His blond hair was dirty and matted. He never told us much about himself. Like Haigler, he was a Guam veteran and landed on Okinawa on Love Day. He was shot in the arm during a short skirmish on the north end of the island. He had recovered from his wounds enough to demand his return to Love Company. There was still a bandage on his arm above the elbow. He had been through the ringer, but still had a leader's posture. It was easy to tell by looking at him he could throw his weight around. We soon learned he was the type to demand respect instead of command it. He used intimidation to lead.

Lt. Pope was from St. Louis, was in his mid-thirties, and had seen a lot of action. Before Guam, he fought on Guadalcanal where his finger was shot off. Fortunately, it wasn't his trigger finger. It was the pointer finger on his left hand. He flashed me a warm smile but didn't speak.

I wasn't in good form, and it took me longer than it should have to splice the comm wires and set up communication with field headquarters. It was a standard field telephone, an EE-8, or "double easy-eight." It had a range of up to seventeen miles and was powered by two D-cell flashlight batteries. The Marines had used the MCT-1 alert telephone, but we'd switched last year to the Army's EE-8, because it proved more rugged than the Navy-designed models. With small clips, I attached a cable between it and the BD-72 switchboard.

Once that was done, I lit a cigarette and waited for him to command me further. He picked up the phone, shooed me away like a dog, and gave the handset to the Skipper.

With Folgers in tow, I started toward the rest of my squad. As we squished through mud puddles, someone called out, "Kentucky! Hey, Old Kentucky!" It took me a minute before I could make out who was talking. He looked familiar, but I couldn't quite put my finger on who he was. As I approached, with no doubt a look of befuddlement on my face, he quietly said, "It's me, Bushrod." I was flabbergasted.

Here was a guy I had gotten to know pretty well at Pendleton, but he was so ragged and pathetic. Like the rest of Love Company—beaten to hell. His face was sucked in and his cheekbones protruded freakishly. His jaw line had grown sharp, angled. Blood stains and crusted mud covered the parts of his dungarees that weren't tattered. It was hard to decipher what the hell color his uniform was supposed to be. Dark, leathery smudges of blood were stuck to his head and chin. His baby blue eyes, sunken into his face like a skeleton, showed no life.

"How you been, Kentucky? How's the ole leg?" he asked as I sat beside him. Folgers continued walking back to our log and made himself a coffee.

"How you been old buddy?" he asked me again.

It took me a minute to shake off the horrible sight that sat next to me. "I...I'm fine." I finally spit out. Trying not to act like his ghastly presence bothered me; I nudged him with my elbow and said, "You look like shit, my friend. So nothing's changed, I guess."

"Nah, just the same ole Bushrod, handsome as ever."

The strange thing was he didn't even seem to acknowledge the mess he'd become. He'd been a fun and witty guy back at Pendleton, joining me in whistling and playing jokes on the guys. A swell fellow.

We'd hit it off at boot camp right away, because I was the only guy around that didn't give him hell about his name—Bushrod Clement. He was named after Bushrod Johnson, a Confederate General. It was his grandfather or great uncle or some damn thing.

With an unfortunate name like Bushrod, he didn't need a nickname. Everyone just called him Bushrod. If he hadn't been such an easygoing guy, he would have been given more shit from the other guys than he did.

I found myself staring at his hands. They were trembling. They weren't shivering from cold. It was different. It was like he had something wrong with him. Nerve issues or something. He was trying to hold a coffee, but the quivering sloshed the liquid in his steel cup. Black filth covered his hands. His fingernails were long, broken, and housed dark grime underneath.

He interrupted my examination of his hands. "Replacement, huh?"

"Yep," I said.

"Don't let these vets get to you too much. They'll give you trouble about joining the fight so late, but you tell 'em it's not your fault. Tell 'em about the car accident. No, don't. They'll think you did it on purpose."

He took a labored sip of his coffee and leaned in. "Don't mention you were drafted. Most of these guys volunteered and they don't take too kindly to those who were forced into it. Now, I know you had more problems with your daughter and wife, but these assholes won't care. Say, how is your girl doing, anyway?"

I filled him in on the little I knew about Patsy, and we shot the shit for a while about boot camp, our families, and the damn rain on Okinawa. It was hard for me to talk to him. He just wasn't right. He clearly had that horrendous expression that only a battle-hardened warrior could possess. His demeanor betrayed the tragic and appalling conditions he'd endured.

He and the rest of the Love Company had been pushed beyond the limits of human endurance and it wasn't over yet. Veterans called this look the "thousand-mile stare" or referred to it as going "Asiatic." I was no psychologist, but in my opinion my friend had gone Asiatic.

Seeing him like this added to the dread I was already feeling. It was a damn shame too. Seeing all these kids changed forever by this confounded war. Changed in a real bad way. And what did they get out of it? Fifty dollars a damn month.

I felt stupid as soon as it came out of my mouth, but I asked, "So, what was it like? What was Sugar Loaf like?"

He blankly stared forward. With no emotion whatsoever, he said, "I'm not gonna bullshit ya, Kentucky. It was goddamn awful. We took a lickin' for twelve goddamn days." He looked at me and said, "Just be glad you got hit by that damn car, cause you would've been there too if you hadn't." He paused and stared at the sky.

"I don't know why they called it Sugar Loaf Hill," he said. "It was more like an irrelevant pile of dog shit." He slid his boot back and forth in the mud.

Suddenly, he slapped my knee and stood up. "Well," he said staring blankly into the fog with his back to me, "welcome to hell." With that he walked away.

CHAPTER FIFTEEN
AMBUSH

CAPTAIN HAIGLER GATHERED US TO share the intel. "First of all, men," the Skipper said as he adjusted his crotch, "HQ reported that we took some pretty serious damage from yesterday's Kamikaze attacks. They said over 150 Kamikaze planes attacked yesterday and last night. Fifty-six raids consisting of two to four Japanese planes wreaked havoc on American forces. Nine U.S. ships were hit by Kamikazes including the destroyer Drexler, which sunk at around 0700. Good news is that of the 150 Kamikaze planes that attacked, 114 of those sonsofbitches were shot out of the sky." Some of the guys mumbled soft hurrahs.

"Listen up!" the Skipper yelled. "Battalion says the Japs are withdrawing to the south and that's where we are headed. You have five minutes!"

"Klapheke!" Angier said. "Get the equipment ready to move."

"Yes, sir." As I packed up the radio and reeled the comm wire, I overheard some of the conversation between the Skipper and Pope.

Skipper, pointing at a tattered map said, "The 1st Armored Amphibious Battalion is holding the seaward side of Naha. We are moving to the east side of Naha toward the Kokuba estuary."

I stopped reeling the wire for a minute—the spool was squeaking like a sonofabitch.

"It's my understanding that part of Ushijima's army has moved too and is holding out on Oroku Peninsula," Skipper said. "That's where the Naha airfield and harbor are. We need these, you understand? Our orders are to move to the hills east of the Kokuba River which separates the peninsula from the rest of the island. Get your boys ready, and let's move out."

"Yes, sir," Pope said. "2nd Platoon, drop your cocks and grab your socks!" Pope so eloquently yelled to get us moving.

Folgers downed the rest of his coffee and helped me gather the comm wire and the rest of our gear. We filed into a line. The two of us alternated who carried the spool of wire. I helped him strap the spool pack on his back.

A few minutes into the march, a jackass with a New Jersey accent decided to pipe up. "Fresh meat!" Real clever.

"You guys are pretty little replacements. Look at you in your clean uniforms. Not a scratch on you. That'll change though. I bet you won't make it two days. Most replacements only last a couple of hours."

I glanced back and gave him a look of sardonic gratitude for the encouraging words. He reminded me of Al Capone. Same block-headed shape with chubby cheeks. Of course he wasn't well groomed like Capone. He looked like shit. He was a veteran. I knew what kind of crap he'd been through in recent weeks and decided to let his comments slide. We continued to walk without giving him more notice.

The rain was still intermittent, but the mud was a constant struggle. We reached the Kokuba estuary by 9:00am. A dense fog hung in the air. Piles of debris and remnants of buildings demolished by artillery fire materialized around us. Ghostly symbols of tragic death and destruction served as reminders of what we were getting into.

A patrol was selected to move up the channel to the West and scout out the approach to the Ona-Yama Island situated in the middle of the channel. The island would serve well as a staging area for an attack on Oroku. For some reason I was picked to be part of the party. I suddenly wished I had the wire spool on so I wouldn't have been selected.

Eight of us stripped most of our gear, save for a couple of grenades and our M1s, and headed in the direction Pope ordered.

"Wish me luck," I said as I gave Folgers a pat on the back. I was about to follow the rest of the squad when Sgt. Angier grabbed me.

"I don't know why Pope picked my wireman for this, but keep your damn head down."

He walked me up the path about fifty yards beyond the buildings.

"Here. You see this big-ass tree?" He asked as he pointed at a twisted Ficus tree beside the trail. "You can't miss this thing on your way back. We can't see a goddamn thing out here and we won't know if it's a Jap or your dumb ass coming toward us. So, on your way back, stop at this tree and yell out *Scarlett*. You yell *Scarlett* and wait till you hear *O'Hara* from me before you move any further, you understand?"

I nodded nervously. "Yes, sir, like the actress." My helmet slid down my forehead.

"Yes, like the goddamn actress," he said. "Those slant-eyed bastards can't say Rs. Now get going." He turned to his left. "Baer, you hear that? Make sure Kentucky here yells the password. His gruff-ass voice can't be mistaken."

"Got it, sir."

I was last in the line following Corporal Mike Baer, who incidentally was built like a black bear. We left the concrete rubble and entered what was left of the forest on the estuary's edge. I hoped Baer saw more than me, because all I could make out was the ass of a guy from Illinois named Watkins.

After about a three minute jog through the pea soup, the fog had dissipated a bit. Baer threw up his hand indicating that we stop. He signaled for us to move forward slowly and quietly. As we approached our target area, I had a terrible feeling about it. It was really quiet. My stomach fluttered and my hands shook.

Creeping through the quasi jungle, I scanned every square

inch of the vegetation. Trees and brush were visible up to about twenty yards. My mind raced with what we'd been told during training—and a hundred more times during briefings—about the crazy-ass way the Japs fought. I was waiting for those bastards to run out of the mist at full tilt shooting at us, yelling "Banzai!" like crazy sonsofbitches, and stabbing us with their bayonets.

I looked behind me every few seconds to make sure one didn't pop up from of a spider hole and shoot me in the back. Maybe one would jump out of a tree like a goddamn monkey and stab me with his sword. All of this was known to be true about the Japs. The brass used terms like "unorthodox guerrilla warfare;" I just called it crazy-ass fighting.

We continued forward. Ahead and to our left we could see through a thin screen of trees. The island in question was a couple hundred yards out in the channel. It was only a dark mass among the cotton-like fog.

Farther up, a bridge connected the main island to Ona-Yama. It was hard to make out if the bridge was serviceable or not. We slowed to a snail's pace. Mike looked back and signaled us to get down lower. As he turned back toward the bridge, all hell broke loose.

Machine gun fire erupted from the trees ahead of us. A bullet zipped past my head like a pissed off bee. We dove to the side of the path, landing on our bellies as the assault of machine gun rounds ripped through the leaves.

Thankfully, my training kicked in, because I was in shock. I propped my M1 with my elbows, threw the butt against my shoulder, flipped off the safety and started blasting away from a prone position. I didn't even look through the sights.

The others did in kind. I fired eight quick rounds until my clip ejected with a familiar ping, barely audible over the din of rifle fire. As I rolled over to my back to grab another clip from my ammo belt, Baer yelled for us to withdraw.

He jammed another clip into the top of his rifle, got to his knees and started firing in the direction of the incoming rounds. "Go! Go! Go!"

We went. I got to my feet and ran faster than my legs have ever carried me.

The machine gun fire died down and ceased. We slowed to catch our breath and wait for Baer.

After what felt like an eternity, one of the guys said, "What do we do?"

I didn't even know his name, nor did I have an answer for him.

"I don't think Baer's coming," another fellow said. "Should we get back to the others?"

These guys were clearly younger than me. One looked like he hadn't even shaved before. I sort of took charge.

"Let's get back," I said. "Follow me."

We started off in a sprint until the ficus tree came into view. I made the same hand signals Baer had made to get us to stop. With them following, I crept behind the tree. I yelled "Scarlett" and waited. They gave me a "what the hell is wrong with you" look. A second later, we heard a distant "O'Hara." I waved them to come on and we ran back to our outfit.

Everyone was pretty well hidden from sight except Sgt. Angier. I ran right up to him and told him what had happened. He told me to get on the radio and communicate to headquarters where we were and what we learned on our reconnoitering. I found the portable field telephone and did as he said while he gathered another group to go back and find Baer.

We waited about twenty minutes and the group emerged from the thinning fog. Four of them were carrying Baer's body, using a poncho as a litter. They sat him down on the ground beside the ruins of a small building. A morbid curiosity compelled me to look at him. With Angier on the phone with HQ, I went to Baer.

After moving a dozen bodies of dead kids when we first arrived on this evil island, I was almost used to the sight. This was different. I hadn't known any of those kids. I didn't even know what their voices sounded like. I didn't know Corporal Baer all that well, but I had heard him speak. There was something about knowing what they sounded like that made losing them harder. I knew him enough to consider him a friend. Enough of a friend to cover us so we could escape the ambush.

Looking at his body lying on that foreign soil next to a blown out building, ten thousand miles from his mother with a bullet hole above his left eye and dark red blood matting his hair, my eyes welled with tears.

I'd always remember the image of my first friend to be violently taken from this earth by those goddamn Japs. I kneeled down and said *thank you*. Placing my hand on his thigh, I gave him a little pat of gratitude and farewell.

"Get his tags," Pope said. "And cover him up. Get ready to move!"

Capone crept up. "You're next, fresh meat."

Ignoring him, I went back to the comm equipment. Folgers asked me how I was doing.

"Swell, real swell."

Only a few steps from the phone, Angier was telling Pope what he learned from HQ: "They said we'll save Ona-Yama for another time. We are to clear the northern bank of the Kokuba River all the way down to the base of the peninsula."

We moved out. Folgers and I stayed close to Sgt. Angier. I don't know what they did with Corporal Baer's body. The fog was navigable, but continued to linger. The rain started again. It was coming down in sheets. My feet felt raw and painful. The mud. Oh, the damn mud.

CHAPTER SIXTEEN
FIRE FIGHT

LOVE COMPANY CONTINUED ALONG THE muddy remnant of a road toward our objective to the south—the Kokuba River. Marching in our platoon columns with our required five-pace distancing, we moved into terrain that became increasingly rocky and undulating.

To our left was the 1/22. To our rear, the 1/29. Around midday, we split off from the other regiments. They headed east, and we continued south into a narrow ravine with rocky escarpments on both sides. Dead trees, barely clinging to the canyon walls, hung precariously over our heads.

"Hey Mac." A guy named Harold broke the monotonous sound of our feet sloshing through the mud. "You don't have to bend over, you know. The Japs aren't around."

Until he pointed it out, I hadn't realized I was half bent over as I walked, as if we were already under attack. Almost as soon as I straightened my back, a shot rang out in the rocky corridor.

"Get down!" somebody yelled.

Everyone in my platoon dove behind boulders or tree stumps. A racket of rifle fire erupted. Bullets ricocheted around me. Behind me, Harold lay on his back. His body contorted. About a third of the left side of his head was nothing but a stringy, bloody pulp.

While the rest of my platoon fired into the hills on either side of us, I fumbled with my rifle. I didn't know which way was up. The noise of the M1s and Thompson sub machine guns was deafening. The sound pressed on my brain. I was so disoriented that I couldn't find my ass with both hands.

Realizing I was useless as far as the rest of my company was concerned, I tried to pull myself together. The safety on the M1 was inside the trigger guard. All you had to do was flick your trigger finger forward to flip it off. Quick and simple. But for some reason, I had a hard time with it. As soon as I got the safety off and the butt to my shoulder, a couple of Japs ran along the ridge line to my right. With them in my sights, I squeezed the trigger and fired off five or six rounds. One fell and the other moved out of view.

Shots continued from the hillside to our left. "In the tomb at ten o'clock!" Sgt. Angier yelled.

Flashes of light blinked out of a small opening of the tomb about three-fourths of the way up the hill. The efforts of my platoon concentrated on the position. By that time, most of the enemy fire from other directions had died down. The machine gun nest let out another barrage of white light and hot lead.

"Stevens! Walker!" Angier yelled. "Get your asses and some grenades up to that hole!" They took off toward the tomb.

"Covering fire!" Angier screamed.

We directed all our fire toward the tomb. I watched as Jonathan Stevens and Tommy Walker crept up to either side of the gravesite's entrance.

Between bursts of Jap machine gun fire, Stevens and Walker threw their grenades into the opening. A second later, two suppressed concussions echoed through the ravine. Smoke billowed from the machine gun nest. Like a huge ghost leaving the crypt, the smoke slowly dissipated into the rainy atmosphere. Stevens and Walker each unloaded a clip into the vault. A silent minute passed.

Pope's voice called out, "All clear!" He walked toward the rear, checking everyone's status as he went.

Smoke and fog filled the gorge, lingering heavily in the still, wet air. I leaned against a cool rock and heard nothing around me but the drum beat of rain on my helmet and my heart thumping in my temples.

It took me a moment to come to my senses. I could hear muffled screaming. My ears hurt and weren't performing their duty well. They were ringing from the mayhem. Men ran past me, on my left, toward the front of the column. One was a corpsman. As they passed, I saw Harold's lifeless body lying in the mud behind them.

Panning left, I saw the ridge I had shot at. Then it dawned on me. *Did I just have my first kill?* It was hard to say if it was the round from my rifle that took that Jap down. Dozens of us were shooting in that direction. There was no way to tell for sure. I looked at Harold's corpse and decided I didn't care either way. If I was responsible for that damn Jap's death, so be it.

I finally got to my feet and looked for Folgers. Not seeing him, I headed toward the commotion at the front. The corpsman, Andy Michelson, was kneeling over one of our guys trying to apply a leg tourniquet. I couldn't tell who he was. A bullet had torn through the guy's upper thigh and red poured from the wound.

I was happy to see Folgers on the opposite side of the poor fella who was bleeding to death. Michelson had instructed Folgers to keep pressure on the pad that had been tied around the hemorrhaging leg. The wounded kid sat in a puddle of his own blood. He hollered for his mom. Two mutilated bodies lay within yards of him. A tangy, metallic smell and the incessant odor of mud hung in the stagnant air.

Pope yelled to Angier, who was sitting on a rock behind me loading another clip into his Carbine. "What do we have?"

"Three dead, four wounded," Angier replied.

Pope walked past and sat beside Angier. "Did we clear that goddamn tomb?"

Sgt. Angier glanced up the hill and returned his gaze to his Carbine. "Yes, sir. It's clear."

Pope pointed in the direction we were heading. "Beyond this

ridge, are the Kokuba Hills. The yellow bastards are reported to be making a stand there. We have to get out of this goddamn ravine before we lose all our guys."

"Prepare to move out, boys!" Pope yelled as he jumped to his feet.

Two sets of stretcher bearers gathered the wounded and started toward the rear. There was no time to bury the three dead Marines. Pools of crimson and brown water lapped at their elbows and boots. Even if we had time, I doubt we could dig much of a grave for them in this damn muck. The conditions made it impractical to move them to the rear.

It broke my heart to leave them. I kept looking back at their pitiful bodies covered with ponchos until the terrain obstructed my view of them. We had to get out of the ravine, or we'd be sitting ducks. We moved slowly and cautiously. All eyes were on the hillsides on both flanks. After assisting the corpsman, Folgers caught up with me. He slapped me playfully on the back of my helmet.

"I guess we're combat veterans now, huh Kentucky." He had an enthusiasm in his voice I didn't share. He was a sweet kid, that Folgers, he really was. I liked him a lot, but he may've been too dumb to be scared. He was young and didn't have a wife and kids. Me on the other hand, I was scared shitless. Pardon my French.

"Who was that guy you were working on?" I asked him softly.

"Do you remember that silly bastard who had to make a comment about every damn thing during the movies on Guam?

It was him. I think his name is Durrell or something."

"Is he okay?"

"Hell, I don't know. I'm no doc. It didn't look too good though. Lost a lot of blood."

"Spread out! Keep your distance!" Angier told us in a suppressed yell. "And shut the hell up!"

Folgers dropped back into formation. A minute later, everyone squatted and fell silent.

After a short stint of stillness, save for the rain, I craned my neck to see what all the hubbub was about, but visibility was poor. From what I could tell, we were coming up to a hill that had a number of tombs embedded in it. The NCOs (Non Commissioned Officers) were trying to make a plan.

Now, I heard some guys say this entire island was a graveyard, but I thought they were speaking of all the casualties. If that's all they meant, they wouldn't be too far off the mark. I realized then there was more to the analogy. The whole island, it seemed, was a giant cemetery. They took their burials seriously, those Okinawans. Elaborate tombs riddled the numerous hills of this damn island. Each looked like they were fit for a king.

The tomb we just cleared had what I would describe as a stone courtyard with small walls running on either side. At the end of the courtyard was a wall that rose about ten feet. Columns supported a rounded stone roof that protected a small doorway like a front porch back in America.

Tombs with the arched roof, I learned, were referred to as "turtlebacks." The entrance was smaller than a normal door. Just big enough to slide a body into, I guessed. I had yet to see the inside of one, but there was apparently enough room in there for several Japs, a heavy machine gun, and enough rounds to take out an army. What they did with the former occupant's remains, I didn't know. I didn't want to know. Those creepy, Jap bastards.

Pope signaled for Angier to move up to his position. Angier made Folgers and me come with him.

"You see those sonsofbitches?" he asked Angier while pointing at a hill beyond the ravine in front of us. "That's where we're headed. I want to get on top of this ridge so we can have a good point of observation of that damn hill."

We all made for the top of the ridge.

CHAPTER SEVENTEEN
UNDER THE SKYLINE

OUR PLATOON MOVED UP THE side of the hill on the left of the ravine while the rest went to the right. It was slow-going. Slippery as hell. Steep too. Just before the peak, we stopped. Pope, who came along with us, ordered a couple of guys to do some reconnoitering. One went over the top of the hill and the other around the front—the side facing the fortified hill forward of us.

Pope, with his cigar dangling from his mouth, pointed at the hills before us and then to the map. With Folgers and me within earshot, he explained the topography to Angier. "I believe this hill in front of us is Hill 27, and that one on the other side of it is Hill 46. These are the hills Colonel Shisler wants us to take. 27—with the radio towers on it—looks fortified and you can bet your ass 46 is too. We may need support."

The fog had lifted enough for visibility to be limited only by the rain. I looked across the gorge that separated us from Hill 27. It had a few small trees and shrubs dotted around it. The hill had patches of green grass with large boulders jutting from the side and maybe twelve tombs scattered around its face. It was small. The men of Love Company decided to call it Knob Hill. The Okinawans called it Mount Jokagu.

It was called Hill 27 because it was said to be 27 feet tall. Now, how they knew that for sure, I had no idea. It was short, but it capped off a long slope. I couldn't see how such a small hill could be a big deal. I could make out the silhouette of its ridge. My eyes followed its outline as it meandered to the right, or west, and dipped slightly, then rose again to form Hill 46.

When the recon guys got back, they informed Pope that it looked like there were tombs ten to fifteen yards below us on the opposite slope. They probably had Jap guns inside that were more than likely supporting Hill 27.

At this point, we were seated in the relative safety of mounded earth, boulders, and shaggy bushes. It was unsettling to know there were probably Japs under us.

Pope stood and put his binoculars to his eyes, the cigar in his hand was perilously close to igniting the hair poking from his helmet.

He scanned Hill 27 left to right, and back. "We're going to need support. I can make out two, maybe three Nambu machine guns. I guarantee there is support in the hills on either side of it," he said without taking his eyes from the eye piece.

Just as he lowered the binoculars, bullets strafed the mound in front of us and the air around our heads.

Pope dropped to his stomach. "Son of a bitch! Where's my goddamn cigar?"

"God damn it!" Angier yelled at his superior officer. "If you endanger yourself like that again, I'll kill you myself."

Pope didn't mind Angier's insubordination because he knew where it was coming from. They served together on Guadalcanal and knew each other well.

We dove to the deck while Pope crawled around looking for his cigar like he had lost another finger or something. We slithered like alligators to the edge of the hill and started lining up our sights.

Round after round, we unleashed a flurry of bullets toward the tombs on Hill 27. Shortly thereafter, Item Company to our right followed suit.

A most peculiar sound came from my left. A loud thump and whoosh, then a whirr. An instant later a white puff of smoke belched from the side of Knob Hill spewing debris with it. A half second later the report of the explosion reached my ears. What a sight. The M1 Bazooka.

We continued firing. I unloaded two clips at anything that moved on that hill. Whether I was actually seeing the enemy or just figments of my imagination, I didn't know. Visibility was terrible.

"Get that machine gun unit up here!" Pope yelled.

Already on their way to the front, the machine gun squad set up their Browning M1919 and started blasting away at Hill 27.

Even during all the confusion, I paused for a brief second when I realized I was on the front line. I was Headquarters Company. I was supposed to be in the rear. I crossed myself and continued shooting at those tombs.

"Get those stovepipes up here!" Pope screamed. A mortar squad a few yards away tried to set up their barrels. I rolled over onto my back to reload. As I struggled to pull another en bloc clip from my bandoleer, I could see the mortar squad to my left. Two men were having difficulty leveling the base plates in the mud, while a third guy was using his compass to determine the range and azimuth.

They stuffed rocks underneath the base to get it somewhat level. After hearing the coordinates, they lined up their sights. One held a shell over the mouth of the barrel and yelled, "Hanging!" The other yelled, "Fire!" and the shell was dropped into the barrel. A thump indicated the launch. After hearing a muffled report, they decided they were off because the bi-pod legs knifed into the mud upon firing and changed the trajectory.

I got back behind my sights and squeezed the trigger. All around me, heavy machine guns roared in bursts, Browning Automatic Rifles (BAR) and Tommy guns screamed, carbines and Garands barked. It was dissonance at its worst.

"Grenade!" someone yelled from my left. I turned to look, and the men of the mortar squad were spat from the ground in an explosion. The blast threw up a red spray, a swarm of shrapnel, and body parts. One of the guys was thrown up and to the right, his legs to the left. Thankfully, he was unaware his legs were in the mud a yard or so from his dead body.

I was appalled. The closest I'd seen to a sight that despicable was on the floor of the butcher shop in downtown Louisville. If I would have had time, I probably would have vomited.

"Move back!" Angier yelled as he grabbed my arm and pulled me. We moved away from the ridge.

"Where'd that goddamn grenade come from?" an exasperated Pope asked.

"Must be from the tomb below us," returned Angier.

Just as they spoke, three guys with Tommy guns ran in a crouch back toward the ridge of the hill. They peeked over the edge and fired off a few bursts and retreated a few steps. One belly crawled forward to see if any Japs were scaling the hill toward us.

We watched as the Marine unclipped a grenade from his belt, pulled the pin, and rolled it over the edge. He buried his face and waited for the blast. It was hard to distinguish from all the other commotion around us, but a thump and then a small cloud of white smoke lifting into view suggested it had gone off.

The grenadier inspected his work and determined another grenade was necessary. The slope was too steep to throw the grenade as it would overshoot the target, so he rolled another as if he were bowling.

As the three men contended with the Japs on the reverse slopes, Angier, who had been kneeling next to Pope, came over to me.

"We have to get some support. I need Captain Haigler." He looked me in the face. "The hand radios won't work with all these goddamn hills. You guys have to set up phone communication with battalion. We can't take this hill on our own."

His words made me tremble and I felt like I was going to puke.

"Yes, sir," I said.

He directed us where to go and wished us luck as he slapped me on the helmet. Folgers and I started off when Angier yelled, "Don't get killed, we need that communication! And hurry!" Several paces away, he hollered one more time. "Keep your asses under the goddamn skyline!"

We headed north along the ridge overlooking the valley we had just passed through that morning. The sound of gunfire and shell explosions slowly faded and gave way to distant rumblings to our right—probably the 1st Marines chasing the Japs down the center of the island.

Remembering what Angier said, we avoided running on the top of the ridge making silhouettes of ourselves from lower vantage points. In other words, we were keeping our asses under the goddamn skyline.

We were supposed to go around some damn hill, down another, and find a beat up, old highway. The post and regimental switchboard was supposed to be located in a small, burned out building, maybe an old shop.

Folgers and I moved cautiously, but swiftly. One thing they drilled into us during communications school was we were targets for both enemy and friendly fire during line work. Keep down, keep alert, keep moving. I carried my rifle in case we had any contact. It was heavy and cumbersome, but it was my security blanket.

The 1/22 had already cleared much of the area we entered, so we weren't in too much danger. As we neared our guess on the command post's location, we slowed our pace. Finally, a small building beside a road came into view a few hundred yards in front of us. It was twilight and the growing dark made it difficult to see if anyone was around. In a crouch, we slowly moved forward.

We kneeled behind a large boulder, where we steadied our rifles. Looking anxious to kill a Jap, Folgers gave me a small nod. My heart was pounding. I had to yell out to what we hoped were our guys and let them know we were coming. That meant giving away our position to anyone within earshot—good guys or bad.

I crossed myself and took a deep breath. "Scarlett!" I yelled. We waited. Nothing.

We moved twenty or thirty paces forward. Behind another rock, I tried again. "Scarlett!"

There was silence for a few seconds, then a very clear, American accent said "O'Hara!" I breathed a sigh of relief. Thank God, they were there.

We pushed our way through a swollen creek, hopped a small retaining wall, and entered the improvised field headquarters. Inside, we were greeted by a tall, barrel-chested guy with a stiff posture. He held a flashlight to his face. His dry dungarees and hair was a peculiar sight to us.

"Good evening, fellas. Lovely night for a stroll?"

Most of the post's roof remained intact, and escaping the rain for the first time in days was exhilarating. By now, it was a foreign sensation. My skin tingled as the rivulets of rain ran off my face and was not followed by more. My skin was acutely sensitive to the process of evaporation it hadn't felt in days.

The man asked us where we were from.

"Kansas, sir," Folgers's dumbass responded.

"Headquarters Company, 3rd Battalion," I said. "We're on an observation point just north of Hill 27. We're getting some pretty stiff resistance and need some support."

"I'm Lieutenant James," he said. "The switchboard is over there."

He pointed to the corner. Wires were everywhere. A hundred wires were twisted and tangled in a spider web. Beside the switchboard was what I assumed was the switchboard operator. On the dirt floor, he leaned against the wall and snored.

"I'm Folgers, and this is Old Kentucky," Folgers said.

I thumbed toward Folgers and said, "That's Leo Walden and I'm Harry Klapheke, sir. Is Colonel Shisler around, sir?"

"No, I don't know where anyone is."

We moved to the switchboard and got to work under the light of our flashlights. It was a six-line BD-71, the switchboard model often used at the battalion level. We spliced and unspooled the comm wire. Lieutenant James sat in a chair just beyond the faint halo our flashlights provided. He dug dirt from under his fingernails with a knife. He paused and shook out a couple of cigarettes from his pack.

"Smoke?" he asked.

"Yes, sir, thank you," Folgers and I said simultaneously.

Light flashed into a flame where James was seated. I continued with the switchboard while Folgers collected the two cigs James had lit for us.

"The tanks and artillery are stuck in the mud," James said. "Can't get you any tank support until tomorrow, probably. The Seabees are trying to drag them out with bulldozers right now. They're doing their damnedest to make the roads passable. They're dumping crushed coral all over this stupid island. I don't know if it's gonna work, but goddamn, they're working their asses off."

That made me think about Earl, my brother-in-law. I wondered what role he had in aiding in the transportation of supplies.

"Not having much luck right now, but I've got my fingers crossed," James continued. "Can't get any supplies right now either. Take it easy on your rations and tell your CO to signal for air drops."

"Yes, sir. Thank you, sir."

Connection made, we unspooled the wire toward the door of the building. I dreaded going back into the rain. Funny how I felt more anxiety facing the blasted rain than the thousand Japs hiding in the darkness.

Our first concern with the comm wire was the creek. Folgers, standing on the retaining wall, reached up and clipped the wire in just under the roof of the building. Helping each other keep our balance, we waded through the creek taking care to hold the spool above the gushing water. Ten yards or so beyond the creek, a serviceable, but bare, telephone pole stood.

"We need to string it up to that pole to keep it out of the water," Folgers said. "I'll keep an eye out, if you'll climb."

"My ass!" I responded. "Why don't you get your skinny butt up there?"

"I'm not good with heights. You know this from training."

There wasn't time to continue arguing. "Give me that wire, you horse's ass." I grabbed it from him and started toward the pole.

I leaned my rifle against the pole and strapped climbing spikes to my boots. With the wire draped over my shoulders, the climb was slippery and challenging. Eventually, I worked my way almost to the top. Clipping the wire in, I paused to take a look around.

For the first time since we'd been on the island, lightning flashed. It scared the hell out of me, I tell ya. I wasn't expecting it. But, the more frightening thing was when its blue-white light temporarily lit up the landscape, the shadows of dead trees and boulders resembled people. Maybe I saw our guys, maybe I saw Japs, and maybe and more likely I saw nothing but shadows. The imagination was much more fertile on a dark battle field. It was unsettling nonetheless.

I scampered back down the pole. "Keep your eyes and ears on

alert. Let's get the hell out of here."

The rest of the comm wire detail was uneventful. We laid it pretty quickly. For the most part, the landscape only provided large rocks to hide the wire behind and mud to bury it under. For once the rain made life easier. We could simply press the wire into the sludge to conceal it and move on. Every twenty or thirty yards, I checked to make sure we still had a good connection.

As we approached our unit's locale, it had grown quieter, save for, of course, the pattering of the rain and intermittent rifle fire. Flashes of lightning penetrated the clouds in the distance. There was no way to tell if the subsequent booms were heaven's thunder or man's.

Focused on the wire, I had forgotten about the signal. From a few yards in front of us, I heard a voice. From the darkness, I heard "Scarlett." Almost immediately, and automatically I puked out "O'Hara." It scared the hell out of me. First hearing an unanticipated utterance from the pitch black, but also that Folgers and I could have been mowed down by our own guys.

"Damn it, son!" The voice said. As we neared his position, he rose and became a standing silhouette. "You almost got your ass shot!" He said.

It was a guy I learned was named Stewart Beech, a.k.a. "Son of a Beech." Creative, I know. But what can you expect from teenagers?

"Thank you for not offing me. I owe you. Where's Lieutenant Pope?"

He pointed to the left where I could barely make out a grouping of large boulders. We finished stringing the line to the field phone. It was among a cluster of rocks. Pope was inside resting.

The spool was light, we barely had enough to make it to Pope. I bet we strung a mile of the assault wire. I clamped the wires to the phone unit and checked the connection again. It was good. Pope stirred. Without a hint of gratitude, he took the phone in hand and told us to dig in for the night. "Stay in your hole," he said. "But if you absolutely have to piss, make sure you use the password."

"Yes, sir."

We stopped and turned back. "Sir, what's the password tonight?"

"Lullaby."

The combination of flares and flashes from the approaching lightning storm, provided fleeting light for us to negotiate through the camp. All around us, men were hunkered in their fox holes. Some sat on rocks as if they hadn't a care in the world. As if it wasn't pouring rain and they were on a smoke break at a construction yard, they tugged on their cigarettes. At the edge of the hill, overlooking Hill 27, a string of men lay prone with their eyes peeled, looking for Jap movement in the glow of the flares.

Folgers and I found a location that was the required five yards apart from other holes and began digging our own foxhole. It was tough work. Every shovelful of mud we removed immediately refilled with rainwater. Twenty minutes later, we gave up. What was the use? If we did succeed in digging an adequate hole, we'd just be sleeping in a bathtub of mud water.

We crawled over to a boulder and leaned against it. Pulling my knees up under my chin, I tented my poncho over my legs and feet, leaned my rifle against the rock to keep the mud out of the receiver, and crossed my arms on top of my knees to serve as my pillow. Folgers sat beside me, his shoulder against my left. I didn't mind.

I then realized how exhausted and hungry I was. I didn't get any sleep to speak of last night and hadn't eaten anything but a dried fruit bar and a bite of oatmeal cereal from my K-ration at some ungodly hour this morning. Since then, I'd hiked God-only-knew how many miles, been ambushed in the forest near the estuary, fought in a skirmish in the canyon and one on the hill, strung a thousand miles of comm wire, and lost a few friends to enemy fire. You could say, I was pretty worn out and famished. Not so much though that I dare move from my position to get food. I needed to try and get some sleep.

As I sat there, I entertained the thought of feeling pity for myself. I already didn't like what the war was doing to me. I'd never been one to complain or feel sorry for myself. That night, I vowed to restrict my whining to that of my internal dialogue. No one needed to hear my griping. It didn't do anyone any good to hear it. Everyone around me knew how awful their situation was.

"Can you take first watch?" I asked Folgers.

"Yep."

CHAPTER EIGHTEEN
PROWLING SHADOWS

EVERY TIME I DOZED OFF, the crack of sniper fire, the crash of mortar explosions, or the burst of machine guns jolted me awake into an unrelenting hell of exhaustion and misery. No one in our unit was firing, but nearby companies still engaged the enemy. I prayed for them. And I prayed the fighting wouldn't start up on our ridge again until I got some sleep.

After perhaps an hour of listening to the chorus of scattered rifle fire and distant artillery, the crashes of battle gave way to a new clamor. A storm raged down on us. The lightning flashed, blinding and chaotic. The hairs on my arms rose and the metallic scent of the gale swamped my senses. The rain poured harder than ever. It was a high-pressure garden hose spraying on my head.

Like a howitzer firing inches from my ears, the thunder

blasted. I had never witnessed a storm of such magnitude in all my life. None of us had protection from Mother Nature's fury—just a helmet and a poncho. I yearned to be back in Lieutenant James's derelict field post.

The storm roared for what seemed like hours. It was so fierce that no man-made explosion or flares went off during its assault. The storm lost much of its fury in what I guessed were the small hours of the night. Folgers and I didn't even attempt to exchange words until God's offensive passed.

"Well, I guess it's your turn to keep watch," he said.

I couldn't sleep anyway, so I didn't argue. I just sat in the pouring rain in a trance. My mind had grown as numb as my soaked body. I prayed for dawn.

At some point I heard a faint "Lullaby" mixed with the pummeling rain. I thought nothing of it until it was within a few yards of us. "Lullaby!"

I heard the voice again. This time it was in my face and it was Angier yelling "Klapheke!"

I tried to shake the cobwebs from my brain.

"You have to go back out!" he yelled over the rain. He squatted next to me. "We lost communication with Battalion. Must be from the electrical storm. I hate to do it to you all, but you need to troubleshoot. Got it?"

I felt like crying, I was so tired and miserable. "Yes, sir," I mumbled. I shook Folgers awake and filled him in.

With great labor, we clumsily got to our feet. I was too tired to carry any extra weight, so I left my rifle behind. That's how drunk I was with exhaustion. I weakly yelled "Lullaby" before we started off. I called it out two more times before we were behind the lines.

He didn't say it, in fact he didn't say anything, but I could tell Folgers was feeling the same dread I was. For the second time tonight, we were potential targets. Only this time it was nearly impossible to keep alert. We were zombies.

Before we made it to the rear of the line, we ran into Captain Haigler. He asked me where my piece was and I explained that it was too heavy.

"You can't go anywhere on this damn island without a piece," he barked in a fatherly tone. "Japs are everywhere, and they're real eager to kill you."

"Yes, sir." I turned to go back for my rifle.

"Hear, take this." I heard a buckle clink and leather slap.

I turned and the Skipper was holding out his holster and pistol. It was a Colt M1911 pistol. It was a single-action, semi-automatic pistol chambered for a .45 cartridge fed by a seven round box magazine. I strapped it to my waist. It felt good having it there. Before I could thank him, he was gone.

"Lucky sonofabitch," said Folgers.

"Let's just get going."

We didn't know what to look for or how to repair a line damaged by an electrical storm, so we were told to replace the entire thing. I grabbed a new spool of assault wire. It felt like I was carrying a bulldozer.

Around ten minutes into our delightful walk through mud in

the pouring rain, Folgers noticed something. Periodically, he had been turning on the flashlight, shining it through his blouse to dim the stream of light, to make sure we were on our former path. After a quick flash, he crouched down and pointed at the ground. He didn't need to say anything. I knew what he was looking at.

I picked up the line we'd strung earlier and slid it through my palm until the severed end passed through my grasp. It was a clean cut. On our hands and knees, we tried to locate the rest of the wire. It was in a dozen pieces. It had clearly been cut by the Japs. We both froze with fear when we realized the implications of what we had discovered.

The Nips slashed our communication wire and were very likely still in the area. Instinctively, we both lay on our stomachs with our weapons drawn. I could hear the faint click of Folgers flipping the safety off. I readied the .45.

We inched close to each other. Face to face, I whispered, "What the hell do we do now?"

"Beats hell out of me," he returned.

Without further conference, we slowly rose to our knees to have a look around.

"If we can't see them, they probably can't see us," I said as I pivoted my head back and forth. "We just have to keep low. Let's get to the switchboard."

We half crawled, half slithered from boulder to boulder toward Lt. James's post. The squish of the mud was painfully loud. Not even the rain drowned it out. I prayed the Japs didn't have good hearing.

I was crawling ahead of Folgers when I felt his hand squeeze my right calf. I froze. As slow as possible, I turned to see him pointing to our right.

A shadow moved ten to fifteen yards away. My heart raced. My veins filled with ice. The dark mass darted from behind a boulder and disappeared behind another like a ghost moving behind tombstones in a graveyard. The phantom was making a deliberate effort to close distance on us. I wished like hell it was only a ghost, but we both knew it was worse.

Keeping my eyes in the direction of the specter, I slowly turned my body and lowered to my stomach. Folgers did the same. I didn't take my eyes off the prowling shadow, but I could tell Folgers's head was panning left and right looking on either flank for movement.

My grip on the .45 was like a vice. I wanted my Garand. I was a decent shot with the pistol because they taught us how to use every small arm during boot camp, but I was best with my rifle.

I heard a voice from where the Jap was positioned. My body seized.

"I see you Maline. I know you there."

Folgers and I looked at each other with horror and astonishment.

"You die, Maliney!"

We just stared into the darkness, rain pounding on our helmets. We waited for more movement. The butterflies in my stomach felt like eagles. Then it happened. Two silhouettes began running toward us. "Fuck you, Maline! You die!"

Rounds poured from my pistol before I realized what was happening. Folgers's carbine raged on my right. Each silhouette dropped in a slump. We looked around for more intruders. Our hands quivered while we both loaded another clip in our pieces. We lay there in silence for a good ten minutes before we nodded to each other and took off toward Lt. James's command post.

We attached a new line. Only this time we operated at a new level of terror. Fortunately, we didn't have any more run-ins with the Japs for the rest of the night. We made it back to our sorry excuse for a foxhole.

I collapsed in a pile and curled into a fetal position and reminded Folgers it was his turn to keep watch. I pined for Hody and the girls, imagining we were together, cuddled up in our bed in our small house on Colonial Drive. In my make-believe world, I briefly forgot about the rain, the mud, and the Japs.

CHAPTER NINETEEN
JUMP OFF

I WAS IN A FOG. I couldn't tell if I was asleep or awake. If I had been dreaming, it was of mundane things like people walking past me, Folgers kicking me in the ass, whispered conversations, my poncho slipping off my head.

The sound of airplanes penetrated the rain's relentless pelting. I wanted it to be a dream. I tried to dream. I wasn't ready to take on what promised to be a rough day. Unfortunately, the sound grew louder, forcing me to raise my head from my pillow of mud.

A strange mist floated through the gray light of dawn. A hundred yards to my left I could make out a cloud of orange smoke spewing from the ground. Again, the airplanes roared above. Looking up, I caught a glimpse of the underside of one knifing through the clouds like a barracuda through cloudy water. I couldn't tell what kind it was, but could easily determine it was one of ours. It didn't have the whine of the Jap planes.

It finally occurred to me they were dropping supplies to us. The orange smoke grenades signified our position.

"Good morning sunshine," Folgers said.

How he could have any enthusiasm in him, I didn't know. I rubbed my eyes. He was handing me a cup of coffee he had made with the Coleman gas stove he carried. He kept it clipped to his belt. He loved that stove like a child. He cleaned it and nurtured it more than his rifle. You can bet your ass he took better care of it than he would his own kid, if he ever had one.

"Good Lord, thank you." I cradled the tin cup of joe like a wounded bird. After a couple of sips, my next aim was to get a cigarette in my mouth.

We were eating some breakfast rations when Corporal Hutton, aka Hut, and that asshole, Capone came over to join us. "Rough night, Fresh Meat?" Capone said. He was juggling balls of mud.

I wasn't in the mood. I remained quiet. Folgers didn't say anything either."Too much for ya, huh princess? Can't say I'm surprised."

"Hey asshole!" Folgers piped up. "We had a pretty awful night, so why don't you back off?"

"You don't know what a rough night is, girls. If you make it much longer, you too might learn what it means to be raggedy-ass Marines. Right now you're a couple of girls who haven't had your cherries popped." He went on jawing.

"Say, weren't you fellas drafted? What kind of Marine gets drafted?" He dropped his balls of mud and got in my face as he said this.

"Hey, Capone," I said as I tried to stifle a yawn.

"Are you talking to me? What the hell you calling me Capone for?"

"What's your name?" I asked calmly.

"Billy Spencer. You can call me *The Kid*."

I held back a chuckle. "I'm gonna call you Capone. I like that better. You look like an ugly Al Capone."

"Now you wait..."

He stood like he was going to charge me or something. I didn't flinch. Not because I was overly brave, but because I was so damn exhausted. I just gave him a look that indicated it would be a grave mistake to cross me. I didn't have much to back it up, but it was enough. Hut, put his hand on Capone's chest and told him to take it easy. Capone sat down. I knew his type. A bully. That's all he was. I couldn't figure out why he picked that moment to be a bully and why he picked Folgers and me.

"You do realize we are on the same team, right?" I said. "Why are you being such a horse's ass?"

"Cut it out, you two," Hut interjected.

Capone stood and left.

Hut sat beside Folgers.

"What's his goddamn problem?" Folgers asked.

Hut was chewing the hell out of his gum. "The last two wireman that got killed on Sugar Loaf were his good buddies. I guess he's having a hard time with it and has to take it out on you two. Hell, he's been in combat for two years."

"Well, he needs to grow up," Folgers said.

I ripped open a breakfast C-ration. Canned chopped ham and eggs, something resembling a dog biscuit, and a cigarette. Already difficult to eat, the rations were even harder to swallow when suffering through intermittent waves of the tangy stench that wafted into the area. It was the bloody smell of fresh death mixed with the product of dysentery. The smoke from the cigarette was my only defense against the odor. Each bite was tainted with the smell of human blood and excrement.

"Gather around girls!" Angier yelled.

We pulled ourselves out of the mud and trudged toward a gathering of Marines seated on their helmets. Captain Haigler was standing in the middle. My leg was really stiff. I attempted to hide it from the others, but I had to walk in a half limp.

"Alright, listen up," the Skipper said. "We get the privilege of taking out the hills in front of us and securing the northern bank of the Kokuba River. That pile of shit right there," the Skipper indicated with his fingers, "that's Hill 27. We have to take that today. If recon is to be believed, there are a bunch of pillboxes and tombs on that sonofabitch.

"As of now, we have no armored support. Tanks are still stuck. But we're going without them. 1st platoon on the left, 2nd Platoon up the middle and 3rd stays back.

"King and Item Company are coming up behind us on the

left. Every man needs at least two grenades, more if possible. Fix your bayonets, cause it could get up close and personal. Jump off is 0900. Eat what you can, say your prayers and be ready. That's all."

Walking back to our boulder, I noticed five or six bodies covered with ponchos spread throughout the camp. A depression in the mud with body parts submerged in red/brown water indicated where the grenade claimed the lives of the two mortar men last night. A Jap wearing nothing but white underwear and a gag had his hands tied behind his back and was seated against a rock. A young Marine was keeping guard.

He was strange to look at. Here he was, a member of our mortal enemy. He didn't look so tough in that loin cloth. He looked kind of pathetic. Somehow, though, he was like a wild animal. He appeared skittish and could attack you any minute. His eyes were wild. Alien.

"Does anyone know what time it is?" Folgers asked as he sat down.

Hut and Capone sat down against the boulder we had cuddled up against the night before.

"Hell, I don't even know what day it is," Capone said. He acted like we never had a tiff.

"It's Wednesday, May 30, and its 0730," Hut said.

Behind us, a voice called out, "Mornin' boys!" It was Bushrod. His squad had caught up with us.

I felt the caked mud on my face separate as I smiled. It sure was good to see him. He looked better than he had yesterday. I guessed a day off the front line does you some good.

"Want a smoke?" he said as he slid in beside me. He was holding a damp pack of Lucky Strikes.

"Of course," I said.

I held my helmet so he could light the cig under its shelter from the rain. With great effort, he was able to get it lit. He handed it to me. To smoke a cigarette in this weather, you had to pinch it between you thumb and pointer finger and keep it tucked under your palm to keep it somewhat dry.

"You doing okay?" I asked him.

"Happy as a possum in a pumpkin patch to see you."

"This is Folgers and Hut." I said. "and that there is the one and only, Al Capone." Despite his annoyance, Capone seemed surprised and impressed I knew a veteran.

"Don't call me Capone, asshole!"

"What's the dope?" Bushrod asked.

"We're taking that hill." I pointed toward Hill 27.

"Bushrod? What kind of name is that?" Capone asked.

"Named after my granddad. What kind of name is Capone?

"Only these creampuffs call me that. The name's Spencer, Billy Spencer."

"I like the name Capone too," Bushrod said.

"Your granddad wasn't Bushrod Clement was he?" Hut interrupted. "The Confederate General?"

"Yeah, on my old lady's side. How the hell did you know that?"

"I'm a history nut," Hut said. He pulled out a piece of gum

and threw it in his mouth. “Particularly Civil War. History was my major at Alabama before Pearl Harbor.”

“I don’t know much about my granddad. I just knew he was a general.”

“Yeah, he was with General Lee at Appomattox.”

“You don’t say?”

Folgers for some reason took interest in Hut. “Did you finish college?”

“No, Pearl happened during my senior year. I wanted to kill some damn Japs! So, here I am.”

“What about you, Kentucky?” Folgers asked. “You’re an old man, did you go to college?”

“I did a year at St. Joseph College in Indiana,” I said. “That was ‘38. The Depression kicked my family’s ass around a bit, so I went to work.”

“Yeah? What did you do?” Folgers said.

I looked around to see if anyone opposed the telling of my history. Hut and Folgers seemed interested. Bushrod was cleaning his rifle, but appeared to be listening. Capone was drawing in the mud caked on his pant leg.

“I was what you call an I.B.M. Tabulating Machine Operator at the Mengel Company in Louisville.”

Folgers’s face held the same look of confusion a squirrel might have if you told it how the combustion engine worked. “You were what, now? What the hell’s a tab-ur-nating machine operator?”

“The tabulating machines were what you might call a super

computer. For accounting. I made repairs and adjustments on equipment. I even did some wiring on them. If you can believe that."

"Wiring?" Folgers said. "You don't say."

I took the opportunity to let these kids know I was a grown up. They might be able to bark orders at me now, but as a civilian, I could throw my own weight around and be a boss too.

"I actually supervised ten operators," I said. "I set up pay roll, did some sales analysis, and some accounting."

"Clean your rifles and tighten your laces." Angier jerked his head at us.

We did as he said, and then moved off the ridge into the ravine, starting toward the west side of Knob Hill. As we came upon a few houses that were miraculously standing, shots seemed to come from nowhere. Japs popped out of spider holes covered with brush, shot off a few rounds and disappeared again. One of our few remaining mobile flamethrower tanks came from behind and burned the entire village down.

It was a hell of a sight, seeing those houses go up in flames like that. I felt the heat of it a hundred yards away. The crackle of the fire was nearly as loud as the people inside screaming. The atrocity made my chest tighten. I had to turn away.

Leaving the tank behind, we crossed a canal that cut through Naha connecting the Kokuba and Asato Rivers. The temporary bridge was one of those planked jobs. Narrow and rickety. We had to cross in single file, leaving the tank behind.

We hunkered down in a defilade just before Hill 27 and waited with heavy anxiety. As 9:00 approached I asked the three veterans what to expect. They all concurred that we should expect hell.

"Those bastards are ruthless and sneaky," Hut said. "No prisoners, you hear? They'll be hiding a grenade in their ass or something and blow you to smithereens."

Those around me were dealing with the dread of the upcoming battle in their individual ways. One fella flipped his wedding band through his fingers. Another repeatedly made the sign of the cross. A guy to my right was sharpening his Ka-bar knife. Folgers obsessively messed with the sights on his M1, unable to find satisfaction in them. I ran my sister's rosary between my thumb and pointer finger repeating Hail Marys. I have never been more anxious about anything in all my life. I felt like a death row inmate waiting for execution. I think all of us replacements felt that way.

9:00 came and went. Angier came over and kneeled down. "Jump off has been moved to 10:00."

"I'm not complaining, sir, but why the delay?" Folgers asked.

"They're using the prisoner and one of our interpreters to offer the Nips a chance to surrender."

"You think that will actually work, sir?" I asked.

"Not a chance in hell."

Shortly thereafter, loudspeakers broadcasted surrender inducements across the ravine. We all waited. Silence. Did anyone really expect the Japs to give up? One thing I did know about the Japanese was they never surrendered. Surrender was dishonorable in their culture. Those crazy bastards would rather die than give up.

Suddenly there was a scream in the air above us.

“Incoming!” Someone yelled.

Shells began exploding all around us.

“Get down!”

We scrambled for the nearest boulder or hole. Nearby blasts knocked us off balance as we ran. I didn’t know who was with me, but I made it into a depression with two other guys. I balled up in a fetal position. My face partially in mud water, I pressed my helmet to my head as if it would fly off if I didn’t. I nearly wet myself. My heart pounded. I could hardly breathe. Mortar shells blasted around us. Nambu machine gun and Arisaka rifle rounds pelted the surrounding landscape.

“I guess that means they don’t want to surrender!”

It was Bushrod yelling into my ear as if the whole thing was a game. Minutes—that felt like hours—later, the barrage ended. We slowly emerged from our holes to assess the situation.

Smoke lingered in the saturated air. Silhouettes crawled from the earth and crept around looking for wounded. Angier came to our hole to check on us. We reported we were okay. “Stay here,” he said as he jogged off toward the direction of Lt. Pope.

I didn’t have a problem with staying put. I tried to catch my breath and collect myself. Then it occurred to me: where’s Folgers? As if he read my mind, I heard his voice from a few yards away. “Kentucky, you all right?”

“Yeah, I’m alright, you?”

"Sure."

A couple of minutes later Angier came back and told me and Folgers the comm wire must have been hit because there was no signal. Of course. I crawled out and started toward Angier. Folgers caught up with me and we followed Angier back to the field phone where he told us we had better hurry.

The wire was mangled, but fortunately it was only about a hundred feet from the phone. We repaired it and Folgers checked the connection. With the phone operational, the Skipper yanked the receiver from Folgers and started barking coordinates into the mouthpiece.

A minute later numerous rounds screamed overhead from behind. From our right, a storm of shells launched by the Navy roared through the fog like freight trains. It was quite a spectacle. Hill 27 was suddenly consumed with explosions. Even from our distance, each concussion felt like a punch in the chest. I couldn't imagine what it must have been like for the Japs. I hoped I never would.

I was in awe of the U.S. Military's immense power. It took no more than a simple phone call for a well-placed, long distance barrage of heavy artillery to pound the enemy. And Folgers and I had a part in it.

Our heavy artillery put on a show for fifteen minutes. At 10:10, we were told we were moving out. I took a deep breath.

CHAPTER TWENTY
HILL 27

OUR 60MM MORTAR SQUAD LAUNCHED several phosphorous rounds into the ravine ahead of us. Smoke grenades followed. Coupled with the lingering smoke from the artillery explosions, the entire valley was covered with a dense blanket of protective cover.

We moved from our position and across the basin that separated us from Knob Hill. Going south, we doglegged back hitting Knob Hill from the west. Splitting up, my platoon headed north around the hill while 1st Platoon went south. We cautiously advanced under the shroud of smoke. Angier had told us not to worry about stringing wire until dark.

About twenty yards to my left, someone screamed. Two shots rang out. Then about six more. A Jap, hiding in a spider hole on the south-facing side of the hill, had waited until our guys passed to shoot them in the back. Two Marines were hit. One killed and the other shot in the arm. I didn't know either one of them.

The two closest Marines retaliated with several rounds from their M1s and killed the bastard. Another guy threw a grenade into the hole sealing it off for good. With the casualties tended to, we continued across the valley toward the south of Hill 27. In the ravine, we were sitting ducks. Our only cover was the fading smoke, so we picked up the pace and ran in a crouch. No one fired a shot. To do so would slow the pace and give away our position.

As we reached the base of 27, bullets zipped past my ears. Mortar shells burst nearby. Men ahead of me were already moving up the hill, darting from the cover of a boulder to another. I did my best to follow. With my back to a sharp, volcanic rock, I saw Folgers nearby on my right. His face was a picture of terror. I'm sure mine was no better.

All of Love Company started shooting back. I was afraid to fire my weapon as I couldn't tell who was in front of me—my guys or Japs. I decided to keep pressing forward. The mud continued its torment. I slipped at least a hundred times. On one occasion, I nearly gave myself a lobotomy with my own bayonet. Just barely missed. For several minutes, I felt alone. I was like a kid who lost sight of his mother in a crowd.

The chaos was overpowering. With every explosion, I felt like my head was splitting open. Each bark of a rifle was like someone boxing my ears. Rocks and metal chards smacked into me, thudding against my dungarees and pinging on my helmet.

The smoke made it difficult to breathe. I was suffocating. I couldn't see or hear anyone. I could only feel the presence of the other guys. My lungs tightened. Somehow, I knew they were nearby.

I continued up the hill, firing a few rounds as I went. The smoke began to clear and I could make out more men of my platoon. I had caught up with a half dozen of them. Our advancement stalled because the smoke had become a hindrance to our progress. The Japs were well hidden in their pillboxes and tombs. Even in broad daylight, their little hideaways were hard to see. Someone could walk right up on one without realizing it was there.

Rifles became nearly useless. Getting a shot at the Japs was almost impossible. They would pop out, rain machine gun rounds on us, and pull back in. For hours, we engaged in a sort of grenade-tag. The Japs would toss one out so it would roll down to our position and explode. We were so close I could hear the Japs arming their grenades by hitting them on their helmet before throwing them. The tapping of grenade to helmet was unmistakable.

We all took turns lobbing our grenades back at them. If the toss wasn't just right, the grenade could roll back down on us. In most cases though, they'd stick in the mud or get lodged behind a tree stump or rock. We got lucky. After scoring a direct grenade hit in a pillbox, a flamethrower operator raced forward and sent a stream of fiery death into the opening.

Several times, I had a front row view of the spectacle. It was impressive and horrifying. Around mid-morning, Joe Tomlinson, our flamethrower operator opened up on a Jap hideaway near me. Perhaps thirty feet to my right, he had his forward knee on the ground and his back leg was stiff and braced for balance on the hill below. He held it at his hip. He pulled the trigger and unleashed a serpent of flames toward the hideout above.

The M2 flamethrower used a mixture of thickened gasoline, or napalm, and nitrogen propellant. Its effective range was about sixty-five feet, but could spray as far as a hundred thirty-two feet. It could shoot jellied flames for seven seconds.

Joe used all seven seconds on the pillbox near me. The weapon had its own distinct sound. It was half roar and half hiss. Almost like the sound when you blow on a hot fire with your mouth—only much, much louder and more sinister. Nothing like it.

I could feel the flamethrower's heat. The air around me thinned as the fire consumed oxygen like a vacuum. The smell of gasoline gave way to the smell of burning flesh. It was a god-awful stench. Like burnt pork. A scent that I'll never forget. Japs ran out from their nests screaming in flaming agony. Our guys often refused to shoot them so the Nips could suffer.

We continued with the grenade-throwing duels for the rest of the morning and much of the afternoon. Around noon, I caught up with Folgers. He was helping Lt. Pope light his cigar. Pope told us to replace the stretcher bearers. He pointed downhill and said they were hit and we needed to get those "damn litters" and start moving men down the hill to safety.

We scooted on our asses, then crawled to the stretchers. The former stretcher bearers were lying on either side of it. One looked as if an alligator took a bite out of his neck and the other might've had a round in the back. I couldn't tell what had happened to him.

There was still a Marine on the stretcher. His chest heaved. He was alive—barely—but alive. With the help of two other passing Marines, we grabbed the stretcher and slipped and slid our way downhill. When we found a corpsman, we carefully dropped the wounded guy off with him, then made our way back up hill. Hunting screams, we moved toward the sound of men hollering out in pain or crying "Tallulah!" as in Tallulah Bankhead, the actress.

The Japanese learned early on that if they yelled "corpsman," they could draw out one of our most valuable guys and gun them down. They even waited for a corpsman to aid one of our wounded and would pick him off. The more corpsman we lost, the more wounded we'd lose.

Marine corpsman had to be careful about responding to the call. To be safe, we decided on "Tallulah" instead of "corpsman" or "medic" (like the Army). The Japs had a hell of a time saying all those Ls.

For at least two hours Folgers, two other riflemen, and I served as stretcher bearers. We moved at least a dozen men. I thought stringing wire made you feel vulnerable, but carrying a wounded man during a firefight was like being a fish in a barrel with a shotgun pointed at me. Moving a cumbersome stretcher in mud was slow and awkward. If I was a Jap, I'd have shot us a hundred times. One time a rifle bullet found its way into the body of a wounded Marine we were moving. He died right there, in our grip.

We contributed to the fighting when we weren't carrying wounded. Love Company was making little progress. The hill was riddled with fortified tombs and pillboxes. Many more than the Skipper had guessed.

In the late afternoon, the thumps of explosions changed pitch. Blasts seemed to slam into the ground with more force. Looking back, I was relieved to see tanks churning through the mud toward our position. The armored division had finally arrived. Sherman tanks unloaded rounds on the hill above us. Nervous about the tank rounds, Folgers and I slid back down the slope a few yards.

"It's about damn time!" I heard a guy near me say.

Another fella I didn't know said, "Of course! They get here when we're almost done!"

I didn't care they were late, I was just glad they were there.

I'm not sure how I noticed, but between blasts and rifle fire, I felt and heard a more powerful concussion. It had a different kick to it than the rest. It was nearby. It felt and sounded like a B-29 dropped a bomb on us.

The whole island seemed to quiver constantly, but I swear I could feel a separate rumble from this blast. I glanced to my left and saw what looked like a volcano erupting.

What appeared to be the entire east side of Knob Hill was spewing smoke and debris. Boulders the size of a Volkswagen were flying into the air and tumbling downhill. I dismissed the blast as part of the bedlam of battle.

To my right, another large explosion lit the sky. A Jap artillery round hit the ground next to Captain Haigler's position. Mud and a mist of human pulp spewed from the ground. When the smoke dissipated, I was relieved to see the Skipper stand up. The blast killed three men at one time. One man I didn't know, but the other two were Private Frank A. Blackwell and Sergeant Donald A. Booth.

It was late afternoon before we secured Hill 27. As the calamity abated, we had to move more men and search for pillboxes we missed. Every once in a while, I'd hear gun fire from someone who'd found another occupied hole. Folgers and I stumbled across a tomb as a Marine from Item Company was crawling out.

"Hey, you guys. You should see this shit." He waved us toward the entrance.

Folgers and I looked at each other incredulously and gave each other a "what the hell, why not" look. We got on all fours and followed him in. As soon as we were inside, I regretted going. The smell was oppressive. Burnt pork and hair. Getting out of the rain was almost enough to persuade me to stay inside, but I saw from this guy's flashlight beam that the tomb opened into a passage in the back.

As we headed into the tunnel, I tried to convince myself I was just crawling through barbecue pork ribs and chicken thighs. We followed the rabbit down its hole like Alice in Wonderland where the tunnel grew tall enough to stand. Several paces in, the tunnel met other passages that ran to the center of the hill. It was a maze.

"It's like a goddamn hive in here," the rabbit said.

He wasn't wrong. From what I could see, all of the pillboxes and tombs were connected by manmade passages. I'd heard the brass say the hills were honeycombed with secret passages on Okinawa, and now I understood what they meant.

"There could still be Japs in here," Folgers whispered.

"Yeah, let's get the hell out."

We stepped aside to let the guy with the flashlight turn around and go ahead toward the exit.

As a youngster, when I would turn off the lights in my parents' basement and head up the stairs, no matter how hard I tried, I couldn't walk all the way up those damn steps. Like a monster or murderous madman was chasing me, I'd always end up running the top half and burst through the door into the kitchen. I'd say leaving that dark Japanese tunnel was similar to that feeling, but I'd be underestimating it by about a million.

As soon as we were clear, the rabbit yelled "Fire in the hole!" and tossed a grenade into the passage. When we emerged, Lt. Pope saw us and told us to move the dead behind the lines.

The three of us got to work. It was terrible, I tell ya. Carrying young men who were brutally murdered only a few minutes before was tough to swallow. The expressions frozen on their faces made it even worse. Some looked terrified and some utterly sad.

I choked up thinking how these young guys would never get married or have kids. Their parents would get a letter from the government telling them their baby was dead. A thought of my girls flickered through my mind. I looked to the dark clouds and prayed they would never get that news.

We were heading back to find our unit when a guy asked us for some help. He led us a hundred yards or so to the east side of Hill 27, where a huge crater penetrated deep into the rise. Debris and boulders littered the ground. White fragments of stone led me to believe it had been a tomb.

"One of our guys threw a grenade in there without knowing it was a cache of Jap ordnance," he said. "Must have been a ton of explosives. Twenty-five casualties in Charlie Company."

I'd figured this was the anomalous explosion I'd heard earlier. Turns out the only man who died was the one who threw the grenade, one of our guys from Love Company. Herman Walter Mulligan from Greenville, South Carolina. He was about a month away from turning twenty-two. When the Jap arsenal detonated, a large rock broke free and crushed the poor guy.

We helped move the wounded down the hill to an aid station. Some of the men from 1st Platoon that were near the blast were still being treated. Shock was etched in their faces.

We sat down to catch our breath. Another replacement, Ed Hoffman, sat beside us. He'd landed on this damn island with us. He was a tough kid. And I mean *kid*. He wouldn't even turn eighteen until September. He'd enlisted in the Marine Corps when he was just sixteen. Crazy son of a gun had more balls than me, that's for sure.

Just across from us, two Marines engaged in an intense back-and-forth. Seated beside each other on a log, one pressed his bandaged forehead into his arms he had crossed on his knees. The other man wasn't arguing, but was trying to convince the enraged Marine of something. He attempted to console him by rubbing his upper back.

But we were in the middle of a war. Everyone was upset. Guys were cracking up all around us. I didn't pay these guys much attention until the grieving Marine shouted, "It doesn't matter! I should have known to check first!" he stood and stormed off.

Ed Hoffman noticed my staring and spoke up. "He and Herman were real good buddies. He thinks it's his fault."

I handed him a cigarette.

He pinched it between his fingers. "Thanks. He's the squad leader. Might have told Herman to throw the grenade. If it's anyone's fault, it's battalion's."

"How's that?"

"Disorganized. Shisler claims we were told to check the tombs for ammo before throwing explosives in. I don't know if he ever heard that directive or not. I didn't. FUBAR."

Ed told me the man walking away was Sgt. Steve Maharidge,

a twenty-year-old from Cleveland, Ohio. In his short life, he'd already endured a lot of hardship. He faced the onslaught of multiple Banzai attacks on Guam. During the attack, the ground was too hard to dig in, so he took cover behind stacks of dead bodies. For most of the night, he and Love Company ferociously fought hand-to-hand with the charging fanatics.

An artillery round exploded beside him and he nearly lost his life. It littered his back with fragments. There was no way to evacuate the wounded that night. Steve nearly bled to death from his wounds as he lay in a hole until dawn.

After recovering, he returned to Love Company, landed here on Okinawa on April 1st, and fought for his life on Sugar Loaf Hill. Now, on Hill 27, he suffered head trauma from the blast that killed Herman Mulligan, and he'd lost his best friend.

Angier found us and told us to get off our asses. "We're moving!"

Colonel Shisler ordered Haigler to take the valley between Knob Hill and Hill 46 before dark. When we caught up with everyone else, they were sitting around waiting.

"What's the dope?" Folgers said.

"There's a hold up," Hut said." Apparently the machine gun section refuses to go into the valley."

"Why?"

Hut shrugged his shoulders.

Another private overheard the questions. He'd taken his helmet off and was looking toward the sky as rain rinsed mud from his face. He wiped his eyes and plunked his helmet back on.

"Couple of guys from the machine gun unit are stuck in the gorge about a hundred yards up. Apparently they're wounded and pinned in by a Jap machine gun nest."

"And..." Folgers said.

The Private scraped mud off his trousers with his Ka-bar. "The rest of the unit refuses to go up there. Skipper's pissed."

We used our helmets as chairs and waited. I was almost finished with a cigarette when Sgt. Angier filled us in on what had transpired. He said Captain Haigler had a conniption fit when his men rejected his orders. After cussing everyone out, he ran into the valley alone to get the two men out, but learned real quick what they were so afraid of. The Japs opened up on him. A bullet passed through his shirt, but by some miracle it didn't hit flesh. Realizing the folly in an officer exposing himself like that, he hauled ass back to us.

Raging to the rear, he found Colonel Shisler and told him they weren't going up the valley without support. Shisler said there was no support available, and they had to do it anyway. Haigler again refused, saying that without flank protection or tanks, the mission would be suicide.

The Skipper wasn't about to give in. He knew Shisler was one to make rash decisions. Decisions that got his men killed. Love Company's former captain, John P. Lanigan, had warned Skipper of Shisler's suicidal orders on Guam's Orote Peninsula.

He said the colonel ordered Love Company down a road thought to be guarded by Japanese. Love Company's captain at the time, Harry D. Hedrick, suspected it was a suicide mission and wanted tank support. Shisler refused.

Captain Hedrick was forced to continue the march. When he reached Road Junction 15, a Nambu machine gun caught him in the head. That was the same night Steve Maharidge was wounded and many Marines were killed.

Now, with this knowledge about Shisler, Captain Haigler stood his ground. He wasn't about to expose his men. Scuttlebutt had it that there was quite the squabble between them. We didn't know exactly what went on, but Colonel Shisler eventually capitulated. He agreed to blow the hell out of the valley early the next morning with an artillery barrage. He said he'd somehow get tanks in there too.

Since we had to hold our position, Angier told Folgers and me to string wire to the west side of Hill 27. We climbed back up to our camp from the night before, found our gear and got to work. It was an uneventful trip, thank God. The only noteworthy moment was when we passed the armored division still stuck in the ravine north of Hill 27.

The night was chilly, and of course, we were saturated.

"At least these tanks are good for something," I said to Hut as we warmed our hands in the exhaust of an idling M4 Sherman Tank. "Let's check this thing out."

I climbed onto the tread, yelled out the password, and then knocked on the driver's hatch. I hadn't been in a tank before and didn't want to pass up the chance. The hatch opened a few inches. The driver peered through the opening and greeted me.

"Evening. Can I help you?"

"Can I check this thing out?" I said.

"Not like we've got a lot to do right now."

He climbed out of the driver seat, over what looked like the drive shaft, and squeezed his way toward the back.

I turned to Folgers, who was skittishly surveying the landscape. "Stay outside and keep an eye out for Angier."

"Wait, what the hell?" He started climbing up to join me.

I squeezed myself into the tank. "Claustrophobic, aren't you? It's tight as hell in here." I ducked my head inside.

Before I closed the hatch, he sat on the roof and leaned against the turret, patting his pockets, hunting cigarettes.

The tank's driver moved to the gunner's seat as I closed the hatch. I took his spot and breathed in the warm, dry air. The idling engine made the whole metal beast vibrate, and it smelled of grease, fuel, and body odor. A young guy with a deep scar on his face sat in the assistant driver's seat. The mark on his lower cheek was a swath of bare, pink skin, accentuated by his dark stubble. A third guy was asleep in the turret seat.

"I'm Elmlinger," the driver said. He pointed at the kid with the scar. "That's Adams."

They both had a cup of coffee and offered me some, but I told them I couldn't stay long.

It was cramped. Knobs here, levers there, a bank of gauges to my left. Wires were all over the place. 75mm shells stood on end in rows on either side of the compartment and stacked on ammunition racks. It was uncomfortably confining, but a thousand times cozier than my more recent lodgings.

With his pointer finger, Elmlinger gave me a full tour of their metal sanctuary. Adams asked me if I wanted to drive it. "Won't go anywhere, but you can give it a whirl."

Hell yeah, I thought. He showed me how all the contraptions worked. I fooled with the pedals and the steering levers. The roar of the engine was deafening inside that metal box. I felt the huge gears at my feet turning in vain. We were stuck.

I eventually got it to move forward about six inches, then back. Elmlinger showed me how to swivel the turret. I switched places with him and grabbed a hold of the hand crank. I turned it tentatively at first, but Elmlinger told me to "give it hell." So, I gave it hell. I cranked that sonofabitch like nobody's business, purposefully turning it to the left hoping I'd knock Folgers around.

"Watch it, damn it!" he shouted.

Got him.

"You can shoot it tomorrow if you want," Adams said. "I'll take the day off."

"I'll leave that up to you guys. You think you'll get moving anytime soon?" I opened the hatch and climbed out.

Elmlinger took the handle. "We're hoping the engineers can get us out of here." He dropped out of sight inside. The latch clinked.

Jumping off the tank, my feet speared into the mud. It was up to my knees, over my boondockers. I tugged on my right leg—nothing. Tugged on my left—didn't budge. I was stuck like a hair in a biscuit.

Folgers laughed. "Serves you right, asshole."

"Hell, you're no worse for wear. Now help me get out of this goddamn glue."

After we liberated my feet from the vice-like grip of Okinawan sludge, we got on our way. We finished stringing the lines, doing our best to hang them on poles or in what was left of the trees. If the tanks did get moving again, their treads would cut the lines if we didn't get them off the ground.

Back on the west side of Hill 27, Pope told us to dig in. We found the rest of our squad near the apex on the opposite side from the next hill—Hill 46. Capone and Angier were sharing a hole our artillery had made. Hut and Bushrod sheltered in another shell crater nearby, and Folgers found one for us a few yards away. We sure had shelled the daylights out of this hill.

We dug a trench on the downhill side of our crater to allow the rain to drain so we wouldn't wake up with water up to our chin. Damn Okinawa rain.

Capone hollered out the password so he could go relieve himself and returned a few minutes later to report a tomb was a few yards behind us.

"You all wait here and cover me." Angier took his Colt .45 from his holster and made his way to the tomb.

"Don't get killed," Capone said. "You owe me five bucks."

We just looked at each other and pointed our M1s in Angier's direction.

After three or four minutes he came back. "Creepy as hell, but nothing in there but a couple of dead Japs. There's no tunnel in back so there's no need to worry about more of those assholes reoccupying it. Take turns watching just in case."

I told Folgers I'd guard first if he wanted to sleep. He slept for an hour, then gave me a chance. By some miracle, I dozed off for what felt like a few minutes before I was introduced to the worst way a man could ever be roused from a much needed sleep. Four or five massive explosions hit the hill nearby. All six of us thought the same thing. Without conference, we darted into the tomb.

The interior was the size of a small bedroom with a low ceiling. Three of us sat against the wall opposite the other three, the sharp smell burning our nose and crushing our lungs. Our options were to stay inside with what appeared to be two scorched Jap corpses or face the artillery barrage. It was a tough decision.

The explosions stopped after only a minute or two. I was told the Japs operated that way. It was just a harassment shelling, mostly to keep us awake. If they weren't shelling, they'd pop off sporadic rifle fire, or yell things—anything to keep us on edge and push us toward going Asiatic. They knew if they kept us awake for extended periods, we would get slow and sloppy. Those bastards.

We waited a minute before Angier told us we could go back out, but even then we didn't venture far. We were afraid another barrage would hit soon. It was nice to escape the gruesome vault. The stench and the feeling of lingering spirits had been hard to ignore. I sucked in some fresh air, ignoring the bitter rain's taste on my tongue.

Capone was last to come out. He'd stayed behind to carve gold teeth and fillings from the dead Japs. I found this to be a disgusting act, though a lot of Marines did it. They considered it the spoils of war.

No one said anything for a while. We sat in silence against the low walls surrounding what I'd describe as a patio. I was nearest to the opening, and boy I tell ya, I felt like a ghost Jap would grab me any moment.

Believe it or not, the rain slowed a little. It didn't stop. It only took a break. Angier and Capone had struck up a conversation, their silhouettes shoulder-to-shoulder across from me. I heard "Corregidor" and something about Dugout Doug. Capone was apparently bent out of shape about General McArthur.

"He just left those sons-of-bitches," he said. "And did you see how they staged that picture of him strutting out of the ocean onto the beach at Leyte? Oh, and let's not forget the radio announcement he made saying, 'People of the Philippines, I have returned,' like he was Jesus himself."

"I don't disagree with you, Capone," Angier said (Angier started calling him Capone too. This killed Capone). "But he did have orders to leave his men in the Philippines. Roosevelt himself commanded him to leave."

Angier knew better than to push it. Hut told me later that Capone's older brother had been a victim of the Bataan Death March where the Japs forced something like eighty thousand

American and Philippine POWs to march over sixty miles. They were tortured every step of the way. Thousands were brutally killed.

The Japs didn't see us as humans. As far as I was concerned, they weren't either. I couldn't imagine how Capone must have felt. He lost his brother in one of the most awful ways. He lost his two best friends and he'd been fighting the Japs for I didn't know how long. I couldn't see him too well through the darkness, but I thought he was on the verge of breaking down. His slouched posture showed defeat. He continually shook his head like he was telling some evil force "no, leave me alone."

A sniper's rifle cracked from the east.

"You have to hand it to him." Angier said. "McArthur was a damn good battlefield General in WWI."

"He's a goddamn pansy now," Capone said. "Why the hell else is he called Dugout Doug? Because he's a chicken shit, that's why."

"His father had a big set of balls," Hut interrupted.

Angier and Capone stopped and just stared across at Hut who was sitting beside me. Breaking the few seconds of awkwardness, Capone said, "Hut, now what the hell are you talking about?"

I don't think it was his intention, but Hut released a little of the tension.

"Go on, dipshit," Capone barked.

He unwrapped a fresh piece of gum. "McArthur's dad, Arthur..."

"Wait," Capone interrupted. "Are you telling me his dad's name is Arthur McArthur? Good Lord, I've heard it all."

"Yes, and what's better is he was Arthur McArthur Jr., so *his* dad had the same damn name."

"At least Jr. had the sense not to burden his son with that bullshit."

"Anyway, General McArthur's dad, *Arthur*, earned the Medal of Honor in the Civil War."

"Yeah, well that doesn't change the fact that his son was a piece of shit," Capone retorted. The topic was dropped momentarily.

I should have let the conversation remain dead, but I was too proud of my little brother. "My brother Charlie was there when they liberated the Philippines."

"Good for him," Capone said as he kicked a rock with the heel of his boot. The rock slid across the smooth stone like a hockey puck and hit the wall to my right.

Everyone was quiet for a few minutes. "My brother was in France," Hut said. "Talk about a different war."

"No, shit." Capone said. "The boys in Europe didn't have jungle rot, malaria, monsoons, mud, and fanatical Jap bastards to deal with."

"They did have frost bite and a lot of marching." I said.

Angier chimed in. "I'd take that over this shit."

"My brother said he lost his little toe from frostbite," Hut said. "Hell, he wrote that some guys would wake up with half their legs stuck in a block of ice."

"Shit, I only have two toenails left," said Capone. "All but the ones on my big toes rotted off. Do I get a Purple Heart for that?"

Angier snapped a small root he had been swatting the air with. "I tell you one thing, I'd trade the Pacific for France any day. They didn't have as much guerrilla fighting as we do. They shot each other from a distance, and usually with tanks and artillery. They didn't wake up with a maniacal Jap in their foxhole. Or deal with crazy, fucking banzai charges.

"The Normandy invasion was important and all, but you don't hear a lot about the dozens of amphibious landings we've done. Hell, our landing on Okinawa was bigger than Normandy. And we had to do it across a big-ass ocean. They just jumped across the English Channel. Statistically, we lost more men on the Saipan and on the Iwo Jima landings then they did at Normandy."

"Captain Haigler landed on Normandy," I reminded him.

"I didn't say it wasn't a hellish battle. He told me all about it. Said it was a goddamn nightmare. He also said he'd seen worse here in the Pacific."

A short burst of machine gun fire echoed through the valley.

"In a letter from my brother," said Hut, "he told me his unit got furloughs in Paris. They got to take shelter in churches and shit. He said they even stayed some nights at French farmhouses. He claims he made it with a French girl. You know how many girls I've seen here in the Pacific? Two. Two nurses on Pavuvu. And they weren't much to look at."

"Hell, Hut, I bet you've never even given a girl the time," said

Capone. "You wouldn't know what to do with a girl if you did find one over here."

We all let out a little chuckle. Hut didn't say anything in return. A star flare arched overhead lighting the landscape with a creepy glow.

"The Krauts are ruthless bastards, that's for sure," said Angier, "but I heard they sometimes help wounded Allies. Our guys did too. Imagine that. Treating each other like they were human, how novel."

"Himmler's SS troopers killed POWs and Allied soldiers trying to surrender," I heard myself contribute. "They murdered Jews, gypsies, and cripples. You can put them in the same brutal-assholes category as the Japs."

"You ain't seen nothing yet, Kentucky," Capone said.

"Jap assholes wouldn't piss on their own mother if she was on fire," Angier said as he stood to stretch his back.

"I'd give my left arm to have a warm farmhouse to stay in right now." Folgers said.

"Hell, I'd take a barn and a pile of hay."

"Well, we've got mud and charred Jap corpses we can cuddle up with," I said. "And a five-star tomb to do it in." I was surprised I could joke about something so horrible, but humor, no matter how dark, was an important part of keeping your sanity during war—gallows humor, if you will. Everyone chuckled a little bit. I don't think Bushrod did. I don't think he said anything all night.

CHAPTER TWENTY-ONE
BOMBARDMENT

A FLARE FLOATED ABOVE ON its parachute. We quietly watched it burn out. Shortly thereafter, all hell broke loose.

"Incoming!"

The hill became a bedlam of concussions. Artillery shells like freight trains roared toward the ground. We darted into the tomb.

We curled up and buried our faces between our knees and covered our ears. Each blast bounced us around like dice in a cup. The pressure in the tomb changed with every explosion, squeezing the air from our lungs, rattling our teeth. I felt like a heavyweight boxer was punching me in the head over and over. A large urn with Okinawan remains fell from shelves above our heads, bounced off my shoulder and exploded into a cloud of dust at my feet.

It was like the acute confusion and terror you feel when two cars collide. All at once, glass breaks, metal crunches, passengers scream, and bones crack. Things fly at you, while you fly at things.

The bombardment we endured in that tomb felt like being trapped in a repetitive car wreck for hours on end. I screamed and cried and hugged my M1 like a Teddy bear. Hail Marys and The Lord's Prayer flowed from my mouth over and over. Folgers was practically on top of me. We pressed harder and harder into the back wall of the tomb. Hut cried out for his mom.

Between blasts, I scooped up some mud (I hoped it was mud) and crammed it in my ears like earplugs. The cacophony was too much to take. I pressed my hands over my ears and tried to tighten my fetal position.

Shells hit closer and closer. One slammed into the ground in front of the tomb a few yards out. It blew rocks, shell fragments, and mud into our den. Debris shot in at us. Projectiles of all sizes smacked against my legs and butt.

The intensity of the barrage faded for a few minutes, then started up again.

The process continued half the night.

When it was finally over, it became eerily quiet. No explosions and, God help me, no rain. The silence was only broken periodically by someone yelling "Tallulah" or the crack of a sniper rifle.

My body refused to move. For a good part of the night, the

surge of fear and adrenaline tensed every fiber in my body almost to the point of breaking. My whole body was sore.

I said a prayer thanking God for sparing me, for keeping me safe. My thoughts turned to those of Hody and the girls safely snuggled up in a bed thousands of miles from this hell. I fell asleep. It might be more accurate to say I passed out.

The faint light of dawn crept into our chamber. I sat up. My head throbbed like I was hung over from a raging bender. Every muscle cramped. My leg—the one broken by the car—was especially stiff and painful. The rustling of my movement and a nearby sound of sobbing sounded muffled to my ears. As my eyes adjusted, I saw Folgers curled up beside me asleep. A dry river of blood ran from his ear across his cheek and under his chin. It reminded me to dig the mud from my ear canals.

Hut was chewing gum in his sleep. Bushrod cried uncontrollably as he hugged his knees. As the others stirred, we looked everyone over to make sure all our parts were still intact.

"I need a new pair of skivvies," Folgers said when he sat up.

Bushrod continued sobbing. We tried talking to him, but we couldn't get him to stop. It was disheartening to see such a tough guy cry like a baby. He'd obviously been pushed beyond the limits of human endurance and cracked. He'd succumbed to Combat Fatigue and would become a statistic on some government record as a "non-battle casualty." Non-battle casualty, my ass. How else do you acquire his condition from anything other than the bullshit of combat?

Angier and I half dragged him outside and helped him to his feet. We walked him over and sat him down on a large chunk of the tomb's facade that had been ripped free during the salvo. He was inconsolable. The rest of the guys joined us outside. They looked as dazed as I did.

Standing beside Bushrod, cradling his head against my thigh, I surveyed the area. A fetid fog was slowly burning off to reveal a battered landscape. Craters, corpses, and twisted metal littered the hillside. Columns of smoke rose through the sluggish air. Charred stumps of trees looked like black stubble on a giant, muddy chin. The ground had shaken so violently that intact trees had fallen over.

Lt. Pope and a couple of riflemen climbed over to our positions. In a professional tone he inquired about our status. Angier told him we were alright, but Bushrod needed to be moved to the rear for some R&R. Pope ordered the two privates to take Bushrod to a field hospital. Angier helped him to his feet.

I patted him on the back and said, "take care, buddy," as they guided him off the hill like a child just beat up by a bully on the playground.

As they passed out of view, the most wonderful thing happened. The sun peeked through a small break in the clouds. The five of us removed our helmets and let the sun soak into our weary faces.

For an instant, I forgot about Bushrod, artillery barrages, torrential rain, mud, sleeplessness, and even the fact that a Jap sniper could have me in his sights. It was the first time I'd seen the sun in over a week. For a fleeting moment, I was on the beach with my family, a Piña Colada in hand, and had no cares in the world. As quickly as the thought appeared, it was gone.

More screams in the sky jolted me back into reality. Shisler's promised artillery barrage flew overhead and pounded the entire valley ahead of us, shaking the ground beneath our feet. Nothing in or near that valley could've survived the onslaught.

Waiting for the smoke to clear, Captain Haigler brought us all together for a briefing. He sat on a fuel can and had a map in his hands. He reported that we'd lost five men in last night's barrage —a tragic yet amazing number considering the violence of the shelling.

Reminding us even high-ranking officers weren't immune to battle, he reported that Lieutenant Colonel Horatio C. Woodhouse Jr., commander of 2/22 was killed by a sniper on the right of our division line. Woodhouse was the younger cousin of our Division Commander, General Shepard.

The Skipper told us we were moving out at 0730 to take out Hill 46, the last obstacle before the Kokuba River. "Just us grunts again on this one boys," he said. "Tank Companies are still held up. Goddamn mud, flood, and mines. SNAFU."

Right on time, we moved out. I only had time for a cigarette and a piece of chocolate. Folgers drank cold coffee as he walked. A persistent ringing filled my ears. Folgers and Hut both had a ruptured eardrum from the shelling. Capone and Angier, like the hardened warriors they were, carried on like nothing had happened.

We didn't talk about Bushrod. I never heard anyone say anything bad about a guy who legitimately cracked. No one was accused of being a coward if they truly went Asiatic. Bushrod was no pansy; he'd had too much.

I worried about how long it would be before I cracked. I didn't think I could last as long as Bushrod did.

CHAPTER TWENTY-TWO
HILL 46

HILL 46 WAS HILL 27 all over again, only bigger. Terrain and vegetation were similar. The rain was heavy, again. 200 machine gun emplacements were rumored to be in the tombs, caves, and pillboxes on its facing slope. Behind them, an estimated 2,000 Japanese navy troops poised, ready to kill.

For the entire morning, we continued the old blast, burn, and bury treatment. We lobbed grenades and satchel charges into openings and spewed liquid fire into them. Then we'd seal them off with another explosive. We traded rifle fire and carried more wounded to the bottom of the hill. I didn't know where we found the energy, but somehow our bodies performed. We were on auto pilot.

More slipping and sliding in the mud. More tripping over body parts. More stench of freshly killed humans, screams of agony or rage, blood flowing down the hill. More bullets zipping past my head. More goddamn rain.

At one point, I stepped on what I thought was a root until I noticed it had fingers. One of which had a gold wedding band around it. I stifled a gag and moved on, pretending I wasn't in such a hell hole. It couldn't be real.

The tank battalion couldn't get close to the hill as Haigler had predicted. They were still dealing with land mines and knee-deep mud. The same mud us infantrymen were fighting. A damn Sherman Tank couldn't get through this crap, but we were somehow supposed to. Not only were we expected to traverse through it, but we had to expertly battle for our lives in it.

We got stuck about halfway up the hill. As we took out machine gun nests on our side, more Japs poured over the top to replace them. Jap mortar and machine gun support from a nearby hill pinned us down.

Around 1:00pm, our tanks gave us some long distant support. They began blasting away at the top of the hill; bits of mud and rock rained down on us. But even with their assistance, we couldn't cover any ground. By nightfall, we'd only advanced 400 yards.

We were instructed to dig in for the night. Folgers and I got to work with our entrenching tools. I was a jittery sonofabitch. My hands trembled, vibrating the entire shovel. I stabbed at the mud like a man possessed. My hands cramped from gripping the handle so tightly. A strange burning in my nose and behind my eyes ignited at the thought of facing that mayhem again.

I wasn't anxious about the Japs attacking so much as from the reality that Angier may come at any moment to tell us to string some wire. After great labor, we made a foxhole big enough for the two of us to squeeze in to. We made it the shape of a tear drop so rain would flow out the bottom toward our feet. Hut and Capone holed up five yards from us.

Dread overcame me as I saw Angier approach. "Well, no need to run wires tonight, boys. We didn't move very far. Hell, we could communicate with hand signals."

The relief poured through me like warm whiskey. For a while, all we did was shoot the shit and use our helmets to bail water. Our pit design only worked so long against Okinawa rain.

Folgers developed a bad case of dysentery. Probably ten times that night, he called the password, *Lilliputian*, crawled out of the foxhole, and sat on an open ammo can. He got plenty of crap from the other guys about it. I didn't make fun, because I assumed I'd be next.

Again, flares lit up the sky.

The Japs were nearby; we could smell them. Each Marine on the front line had their own interpretation of what a Jap smelled like. Some thought they smelled like wet dog, some thought rice wine, but an inordinate amount thought Japs smelled like toothpaste. I, for one, thought they smelled like horse's ass.

Sleep would not come that night. We alternated watches but neither of us got any rest. It was torture. The anxiety of creeping, murderous Japs bayoneting us at any moment wore us out, but the same anxiety also kept us from resting. The damn flares danced as they floated toward terra firma, casting shadows that moved among the remnants of trees. Each one took on the appearance of an approaching Jap.

In the middle of the night, chaos ensued. Only this time, Americans brought on the pandemonium. Two of our artillery batteries and the Navy's guns launched a frenzy of shells onto suspected Jap positions. It's sad to say, but I took comfort in the barrage of death raining down on our enemy. The concussions weren't as bad as the night before, because they weren't right on top of our heads. Plus, I felt solace in our retribution.

I must have dozed off, because nearby rifle fire jarred me awake, erupting around me. The sun had just come up behind heavy clouds and we were back at it. More fire fights, grenades, flamethrowers, rain and mud. Bodies left from the day before had entered the first stages of decay. They'd become bloated from the gases trapped inside. The smell was tough to stomach. Swarms of large, green blowflies had moved in to feast on the smorgasbord of fresh meat and the pelting rain didn't seem to bother them. If I had any food in my body, I would've puked.

Around mid-morning, we were nearing the crest of the hill when a Nambu light machine gun opened up on Folgers and me. I dove to my stomach. He slid down the hill behind me. Beside me, green flies zipped around a Jap corpse. I held my breath and raised my head to look for a new position. Another machine gun burst blazed past me, heating my face.

I was pinned down. I rolled to my back to look at the dark clouds and catch my breath. I had a heavy feeling of someone staring at me. Reluctantly, I turned my head to see the dead Jap facing me. His swollen eyes, threatening to pop out of their sockets, were foggy and lifeless. Somehow they stared deep into me.

The skin on his face had a green hue. His mouth, wide open as if he'd died in mid-yell, collected rainwater like a bucket. A fat fly crawled out of his nose and flew off. The stench and the sight threw me into a convulsion of dry heaves.

Other guys from Love Company started past me. They must've taken out the Nambu. Folgers, on his way by, grabbed the sleeve of my poncho and helped me up. At the top of the hill, I could see the Kokuba River. We'd made it.

It looked like the dysentery was kicking Folgers's ass, so I took the wire spool from him and strapped it to my back. Each step was searing pain. For the next two hours, we routed out remaining Japs. Item Company moved ahead and easily took Hill 98 just to the south of our position.

The wounded and dead were moved and we finished "mopping up" Hill 46. Folgers, Hut, Capone, Angier and myself found each other in the courtyard of yet another tomb and collapsed onto the rough granite. That's when a miracle happened. Lt. Pope gave us a few hours off and the rain actually took a break too.

The reprieve gave me a chance to treat my hideous feet. I needed new boondockers something awful, but I really didn't want to get them from a dead Marine. James Laughridge made a good argument.

"What ya waitin' for Kentucky," he said as he pointed at the dead man pile. "Get some goddam boots while you can."

You had to love Laughridge. He pointed out that it was spelled *Laugh* Ridge, but was pronounced *Lock* Ridge. The Corps seemed to bounce him between our platoon and mortars.

He was born in North Carolina where he attended a military school. After being drafted, he trained at Parris Island, and then the Corps sent him to Guadalcanal, where he was pulled out of the First Marine Division and placed in the 6th.

Just before Sugar Loaf, they put him in Love Company in the 60-millimeter mortar squad. He had a southern drawl and cussed up a storm. He and I shared an appreciation for vulgarity. I liked him the minute I met him.

We hit it off the first time we crossed paths. Our column slowed to get around a Jeep that was mired in mud. Laughridge had come to a halt to watch the tires spin in an effort to gain purchase. Curious as to what he found so interesting I stopped beside him.

Without taking his eyes off the rooster tail of mud shooting from the back tires, he said, "If General Motors made it, it would get out of there. Wouldn't break down as much neither."

"I don't know," I countered. "I think Ford made a fine Jeep."

"Ain't no GM though."

"Yeah, a GM wouldn't have made it off the beach," I said with a smile.

Laughridge had a point. GM made the Duck, or the DUKW, our amphibious vehicles. One of those would've made it through the mud if they were here. GM also produced the Sherman tank and a lot of our aircraft. I didn't really have a preference between Ford and GM. Before the depression, my dad bought and tinkered with all kinds of cars. I did like the Ford cars and the company's history. I was just in a mood and wanted to be contrary. GM made good products, but I wasn't going to let Laughridge know that.

At Laughridge's suggestion of shoe shopping at a pile of dead kids, I gave him an incredulous look. He raised an eyebrow and gave me a "don't question me, rookie" face.

Apparently, it was commonplace for Marines to get new socks, boots, blouses, dungarees, or what-have-you from the piles of dead Marines—the "dead man" or "casualty" pile.

Keeping my feet out of the mud, I crawled to the morbid stockpile. The bodies were stacked neatly like lumber and covered in ponchos. The feet stuck out as if inviting me to take their boots. I felt very uneasy about doing it, but after guessing which pair might fit me, I worked them off, tied the laces together so I could string them around my neck, and crawled back to the fellas.

Digging out my only other pair of socks, I laid them on a rock to dry while I tended to my feet. After rinsing them off, I applied a powder our corpsman, Stanley Wright, had given me. With my feet taken care of for the time being, I used my Ka-Bar knife to open a can of eggs and ham. It wouldn't have won any awards for flavor or texture, but it was much needed sustenance.

We used Folgers's stove to heat water in ammo cans so we

could wash our faces and shave. I used a small cloth to wash my armpits and private parts. I temporarily felt human again.

The Marine Corps insisted we follow detailed procedures for personal hygiene. Yes, the Corps even made us clean our genitals a certain way. We had to endure lectures on the Marine's "washcloth method." After employing the prescribed process, I reveled in brushing my teeth with my Marine Corps-issued toothbrush. I felt like a million bucks.

Elation might've been the best word to describe how I felt when the sun pierced the clouds and flooded my eyes with its bright warmth. It was like seeing an old friend.

"Maybe we're supposed to endure war's bullshit so we can better enjoy moments like this."

"Maybe so, Kentucky," Folgers said. "I like that."

"Poppycock." Capone said without turning his head.

We all lazed around on the ground and soaked it in. I reclined, used my helmet for a pillow, and propped my sorry feet on a rock. For about fifteen minutes, we were in heaven. We weren't on Okinawa. There was no war, no crazy Japs, no dead bodies, and no rain and mud. Fifteen minutes.

CHAPTER TWENTY-THREE
HELL OF A STORM

THAT NIGHT MAJOR WALKER'S 6TH Reconnaissance Company was sent across the Kokuba River in rubber boats. We were directed to hold off on flares from 10:30pm until 3:00am so we wouldn't illuminate the recon guys' positions. They sent four scouting teams of four men each. They were on the Peninsula for six hours. They reported back that the it was definitely Japanese occupied, but the troops had moved north of the river to another holding line farther into the peninsula.

General Geiger gave General Shepard thirty-six hours to organize a shore-to-shore amphibious landing on the Oroku Peninsula. Geiger figured the Japanese would be facing inward toward the Kokuba (toward us), so he called for a flanking strike that required the 4th and 29th Marines of the 6th Division to make an amphibious landing on the northeastern tip of the peninsula. Basically, my regiment was to serve as a distraction while the 4th and 29th landed on the other side of the peninsula.

The next day at around noon, the 2nd Battalion, 7th Marines relieved us and we went into regimental reserve. The 2/7 crossed the Kokuba on a damaged railroad bridge and engaged the Japs on the hills just west of the river. Playing leap frog, we would catch up to them in the upcoming few days.

That evening, Hut filled in for Folgers and the two of us ran wires to the outpost and set up the phones. When we got back, we decided to dig in. A light rain fell on us as Hut, Folgers, Capone, and I worked together to build a little shelter. Since we were on reserve, we spent a little more time on our evening accommodations. We weren't about to spend another night in a tomb.

Beside a large boulder, we dug a hole about the size of a queen-size mattress. Folgers and I clipped two canvas shelter halves together to make a small pup tent. Hut and Capone did the same beside us. I lay on my back inside while Folgers fooled around with his stove. Water made its way through the seam in the roof and dripped on my face. I decided to see if there were any ponchos on the dead-man pile I could use to bolster the water proofing.

I pulled one off a kid and his ghostly white face stared toward heaven. My chest grew heavy with guilt. Rain drops pelted his exposed eyeballs. He didn't deserve to be rained on like that. I hadn't considered the dead needing their ponchos. I placed it back on him.

"I'm sorry," I whispered.

I wasn't taking any ponchos from dead kids. I was going to make damn sure they were all properly covered.

The wind exposed the head of one corpse on the opposite side of the pile. I went to cover it and noticed, to my horror, that it was Stewart Beech—the guy who nearly shot Folgers and me when we were coming back to camp without yelling the password. The "Son of a Beech" was gone. It didn't look like anything was wrong with him. He actually looked peaceful. His eyes were closed and his stiff face almost showed contentment. I covered his head and said a quick thank you and went back to our shelter empty-handed.

Our shelter wasn't the coziest situation, but it was far better than anything I'd had for over a week. The four of us huddled together and shot the breeze while we cleaned our rifles, grateful the 2/7 were fighting instead of us. The rumble of battle roared over the river.

Shortly after taking cover, the rain picked up. I mean it really picked up. I thought the downpours so far had been heavy, but this one took the cake. In a matter of seconds, a wall of water cascaded over the edge of our makeshift roof. Streams poured through gaps in the roof. We struggled to keep it from collapsing under the weight of the gathering water.

About an hour into the storm, the winds kicked up. We held on to the supports of our shelters in hopes of keeping them from blowing over. A gust ripped both tents from our hands they flew away—probably to Hawaii.

Completely exposed to the deluge, we reluctantly decided to find a tomb. We made it to the one we had rested beside earlier in the day. Charred human remains were piled up outside. Three blue urns stood neatly side by side on the courtyard wall.

It was pitch black inside. Not taking any chances, Capone yelled "Lilliputian" into the mouth. A muffled, but American voice responded.

Once inside, a flashlight blinked on. It was Daniel Swinggate, our interpreter. He was half Jap, but we didn't hold it against him. From Santa Cruz, California, he'd turned twenty-one in March. Because his mother was Japanese, he grew up speaking Japanese and English, and after Pearl Harbor, he rushed to the Marine Corps recruiting office to enlist. At the time, he'd been seventeen so he needed his parents' written permission. Because Japanese-Americans were being hauled off to internment camps, his parents were eager to show their patriotism by granting permission to enlist early.

When the Corps learned he spoke Japanese, he got the job as interpreter. He served on Saipan where he was shot in the right butt cheek. When he recovered, he was transferred to the 6th Marines on Guam.

Frank "The Hammer" Salazar, our radioman, sat beside Swinggate. He came to the war with his own nickname. He was from Philadelphia and had a promising boxing career. Before Pearl Harbor, he'd had three professional fights under his belt. He knocked all three opponents out in the first round, giving him the nickname.

He was a Guadalcanal and Peleliu veteran which was incredible. Radiomen had very short life expectancies. They, like wiremen, were considered sniper bait. He was wounded on Guadalcanal, but not serious enough to keep him out of the war. He must have been invincible or had a hell of a good guardian angel looking out for him. His SCR-300 radio leaned against the wall beside him.

They both encouraged us to get inside quickly, scooting farther back to accommodate us.

The wind howled past the opening of the tomb. You never heard such a noise. It sounded like a jet engine was parked outside revving up, dying down, and then revving up again. It continued all night. I don't recall hearing any explosions of battle the whole night. I think everyone—good guys and bad guys alike—had a lot to deal with without the inconvenience of war. A shiver ran through me as I thought about the dead Marines lying out in the storm.

CHAPTER TWENTY-FOUR
GOODBYE, SIR

BELIEVE IT OR NOT, I think we all got a little sleep during the night. Restless sleep, but sleep, nonetheless. We must have felt a sort of comfort knowing the weather was so intense the Japs wouldn't be prowling around.

In the gray light of dawn, we crawled out of the tomb. Swinggate and Hammer quickly put the urns back in the tomb. I was touched by the respect they paid to the residents of the tomb we borrowed.

The storm was still raging, but not as ferociously as it had last night. Storm damage was present everywhere we looked. Scrap metal hugged black trees. Tent material, ammo boxes, airplane wings—you name it—had been strewn over the battered landscape. At the bottom of the hill a Jeep lay on its side.

Trees that remained standing only did so because they no

longer had branches to serve as sails. They had already been blasted off by ordnance. Between Mother Nature and man, the island was a junk yard.

Scuttlebutt had it that there was a typhoon just east of Okinawa. A typhoon is what we call a hurricane in the States. They said there were winds over a hundred miles per hour and it was doing more damage to the Navy than it was to us. It was also reported that we could expect the storm to last several more days.

My squad spent most of the day re-stringing damaged lines. We waited on replacement switchboards, phones, and other equipment that had been destroyed. When tanks brought our supplies, we hooked everything together to reestablish communication with battalion. It was a great deal of work and the conditions were terrible.

Even with the storm still carrying on, the 2/7 continued to fight on the other side of the river. With binoculars, we could make out some of the fighting. It was difficult to watch our guys fight for their lives knowing we couldn't do anything to help. They were giving them hell though.

We were in reserve, but because of the storm, we didn't get much rest. We became ammo carriers, stretcher bearers, latrine constructors, mechanics, and carpenters. You name it, the brass made us do it.

During rest periods, I tended to my feet. I tried to write Hody a letter to let her know how I was doing, but the ink kept running and smearing. Impossible to keep dry in the miserable rain, the paper dissolved in a matter of minutes.

Other guys, despite being ordered not to, hunted for souvenirs. They searched Japanese dead for flags, firearms, knives, Samurai swords, and the coveted gold dental work. This particular undertaking was their way of investing in their financial future. The private's salary of $50 a month pay wasn't gonna do it.

One of the worst souvenir collectors was Captain Haigler himself. You could say he was obsessed with it. Always picking up flags, helmets, swords, you name it. Anything he could carry, he'd grab. If he couldn't carry it, he'd have one of his runners carry it for him.

Everyone had their own process of dealing with war. Combat had a way of numbing combatants to their barbarous acts. Fighting the Japs presented a unique way of dehumanizing the enemy. When a Marine was forced to kill or be killed, he'd lose a bit of his sense of humanity. Haigler had seen so much combat, that I don't believe he gave it a thought to strip dead men of their possessions.

The propaganda we'd been fed about the Japs for so many years had only contributed to the callousness. It didn't help that the Japs saw us as inferior beings and tortured and mutilated our guys like they were cattle.

Routing Japs out of caves and burning them had become so routine, a Marine could often feel like an exterminator cleaning out rat or hornet nests. You kind of stopped thinking of them as people. People who had families, careers, hobbies. The Japs had just become pests.

The Japanese had become so inhuman to the American populous, that even President Franklin Delano Roosevelt received a ghastly gift from Representative Francis E. Walter. It was a letter opener made from the arm bone of a Japanese warrior. Now, while I understand the animosity toward the Japs, I didn't feel the gift was in good taste. I thought we were better than that. I was glad to hear FDR sent the letter opener back to Japan so it could have a proper burial.

So far, I had refrained from collecting souvenirs. We were told numerous times in training to stay away from Japanese wounded or dead because they could be booby traps. A sword or rifle could have a trip wire that detonated an explosive. Wounded Japs sometimes held a grenade where you couldn't see it and blow you to smithereens if you got too close. That was all the deterrent I needed to stay away from the Japs and their belongings.

The morning of June 3, we started moving out. The rain had no plans to quit anytime soon. Already saturated for the past two weeks, and having lost most of its vegetation, the ground was raging past me in torrents. Every gully was flooded. Every crack in cliff faces became spewing hoses. Streams had become creeks, creeks had become rivers, puddles were brown lakes. Flooding was everywhere I looked. Water gushed and gurgled all around us. All sorts of debris floated past us down the hill toward the Kokuba River.

The River was about a hundred fifty yards across where we were crossing. It was obviously swollen and raised well above its normal banks. Brown water raced by at what looked like a hundred miles an hour.

Crossing a damaged railroad track bridge was unsettling to say the least. Scores of men and machines crossed it without any problem, but Folgers and I were charged with running wire along the sonofabitch. Normally, we'd string lines after reaching our objective, but today we were moving so fast, we had to do it as we went. It was hard to keep up.

To string wire across the bridge, we had to run it along the bottom of the lateral supports. There wasn't enough of the overhead, metal framework left to run a consistent line. Plus, attaching it to the lower trusses allowed us to hide it better.

At times, it was difficult reaching the connecting points. Twice, I had to lie on my stomach and inchworm over the edge. With most of my upper body hanging over the lip of the bridge, Folgers stood on my pant legs to anchor me to the railroad gravel.

The rushing water, only yards below me, flew by with dizzying speed. The blur of the water and the blood rushing to my head made me woozy. I was sweating bullets.

"How's it going down there, Kentucky?" Folgers asked. "How's the view?"

Rain and bits of iron, gravel, and God-knows-what invaded my eyes. I couldn't see and it stung like hell. My dog tags flapped against my forehead and water poured off my poncho into my mouth like a downspout, choking me. Let's just say I wasn't real jolly at the moment.

"Fuck you, Folgers. How the hell did I end up down here and your sorry ass up there?"

"Be nice, Kentucky, you ain't in a very good position to be talkin' ugly." He let out a little chuckle. A goofy chuckle.

If dumb were dirt, he'd cover about an acre. But I trusted Folgers. We'd been through enough nights of keeping watch for each other that I'd learned to put my life in his hands. That's how you get with your brothers-at-arms. You end up trusting them more than anyone else in the world. Going through life-threatening situations together really creates a strange bond.

With the line secured, Folgers helped me back up. Looking upstream, the river widened. For an instant, it reminded me of the Ohio River in Louisville. I'd have given a million bucks to be looking at the Ohio with my girls instead of the Kokuba with Folgers.

We made it over the north fork of the Kokuba, crossed the Naha-Higashi Highway, and started down a dirt road known as number 11. Telephone poles were scattered down the length of the road. Conquering his fear of heights, Folgers and I alternated who climbed them to string our wires. Around two miles from the north fork of the Kokuba, we approached the south fork. Our platoon had just started across a bridge ahead of us.

Folgers and I were busy with the wires when several shots rang out. Everyone hit the deck and fired into the forest on the opposite side of the river. A dozen or so of our guys sprinted across the bridge to engage the Nips that had fired on us.

When the "all clear" was given, we assessed our situation. A commotion of yells and scurrying developed near the center of the bridge. Curiosity forced Folgers and me to run to the scene. When we got there, Doc Wright was applying pressure to a rifleman's hip. He writhed in pain, but looked like he would survive.

Nearby, Lieutenant Pope lay lifeless. He was shot in the head. His teeth still clinched a cigar.

I didn't know what I felt. A fearless leader was dead. He'd seemed invincible. Now he lay there limp and pitiful. It was a somber reminder of how vulnerable we all were—not that I needed reminding.

A moment of silence passed before he was carried to the rear. Angier stepped up and told us to get going and get off the bridge. We got going in a hurry. A few minutes later, we were on the Peninsula.

CHAPTER TWENTY-FIVE
THE TOOL

BY LATE AFTERNOON, WE'D ENTERED the village of Tomigusuku. Dilapidated buildings and houses evidenced the passing of the 2/7. Japanese dead littered the streets. We set up a field post in one of the few homes that had an intact roof. It was an amazing feeling to be indoors for a while, even if it was a ramshackle house.

We set up our communications in the front room. The remainder of the day we prepared for the upcoming assault. We hauled recently air-dropped ammo, large cans of potable water, food, and of course, more spools of wire.

Miraculously, I found a small, upright piano positioned in the middle of the back room. I was surprised there would be any musical instrument in this hell hole. It was quite beat up and sounded terrible, but I couldn't resist the urge to tickle the ivory a little. I enjoyed all instruments, but I naturally took to the piano.

I'd never had any formal lessons. My father felt it more of a priority to provide my six sisters with music lessons, so Charlie and I got the shaft as far as that went. In Dad's defense, the Depression probably had something to do with him not doling out the dough for professional lessons for us.

Somehow I got good at the piano. Friends and family said I had a gift. I guess I did have a knack for learning musical instruments. I could even play a mean accordion. I loved all forms of music. Hearing my out-of-tune music in that abandoned house, in a small Okinawa town, in the middle of a war, was especially gratifying. For a few minutes, I was home again.

My concert was rudely interrupted when a fella I didn't recognize stormed in and kicked the piano over. He slapped me on the helmet and yelled, "What the hell are you doing?"

"I'm playing the piano, Sherlock. Who the hell are you and what are *you* doing?"

"I'm *Lieutenant* O'Toole. I'm replacing Lt. Pope."

I snapped to attention and saluted the asshole. "Sorry, sir."

He told me to get my ass to the front room. I got my ass to the front room.

All the guys from Headquarters Company were there. They were all snickering. If I hadn't felt so embarrassed, I might have felt important to be included.

"Here's the dope, boys," O'Toole started.

He went on to tell us the amphibious landing of the 3/4 and

3/29 was scheduled for 5:45 in the morning. We were ordered to relieve the 2/7 at 5:00am and move west to secure the base of the peninsula. We'd then press north toward the airfield and serve as a distraction for the invasion.

O'Toole tried to come off as authoritative and tough. It was phony, you could tell. A classic example of a guy with a Napoleon complex. Around five and a half feet tall, he tried to compensate for his size by humiliating his men. Overly strict and by-the-book, he was new to a band of brothers, and knew it.

His name was Barry O'Toole. He was probably twenty years old or so and was from upstate New York. He'd earned his rank at Quantico where the Marine Corps University spit out thousands of lieutenants. He had no battle experience. This was typical. Many replacement lieutenants came into the field without experience and tried to run a unit with textbook procedures. The problem was he didn't know how things really worked, like Pope did. He didn't understand how the Japs functioned and didn't know our personalities.

We started calling him the "Tool Bag," or "The Tool." With his introduction, I understood how the veterans viewed us replacements. Now that I'd been enduring the bullshit of war for over a week, I understood what it felt like to have formed a bond with these guys, and then have a new face suddenly thrown into the mix. Folgers and I had lasted a week longer than Capone had predicted, so I felt like I was getting the hang of this battle thing.

My new-found wisdom told me this new guy didn't have what it took to survive. If Lt. Pope couldn't, there was no way this joker would.

Making things worse, The Tool and Angier butted heads immediately. Angier didn't respect him or his rank one iota. He questioned The Tool's every order. Dissension in the ranks was a dangerous thing during combat, but so was stupidity on the part of an officer.

It wasn't just Angier and O'Toole who were at each other's throat. A lot of guys were bickering. You could feel the tension in the air. Everyone felt the overwhelming dread of the upcoming battle. We had a rough day ahead of us.

In an attempt to ease anxiety, we looked for distractions. Hut and I decided to divert our attention by exploring a couple of nearby houses. We presumed we were in a wealthier area. They had more in the ways of furniture and amenities than I would have guessed. In one, we found an old hand crank Victrola and a few records.

We took our loot back to the field post where its music entertained us for a good part of the night. Hut, Folgers, and I laid back and listened to what sounded almost like opera. It was a woman singing in Okinawan, I guess. The scratchy sound of the record coupled with her despondent tone had a haunting effect. Back home, opera was one of my favorite things to listen to. Capone, who had been rooting around for treasure, came in some time near midnight. "Look what I found boys!" He was holding a bottle of sake and two small cups.

When young men are forced into the crappy situation of fighting for their lives in a foreign land, it was almost dutiful that they get plastered each and every time the opportunity presented itself.

Capone handed me one of the small ceramic cups and filled it with the clear liquor. “Give it hell.”

I raised the glass. “To the nip bastards!”

I’d never had rice wine, Jap wine.

I threw that cup back and downed its contents in one shot. I passed the cup to Folgers and he tossed one back too. Everyone did. It tasted like rubbing alcohol, but none of us cared as long as it numbed us a bit.

Capone confirmed my thoughts. “This tastes like horse piss, but let’s drink and be merry, for tomorrow we shall die!” He passed the bottle around. Because the platitude was literal in our case (for tomorrow we shall die) it dampened the mood for a total of about one and a half seconds.

When the cup and bottle made it back around to me, I raised my cup. "See, fellas, if this war didn't suck so much, this wouldn't be such a good time."

Capone raised his cup enthusiastically. "Yeah, what he said."

“Hey, has anyone gotten any mail lately?” Folgers changed the subject. Everyone shook their heads.

“When do you think we’ll get some?” Folgers directed his question toward Capone.

“How the hell should I know? Do I look like a postman?”

“You waiting for a sugar report, Folgers?” Hut asked.

“Nah, it ain’t like that. I don’t have a girl. I’d like to read one of my mom’s letters right about now, that’s all.”

"Well, write your goddamn congressman and let him know how you feel about it." Capone said.

The typhoon must have had something to do with our lack of correspondence. We didn't really need another excuse to drink, but it didn't hurt.

We all took several shots. In no time, I was swimming. A warm sensation filled my skull. Then I had a swell idea. I thought I'd entertain my buddies with some piano.

I stood up a little too quickly and staggered, catching myself on the door frame.

"Damn Kentucky! Drink you a nuthern'!"

I walked in a relatively straight line to the piano in the other room and tried my damnedest to lift it back up to its proper position. Couldn't do it. I nearly passed out from the exertion.

"Someone come help me with this thing," I yelled.

"Go screw yourself, Kentucky!"

Fine, I decided. I figured I could play it sideways and bend over and play the damn thing while it's lying on its back. Bad decision.

When I bent, my helmet fell and bounced off the piano to the floor. My fingers found a good starting position on the ivories. I played about three cords, and passed out. Inverting oneself when drunk on sake is not something I would recommend.

There was about ten minutes of my life I couldn't account for. The next thing I knew, Folgers was shaking me back to life and helping me up. Apparently, I had hit my head on the edge of the piano as I fell. I had a large pump knot and a cut on my forehead above my right eye. That sucker hurt. I glided my hand over the area and smeared blood across my head. "You're a crazy sonamabitch," Folgers garbled.

We walked back into the front room where the others clapped for me. I laid down against a wall and closed my eyes and the world spun. The fellas' conversation faded, but I could still hear the Victrola. The ghostly voice of the Okinawa opera singer lulled me into a fitful sleep.

I had a fleeting dream about Hody, Kay, and Patsy. We were in the front yard chasing each other around in circles. My little Patsy was a normal kid in my dream world. She was laughing and running. All three of them had white, lacy dresses on. Like something they would wear to Easter Mass. Hody tackled me and all three of them jumped on top tagging me with playful punches. To my disgust, the girls' sweet voices calling out "Daddy," and Hody saying "Harry," turned into that of a man's voice. "Kentucky. Kentucky. Harry!"

It was Folgers punching and shaking me awake into a nightmare. The revulsion I felt when I realized I was still on Okinawa, that God-forsaken island of mud and death, was crushing. I slapped Folgers in the chest to get his damn mitts off me.

I couldn't be mad at him. It was justifiable why he'd ruined my dream. Captain Haigler was coming in. It was 4:00 in the goddamn morning. My head throbbed from the sake and the spill I took. Having to wake up early for work with a hangover was one thing, but when you wake up *really* damn early with a hangover to go into life-threatening combat where your life balanced on every move you made—now that was a whole new level of crappy.

Folgers slammed my helmet onto my head to cover my injury. I shuddered with the lightning bolt of pain in my skull. But I guess it was better not to invite questions about my tomfoolery. Captain Haigler and O'Toole walked in and everyone struggled to get on their feet.

The Skipper got on the horn with Colonel Shisler. We heard most of the conversation, but the Skipper gave us a re-cap anyway. He explained we were moving west to Hill 55.

The Japs were using the hill to guard the Peninsula from a southern advance of the Americans. Securing it would have a few functions. It would form a line across the base of the peninsula that would trap the Japs on the peninsula, and it would also get their attention while the 4th and 29th landed on the beach to our north.

After securing 55, we were scheduled to move toward the middle of the Peninsula. There, we'd meet up with the rest of the 6th Marine Division and encircle the Nips. Dope had it that Rear Admiral Minoru Ota was holding out in the center of the Peninsula with approximately 5,000 Jap naval troops under his command.

Leaving the switchboard in the house, we immediately started out for Hill 55. My head throbbed, my knee was stiff, and my feet were on fire. Folgers and Hut help spur me along with jokes about my performance on the piano and how the piano kicked my ass. Playful kicks in my butt kept me moving. I was never going to live that night down.

It was as dark as a struck match and still raining like hell. The 2/7 had fought their way through the valley that now separated us from our next objective. We'd leapfrog them as we moved west.

After only a few minutes of marching, it was evident we were close to the front lines again. At that hour, we could hear mostly harassing fire, but the smell of the front line was discernible. Sounds like I was a blood hound, but any Marine on Okinawa learned to deduce a number of things with his nose. As we continued into the darkness, the stench of battle became stronger and stronger. The unmistakable, sharp odor of blood, the foul stench of decay, and the biting smell of cordite from the shellings. If dread had a smell, this was it.

My stomach churned and my pulse thumped in my temples. The dismay a Marine felt on his way to battle may've been harder to deal with than the actual combat. You didn't have time to think in a fire fight. But the approach of another battle was terrifying and seemed to last forever.

CHAPTER TWENTY-SIX
HILL 55

ITEM COMPANY MOVED TO OUR left flank while King Company came up on our right. We held back as they moved into position to attack Hill 55. Mortars and artillery from our battalion began blasting the hillside at around 4:30am and lasted ten to fifteen minutes. Item and King immediately rushed the hill.

At around 4:45am, thunder erupted to our west. The Navy rained shells on and around the Nishikoku beaches, softening it up for the landing of the 4th and 29th Marines.

Around 5:00am, my company moved toward the fray on the hill. Pillboxes were everywhere. From within, machine guns spit hot lead down on our position. Some Marines say the Jap machine guns sound like a sheet tearing. I can't disagree with that description normally, but on this morning, the *burrrrup* from the pillbox portholes possessed a deeper tone.

It was a new weapon we hadn't encountered yet. We learned later that the Japs had stripped huge automatic 40mm guns from damaged aircraft on the Oroku airfield and were using them to pour rounds on us.

We spent the morning blasting, burning, and burying pillboxes. More screaming, crying, moaning. More death, anguish, exhaustion, and fear. And of course, more damn rain. Around midday, the rain turned into a monsoon-level downpour for the one millionth time in the past two weeks.

During a lull in the firefight, Folgers and I met up with Doc Wright and a fella named Chester at the entrance of a cave. The cave reeked of barbecued Nips, so we knew it had already been flushed out by our guys. We sat together under an overhang to catch our breath.

We sat in silence for a moment or two, knowing what the others were thinking. There was no point in small talk about the weather or how shitty the war was and how tired we were of fighting Japs.

I took my helmet off to check the progress of my cerebral swelling. Doc Wright noticed it and crawled over to have a look.

"Doesn't look too bad." He wiped the cut with gauze and taped a bandage to it. "How'd it happen?"

Folgers and I looked at each other and had a tough time holding back our laughter as we told him the story.

"I'll put you in for a Purple Heart," he said, grinning.

"Hey, Doc," Folgers said, "this dysentery has really done a

number on my ass. Can I get a Purple Heart for that?"

CHAPTER TWENTY-SEVEN
CIVILIANS

HILL 55 WAS SECURED BY mid-afternoon and the 4th and 29th had made it inland and were in the process of securing the Naha airfield. Turns out, the Japs had constructed a bunch of dummy planes. Crafty bastards.

At dusk, Angier caught up with Folgers and me and instructed us to string line from the Tomigusuku house to the top of the hill where Captain Haigler was dug in.

The hike to the village was uneventful, but when we were headed back I stumbled upon a strange discovery.

I was several yards ahead of Folgers as we were sneaking along the ridge of a small escarpment adjacent to Hill 55. The battlefield was quiet and I was moving stealthily along when I heard what sounded like a baby crying.

I froze in my tracks and listened in disbelief. When Folgers got close to me, I motioned him to stop and be quiet. I crawled over to him and filled him in. He thought I was losing it.

"You're just hearing things. Hearing the sound of your daughter crying in your head, or something," he said.

"No, just listen for a minute."

We sat in the dark straining our ears. I almost couldn't hear anything over the sound of my pounding heart. We inched forward and cupped our hands behind our ears to amplify the sounds around us. It seemed to help. We both heard the baby again. Its cry was quickly stifled. Immediately following, we heard a quiet murmur of what sounded like suppressed voices.

Folgers and I looked at each other with astonishment and confusion. "Let's get the wire to the Skipper and tell him about this," I suggested.

I made a mental note of the shape of a nearby boulder so I could find the place again. We high-tailed it back to Captain Haigler's position. When we reported what we heard, he actually believed us. I thought he would tell us to get lost, but he didn't. He ordered a squad of about seven men, led by Corporal George Irwin, to follow Folgers and me back to the location of the voices.

One of the members of the squad was Daniel Swinggate, who was necessary for interpretation. When we got to the location, we found a small entrance to a cave we must have missed earlier in the day. Kneeling beside the hole, Swinggate shouted some Japanese nonsense into the hole. Whatever he said got the occupants scrambling. We heard scuffling and muffled voices deep inside.

"I think they're civilians," Swinggate said to Irwin. "A few voices sounded like they were using an Okinawan dialect to direct people further inside."

"Do you speak Okinawan?" Irwin asked. "Tell them we're Americans and they can come out safely."

"The roots of Okinawan are similar to Japanese. I could probably communicate on a basic level."

"Well, do it."

"I'll try, but I doubt it will do any good." Swinggate hollered into the opening in the very foreign tongue of the Okinawans. Then he repeated it in English so it was clear we were Americans. He told them we were Americans and they were safe to come out. He said we would feed them and care for their wounded.

He stuck his head deeper inside to listen for a reply. Hearing one, he withdrew and told Corporal Irwin that they refused to come out alive.

"Okay, you and the guy with the voice," Irwin said to Swinggate and pointed at me. "You all stay here and keep an eye on things. Don't let anyone in or out. We'll give the Skipper the scoop and see what he wants to do."

With that, he and the others left. In the dark, I could still make out Folgers as he turned back, lifted his palms skyward and shrugged his shoulders. His body language said what I was thinking: "What the hell?"

Again my gruff voice betrayed me. I knew he wanted me there so when they came back they could make damn sure it's still us sitting here, not someone from inside the cave. I wasn't sure what the big deal was or why we needed to stay there.

Looking for answers, I asked Swinggate why we were staying there and why he chose me. "There are Okinawans in there and it sounds like a lot of them," he said. "We can't leave them in there. It's too dangerous for them and us."

"Why won't they come out?" I tried to make myself comfortable in the mud.

He moved a rock from behind him to lean back. "They're afraid."

"Of sweethearts like us?" I offered him a cigarette.

He waved me off. "Imperial propaganda brainwashed these people. Japanese civilians and the Okinawans were told the Americans were white devils whose sole desire was to kill mercilessly and brutally torture. They were told we'd rape the women and butcher and eat their children in front of them."

"We can't tell them they were tricked by their leaders?"

"They were also told the Americans would lure them out by acting friendly. They think we're evil, Kentucky."

We were quiet in thought for a moment. He broke the silence. "Last I heard, since we landed in April, something like 100,000 civilians have already died on this island."

"From us?"

"Sometimes, but not on purpose. The goddamn Japs used them for body shields. Sometimes they forced the civilians to fight us. Over near Shuri, they sent crying mothers clutching their babies into our lines with explosives tied to them.

"Sometimes the poor bastards just got caught in crossfire. The Japs didn't give a shit. They treat the Okinawans like they treat us."

He paused, then leaned toward the hole for a listen. Deciding he hadn't heard anything, he turned back.

"The majority of the civilian deaths is from suicide," he started again. "They'd rather blow themselves up then be taken by the Americans. It's sad; I can't stand it. I saw two ladies dive off a cliff onto rocks when we got near them. Hell, on Saipan, they weren't any different. Some guys there watched hundreds of civilians jump to their death in mass suicides. Can you imagine that, Kentucky? Can you imagine holding hands with your wife and kids and jumping off a cliff?"

I shuddered. "Shit, no. God, that's awful. Thanks for brightening my day. You're a real prince."

"Yeah, the Japs are ruthless assholes and..." His words hung in the air, while we both sat silently. From behind a nearby rock came a voice: "Gehringer."

Swinggate and I looked at each other and thought about it for a minute. "Ah," he whispered, "I got it."

He turned toward the voice and yelled, "Charlie."

He saw me looking at him incredulously. "Charlie Gehringer," he said. "The second baseman for the Detroit Tigers. He was the MVP in '37."

A minute later a runner named Jerry approached.

"What's the dope?" I asked.

"You all have to stay here until dawn," he said while trying to catch his breath. "O'Toole said we'd clean the cave out in the morning. You have to make sure no one comes out before then."

"Are you shittin' me?" Swinggate said.

"Did Haigler agree with that horse shit?" I asked.

"No one knows where he is. Sorry fellas." With that, Jerry ran off.

Swinggate and I sat outside that damn cave in the rain all night. We chewed the fat and acted like the weather was pleasant. For a while, we talked about our families and hobbies we used to have. Between thoughts, we'd listen carefully for any movement in the cave.

Near 10:00pm, we decided to take shifts. Swinggate said he'd keep watch for the first four hours. I was nearly asleep when I was suddenly and swiftly attacked. It was a shot to the gut. Not by an enemy sniper round, but from some heinous presence inside. My stomach growled and turned. It was suddenly very heavy.

"Oh, dear Lord." I clutched my stomach and ran to a nearby boulder. I barely got my trousers down before all hell broke loose. Dysentery!

I had had some miserable nights on Okinawa, but this one was especially memorable. Now, I won't get into the details of what transpired in and around my hindquarters, but it was a wretched situation.

At least fifteen times that night I had to run to a rock, shell hole, or ammo box for relief. It got so bad that I often couldn't tell if I was stepping in mud or the product of my affliction. Between bouts, I'd curl up in the fetal position in a mattress of mud.

Dawn was a welcome sight. With it came Captain Haigler and a number of riflemen. He took one look at me and told me to get some rest. No argument from me, but curiosity kept me nearby. While I lay crumpled beside a rock, I watched the civilian debacle unfold. It was a God-awful mess.

Swinggate continued to make pleas with the civilians to come out. It all went to hell when they started pulling out roots and rocks to increase the size of the opening. Two blasts emanated from inside. Smoke and stench wafted out the opening.

"Holy shit! It's Shuri all over again!" someone yelled.

After the air cleared, screaming, coughing, and crying was heard inside. Swinggate continued yelling into the cave.

"Let's just torch them!" some horse's ass yelled.

Three guys with flashlights and M1s moved in. A handful of civilians came out at gunpoint. A few small children emerged. They looked like skeletons. Their stunned silence and the blank looks on their faces illustrated what they had been through. Their parents, like cornered animals protecting their young, attacked the fully armed Marines with their bare hands. Trying their damnedest to avoid it, a few had to be gunned down.

Suddenly, part of the cave entrance fell in, leaving a larger opening. As daylight filtered into the cavern, we could see the panic on the faces of the remaining occupants. You would've thought we were the devil himself. Swinggate was right; they believed we were demons here to torture them. Swinggate continued yelling into the cave.

A father, hugging his wife and baby in one hand, held a grenade between them. They were all crying hysterically. As Swinggate slowly approached them to assure them of their safety, the father pulled the pin and blew the family to bits. My stomach reared and I vomited, turning away.

Swinggate had covered up and dropped to the deck, but to everyone's horror, shrapnel of bone fragments splintered his back end. It was not serious, but it was sickening.

He climbed out of the cave covered in blood and God knows what else. Doc Wright, who was already administering fluids to an Okinawan child, handed the saline bag to a rifleman and tended to the ghastly shrapnel in Swinggate's butt and legs.

When they were finally able to get some light down in the cave, they found there were perhaps a dozen injured people on stretchers. Some had IVs hooked to them that had long ago run dry. Dark blood had made its way up the lines and clotted. Many wore bandages with old, brown stains. Young women wearing what looked like nurses' uniforms cowered in fear in the farthest corners.

In the back of the cave, severed limbs rotted in a pile. Bloody rags and excrement littered the floor. It looked as if they had been using the cave as a makeshift hospital for weeks. Apparently, when the Japs came through Tomigusuku, nurses and doctors brought some of the injured patients from the hospital to take shelter in the cave. The cave was a nest of filth and stench.

The surviving civilians sat down on rocks and were offered water and medical care. The adults refused to be touched and declined the water. Before offering it to one Okinawan man, a Marine took a sip from his canteen to show it wasn't poisoned. Finally, the Okinawan reluctantly took a draw.

I tried to hang on to my waning belief that there might be a reason for such despair. You can't enjoy good times without suffering miserable ones, right? The civilians in that cave wouldn't see it that way. But maybe it was my place to feel gratitude for the safety of my family.

Hoping to get some rest, I stumbled back toward the rest of the outfit. They had moved past Hill 55 toward the north and camped on the opposite side of a small ridge.

"Hey, Kentucky! What's shakin'?" greeted Folgers.

I was holding my stomach and didn't say a word. He knew right away what was shakin'.

"Not feeling too hot?" Real observant, that Folgers. Sharp as a bowling ball.

"Oh, I see. Got you too! Don't worry, lasts about a week."

I found a spot under a bush beside a boulder. After dealing with another bout of diarrhea, I curled up underneath and trembled in pain and fever until I dozed off.

I don't know what they did with the civilians while I slept. The only thing that could take my mind off the horrible cave scene was the intestinal anguish I was enduring. My stomach cramped and knotted.

I was abruptly awakened by a kick in my pants.

"Get your ass up! I need you to run wire." It was O'Toole. Hell.

"I'm sick and it's the middle of the day! I'm not going out there in broad daylight. That's suicide!"

"I don't care what time it is!" he countered, "get off your ass and do what you're told. That's an order."

Hearing our words, Angier showed up to defend me.

"Listen O'Toole! We don't string in the daylight! These guys are sniper bait when it's dark out. Sending them out at 1000 is murder!"

"You'll call me *Lieutenant* O'Toole, Sergeant! I don't give a shit what you all did when Pope ran your outfit. Communications with Battalion are down and I intend to get it back up."

"That's *Lieutenant* Pope, to you!" Angier yelled. "Send a runner or use your talkies! My guys are not going out there!"

O'Toole pulled Angier out of earshot. I sat up to see what was happening. All I could tell was they were having a heated argument and I needed to find a hole in the ground. Angier's posture weakened. He backed down and stomped over and sat beside me.

"I tried, Kentucky, but we have to repair the work you did last night, and run it to the west side of 55. Apparently it has to be done now. He doesn't have a damn clue what he's doing." He offered me a cigarette. I gladly accepted.

"I appreciate you trying, sir," I said weakly. I meant it too. He was looking out for us.

"Take your time smoking. When you're done, we'll go."

"We, sir?" I asked.

"Yeah, if he's going to send you guys out in plain sight, I'm going to tag along and keep an eye out for you all. I'll get Folgers."

CHAPTER TWENTY-EIGHT
MY BREAKDOWN

YOU DIDN'T HAVE TO BE a meteorologist to predict what the weather was like. Still raining like a sonofabitch. Angier, Folgers, and I set off to string line. To say we felt exposed in the daylight would be an understatement. Since I was feeling pretty crappy, we took turns carrying the spool. Folgers and I left our rifles behind so we could move faster. Only Angier brought his piece—a Thompson submachine gun. He would keep watch while we worked.

By late afternoon we'd repaired the broken line and were running wire over Hill 55. At the top, I had an intestinal attack. Angier could see it in my face. He knew I had some business to attend to.

"Here, take this," he said glancing at my clinched jaw. He handed me the Tommy gun. "And give me the spool. I'll run the wire while you take your shit. Hurry, and cover us when you're done."

I found a little hollow in the top of the hill. A few yards to my left, Folgers was holding the wire as Angier slid down the hill with the spool under his poncho.

Teasing me, Folgers looked over at me with a thumbs up. "Everything coming out alright, Kentucky?" he said with a giggle.

A shot rang out and Folgers crumpled to the ground holding his neck, writhing in pain. I pulled my trousers up and crawled to the edge scanning the ridge on the opposite side of the small ravine.

Folgers rolled and twisted on his back. Angier was near the bottom of the ridge, plastered to a rock face. With his hands, he signaled to me where he thought the sniper was.

I lay on my stomach and continued to inspect the terrain of the valley. My heart pounded in my head and the rain drummed on my helmet and poncho. I trained the Thompson on the hillside. Rain dripped from the receiver on the machine gun and droplets gathered in little balloons on the metal sights.

A faint flash blinked from the ridge. If it hadn't been so dark, I probably wouldn't have seen it at all. The hidden Jap must've had one of those sniper rifle jobs that had a low muzzle flash. I couldn't quite discern where he was. I assumed he'd shot high or I wouldn't have seen the flicker. I waited with great anticipation for another blink to pinpoint his position.

I saw a dim spark from inside the hill. Mud and rock blew out of the ground a few feet in front of me. I aimed the Tommy gun on the ridge and started unloading the first magazine. On cue, Angier climbed up the ridge toward the gunman. I sent a short burst into the rocks above him leading to the sniper. His hand curled around a grenade. I continued to supply covering fire until he reached a small opening. His arm swung in an upward motion, and seconds later, a cloud of dust and debris spewed from the face of the ridge where the sniper was located. Thunder echoed through the hills.

I belly crawled to Folgers. He was in bad shape. He had been hit in the throat. I ripped the small first aid kit from my belt, found an insufficient amount of gauze and began pressing it to his neck.

"Corpsman!" I yelled, looking around frantically. "Corpsman!" I pulled his head and shoulders into my lap. "Tallulah, God damn it!"

Blood soaked the dressing in seconds. Bubbles inflated then popped over the wound. His eyes were wild with fear. His throat gurgled. I was losing him. He was drowning in his own blood. Clinching fistfuls of my shirt, he pleaded that I not let him die. I'd have never seen such panic in a person before.

Angier scrambled up to us. "You're going to be fine, Leo," he reassured him. We both knew he wasn't going to be fine.

"Give him morphine," Angier calmly instructed me. I was so wracked with fear and sorrow that I couldn't think. I found myself doing it automatically. I sort of watched myself dig into my first aid kit for a morphine syrette.

Folgers's face showed a mixture of abject horror and approval.

I broke the glass seal and jabbed it into his leg.

"Here, give him mine too," Angier said as he handed me his syrette.

"Do it, Kentucky," Folgers softly and laboriously said as he looked up at me with his large, innocent eyes. He sounded like he was trying to talk while gargling.

Angier put his hand on my shoulder. "It's okay."

I broke open the second syrette, held Folgers's head tight against my stomach. I stabbed his leg injecting the misery-ending morphine.

"I don't want to die. I don't want to die."

He was trembling violently. I held his hand.

"Tell my mom I'm sorry I didn't come home. Tell her I was brave."

I started with the perfunctory "you tell her yourself, because you're going to be okay," but he coughed violently, spraying blood on my face. His eyes glassed over as his last breath escaped his lips. He became quiet. I cradled his head and pressed my brow into his hair and began to sob. My friend was gone.

I gently pulled his eyelids down. Shaking, I unclipped his Coleman stove from his belt and secured it to my own. I put his helmet back on him and covered him with my poncho.

Sitting beside his lifeless form, I was too heavy with grief to get up and leave him. Here he was, a kid. A kid whose life was over. His body would never leave this bedeviled island.

He'd never see his mother again. She'd never see her baby. He was only eighteen. He'd never voted. Never made love to a girl. He'd never get married and have kids. He wasn't even allowed to drink alcohol legally. Hell, from the looks of it, he hadn't even needed to shave yet. He was only a child. A child who saw horrors and lived in ten days of hell on this island; and for what? What a giant waste of a human life. Of human potential.

How was I supposed to tell his mom he was brave? I didn't even know who she was. I should have learned more about him. All I knew was he was from Kansas City. But I knew he was brave. Very brave.

"Let graves registration take him from here." Angier helped me to my feet. He put his hand on my upper back and guided me back toward the rest of the unit.

"I'll finish the line." Amid my mourning, I couldn't help feeling touched by Angier's compassion.

When I got back to camp, O'Toole asked me where the hell we'd been. Without saying a word, I walked right up to him and buried my right hand in his stupid, ugly face. He fell to the ground and curled up, covering his head with his arms. I bent over him poised to hit him again.

"Get away from me, you son of a bitch!" he yelled like a child. He looked like he was going to cry and then go tattle on me. I backed off. He wasn't worth it.

"You'll be court martialed for this, you son of a bitch!" he carried on as I walked away.

I found an unoccupied half shelter and crawled underneath where I had a full come-apart. I broke down. I couldn't control my sobbing. Folgers had been my only true friend on this hell hole of an island. My foxhole buddy. My backup. My source of levity. My source of coffee. My brother.

I bawled my eyes out for all of the wasted human life on this island, for the civilians that were so afraid that they opted to kill themselves and their families rather than face us, their liberators. I sobbed because it was still raining, my dysentery was wreaking havoc on my body, and my feet were burning with blisters and infection; because I missed my family and friends at home; because this war was an absurdity and no man should have to endure this nightmare.

Like a child, I cried myself to sleep. A few hours into my slumber, the Japs started shelling us again. Of goddamn course. Our mortars and artillery answered in kind. Nothing hit any closer than a hundred yards or so from me. I almost didn't care. I guess if you're meant to die, you'll die. There's not a lot you can do about it when shells are raining down. If there was a day to pass on, this was a good day to leave the earth.

With these thoughts running through my head I began to wonder if I was beginning to crack up. Was this what it felt like to go Asiatic? Did I have combat fatigue? Was not-giving-a-shit a symptom? I curled up and slid my hands under my helmet to cover my ears. Somehow I fell asleep again. As explosions rocked the ground, I barely stirred.

When I awoke again, an unfamiliar sight was before me. My wife and kids aside, it was one of the most beautiful things I'd ever seen. Beyond distant hills, a gorgeous sunrise was developing. Orange and gold reached into the deep blue sky with a spattering of small, white clouds. The sky was mostly clear, but my mind was in a fog. I felt like God, with the urging of his newest angel, Folgers, arranged this for me.

Hut was sleeping in a small depression to my left. As I stood, I was surprised by a quiet clink at my belt line. I had forgotten I had Folgers's stove on my belt. I sat back down, fired it up and placed my metal canteen cup, half-filled with water, on the flame.

I leaned back and lit a cigarette. It felt amazing to start the morning without rain. Before I could get too comfortable, of course, my intestines spoke up and demanded my attention.

The dysentery was taking its toll on me. I suffered from headaches and my muscles were sore because I had become dehydrated. All the extra squatting my affliction required was over-working my bad leg. It cramped often and was very stiff.

Hobbling back from my makeshift latrine, I accidentally woke up Hut. Wiping sleep from his eyes, he marveled at the drastic change in weather.

"Holy crap. The sun shines in hell? How long's it been since we've seen that son of a bitch?" He pulled a wad of gum off the butt stock of his rifle and shoved it in his mouth.

"Got any for me?" he asked as he pointed at my heating

water.

"Yeah, this one's for you." I handed him my cup. In return, he gave me his empty one and I repeated the process of heating more water. After mixing the instant coffee, we let the cups sit until the coffee became tepid so we wouldn't burn our lips on the cup. While waiting we said nothing. Just stared at the sunrise and listened to the peaceful sound of distant shelling.

Holding up his coffee, Hut said to me, "To Folgers."

"To Folgers."

That's really all we said about our fallen friend.

We sat in silence while we forced down a K-ration breakfast and enjoyed the cup of joe. It pained me to know how much Folgers would have appreciated that coffee and the extraordinary sunrise. I felt guilty for enjoying it. It was a damn shame he didn't live to see the sun come out again.

I surprised myself when I began counting my blessings. The sunrise must have inspired it. I thanked the good Lord above for the beautiful morning. I thanked Him that I was still alive and my family was safe.

My reverie was interrupted by my intestines. Apparently they weren't ready for coffee. I paid another objectionable visit to a boulder. When I returned, it was easy to find my spot. My butt cheeks had left an impression in the mud. I lit another cigarette.

"I thought I smelled coffee!" said Doc Wright as he came around a group of boulders. He plunked down beside Hut. "Got any for me?"

"Yeah, here you go." I handed him mine.

"Make sure you stay hydrated, Kentucky," Doc said.

"I'm trying."

"There is a bright side to dysentery," said Doc.

"That'll take some convincing. Go on."

"In combat, or any situation where you feel like your life could be in danger, your body automatically wants to evacuate the bowls."

"You don't have to be a doctor to know that," Hut said. "I have proof of that in my skivvies." We all chuckled a little.

"You know why we shit our pants when we're scared? Why we're scared shitless, so to speak?" Doc Wright continued. "It's a survival mechanism. If we get shot or stabbed in the body with our guts full of shit and bacteria, we would be more likely to die from sepsis because all the intestinal germs would get in our wound."

"Enlightening."

"So, dysentery has a silver lining. If you get shot in the stomach, you won't have any shit in you to infect your wound."

"That makes me feel a hell of a lot better, Doc," I said. "I really appreciate it. You're a real prince, you know that?"

"Hey, I try."

"Let's get going, ladies!" Angier said as he walked by. We reluctantly got to our feet.

"Oh, I almost forgot to remind you," Doc said. "There's a bunch of damn snakes down in those fields. Okinawan Habu snakes. Venomous as hell. Watch out for those bastards. While you're looking out for them, be aware of mines too. Apparently they're finding land mines all over the place."

"Swell," I said. "We really need more things trying to kill us."

"Don't we have *enough* Jap snakes to look out for?" some comedian said.

"Okinawan, shit head. They're Okinawan snakes."

"For chrissake, you know what the hell I mean."

Distracted by war, I'd almost forgotten the prospect of venomous snakes. I could see the snake in my mind. The Corps gave us a small, illustrated guide on those damn varmints. Intimidating bastards. They're described as olive or light brown in color with long, dark green or brown blotches highlighted in yellow. The pattern resembled double triangles. It had a big triangular head and creepy-ass eyes. The sons of bitches could get up to eight feet long.

It reminded me of a rattlesnake back in the States, but without the rattle. Somehow it took on a more oriental look, if that makes sense. The guide said they are numerous and there are a lot of victims. "Death rate high," it said. The Habu wasn't alone. It had friends who were nearly as nasty. All of which enjoyed hanging out in caves, tombs, and jungle vegetation. Oh, and they loved coming out at night. Perfect. I believe a footnote claimed they enjoyed dining on white, American flesh.

"It could be worse," Hut spoke up as we walked.

"Oh hell, what's with the pep talk today?" I said. "Am I the only one not shitting rainbows this morning?"

"Snakes are bad, but at least we don't have packs of wolves hunting us," Hut said.

I knew another one of his history lessons was in order. I stopped and put my hand on his chest halting his advancement. I looked him in the eyes and said in almost a whisper, "Hut, my dear friend, what the fuck are you talking about now?"

We started walking again.

"During the first World War, there was apparently what they called a 'Super Pack' of Russian wolves. Hundreds of wolves started attacking and killing the Russian and German soldiers. It got so bad that the Krauts and Russian armies agreed to a truce so they could work together to hunt and kill the wolves."

"Holy shit," said Doc.

"Can you believe that? Thousands of men who were armed with machine guns, rifles, and grenades were killed by wolves more than they were the enemy."

"That's down-right creepy," I said.

"Just be glad we only have to deal with a few poisonous snakes," Hut continued.

"Venomous," Doc interrupted from behind.

"Venomous, poisonous? For chrissake, what's the difference?" Hut retorted.

"Venom is injected by something like a snake or spider. Poison is something ingested like cyanide or a plant."

"Well, thanks for clearing that shit up. I'd have never made it through the war without knowing the difference."

"Anyway," Hut turned back toward me. "It could be worse."

"Agreed," I said, "but can we knock it off with all the 'bright-side-of-things' crap. All of you people are puking sunshine this morning and it's making me sick."

I knew they were just trying to lighten the mood and I appreciated it. I just wasn't ready to be happy yet.

CHAPTER TWENTY-NINE
NIGHT BATTLE

FROM THE TOP OF A ridge, I could see the landscape to the north. For a quarter of a mile or so in each direction, earthen walls framed flooded paddy fields. A road parted the fields and meandered east, then back to the west, disappearing between more hills. Small houses dotted the landscape. We passed through a bare stand of trees still smoking from the artillery barrage the night before.

The rest of Love Company bunched up at the edge of the field. Angier and Capone sat on their haunches, looking intently at a piece of airplane wing.

"What's the dope?" Hut asked.

"I think mine's winning," Capone said without looking up. "They're so goddamn slow it's hard to tell who's gonna cross the finish line first. But I'm feeling pretty good about my odds."

"The hell you say," Angier said. "Harvey is kicking ass."

Capone turned to Angier, "Harvey? You named the goddamn thing?"

"Yeah, and because of Harvey, you're going to owe me five bucks."

"For chrissake. Harvey sucks."

They were involved in a pretty serious engagement. Maggot racing. Creative, I'd give them that. I leaned over their shoulders to have a gander. No surprises; maggot racing was about as exciting as you'd guess.

"I mean, what's the hold-up?" Hut tried again.

"Mines. Lots of 'em." Capone answered.

Captain Haigler leaned against a tree, the phone to his ear, talking to Battalion. Apparently, Angier and Capone had taken care of things while I was losing my mind. The Skipper tried to get some tank support, but was told they were still bogged down in mud. No surprise there.

Mine clearing crews were hard at work. We sat in wet ashes and charred twigs, and waited for further orders.

"Did you hear about O'Toole?" asked Capone.

My heart galloped. I had forgotten about my imminent court martial for punching his damn face in. I checked to see if there was any swelling around my knuckles. Too dirty to tell. I wondered if he had reported me yet.

"Dead," Capone said.

"Dead?"

"He thought it would be a good idea to kick a tomato can on

the side of the road."

"I don't follow." Hut said.

"It was a mine, shit-for-brains! Damn Japs have mines in everything. Cans, dead animals, cabbage, the bodies of their dead infantry, you name it. Hell, they even put mines in beer bottles. Lousy bastards."

My initial reaction to this news was relief. *Good*, I thought, *now that horse's ass can't report me.* I bowed my head, staring at the mud. Only on a battlefield could one become so numb and hardened that his first reaction to a fellow Marine dying was relief. God, forgive me.

"By the way," Capone started again, "did anyone notice the shiner on the Tool?"

"No!" Angier said emphatically, "no one noticed any shiner on O'Toole. Did we boys?" He shot me a quick wink.

"No sir."

"No sir. Didn't see a thing."

Capone gave me a light punch in the shoulder. "Nah, I didn't see nuthin' either."

It took the better part of the day to cross the mine-sewn field. Mine removal wasn't something you wanted to rush. But we were finally operating under clear skies. The hot sun dried our dungarees in no time. It was damn hot. It almost made me wish for more rain. Almost.

Near dusk, we reached the other side of the field where it butted against a low ridge. 1st platoon had already cleared a row of battered houses that nestled beside the ridge. We set up the command post in the first house we reached.

As the sun fell, a barrage of mortar fire rained down from the ridge.

"Incoming mail!" someone yelled.

Our mortar squads got to work returning fire. The Skipper came in as I untangled wires and connected everything.

"How's that .45 treating you?" He picked up the receiver.

"It's a beauty, sir. Thank you." I started unbuckling the holster to give it back. He waved his hand and patted a new holster on his hip. It looked like a pistol he'd picked off a Japanese officer. He started to say he had a new sidearm, but was interrupted when a voice answered on the other end of the phone line.

"I need the hell blasted out of that ridge," he said. "Coordinates 300 - 310!"

He grinned as the roar of our artillery started over our heads. "Outgoing mail."

We stepped outside to see where the shells were hitting, and the Skipper went back to the receiver: "Left 30 - add 50!"

Our new lieutenant, James Bussard approached and reported for duty. He was a replacement that arrived with Folgers and me. All I knew about him was that he was from Ohio, and like O'Toole, had recently graduated from Quantico.

More cannons fired in the distance and shells wailed overhead and slammed into the ridge in front of our position. Captain Haigler told me to find my unit. I ran into the night toward Angier and the guys. Machine gun rounds smacked the rooftops and the dirt road.

We were thrown into another firefight, but this time it was in the dark. The only thing more terrifying than fighting a fanatical enemy was doing so blind.

The Japs had machine gun nests scattered around the ridge. Light machine guns and heavy. We later learned the heavy guns were 40mm cannons stripped from their planes and adapted for ground use. The crafty Nips camouflaged the openings of pill boxes and set these damn guns back inside, out of sight. Artillery mounted on wheels were rolled out of the mouth of caves, fired, then pulled back into the safety of the cavern.

In the absence of flares, the only thing visible were explosions and the flicker of tracers. Our machine gunners shot a phosphorescent tracer round every fifth round to zero in on the target without betraying the gunner's position. They also loaded two or three tracer rounds in a row near the end of the ammo belt to let them know they were almost out.

Our boys were busy. Thousands of tracers zipped into the hill. The Japs' Nambu machine guns spit out flaring rounds too. The strings of lights flying back and forth would have looked beautiful under any other circumstance.

Once again, the Japs had the advantage of the higher ground. For most of the night, we lay flat on terra firma, slowly inching uphill and firing off pot shots as we went. Periodically, flamethrowers illuminated the side of the hill causing human torches, weaving and flailing their arms, to pour out of their spider holes and collapse in a rolling heap of flames.

The light of a flare showed a kid from our platoon lying in a depression a few yards above me on the hill. He hugged his carbine. I crawled to him and lay beside him. He acted like I wasn't even there. I sure as hell wasn't expecting any pleasantries about the weather, but he didn't even glance in my direction. He was staring into space. There was nothing in his eyes. They were primal and lifeless, the eyes of a mad man.

He mumbled something about getting the tractor started. I thought he meant one of the artillery tractors, tanks, or bulldozers, but, then he went on about pigs. He hadn't fed the pigs. "They's gonna be hungry."

I remembered he was from west Tennessee and grew up on a farm. I think his name was Dwight or Darrell. He had obviously cracked, gone Asiatic. When I pulled at his arm, he only clutched his carbine tighter. I left him there and kept moving upward to find my squad. I found out later he shot himself in the head.

Twice, we were driven backward to the base of the hill and three times we fought our way back up. Finally in the pre-dawn hours, we overtook the ridge. We worked until noon mopping up and tending to the wounded and dead. We sustained fifteen dead and twenty-four wounded.

Hut, Capone, and I explored the caves in the hill—a labyrinth of interconnected tunnels. Some were natural passageways, but most were man made. The slippery Japs could fire from an opening, retreat into the tunnel, and come out on another side to fire on a completely different set of Marines. There was no wonder why it took so much effort to get up that damn hill.

We had to seal off every cave as we went. If we didn't blow the hell out of the tunnels, more Jap assholes would pour out.

Around mid-afternoon, we were able to break for a C-rations lunch. Canned meat among dead bodies, smoking human flesh, diarrhea, and flies the size of a marble made for a delightful picnic. It was nearly impossible to eat. Human flesh, both rotting and fresh, was everywhere. The overpowering stench had a way of suppressing your appetite. When you did finally brave a bite, you had to compete with flies that were relentless in their pursuit to consume and shit on everything you wanted to eat. You had to continuously blow them off each bite. Many of those bastards had just fed on a corpse before landing on your fork-full.

If you did get something in your mouth, it tasted like the smell of decay and dysentery. Chewing and swallowing required an indomitable spirit. Keeping it down could only be done if you looked to the sky and pretended you were somewhere else, smelling Mom's kitchen.

Some veterans didn't even seem put off. One Marine sat in the mud and leaned against the dead body of a Jap like it was a bean bag or something. He shoveled rations into his mouth without a care in the world while flies crawled all over his face. I'm fairly certain he consumed at least two with his food while I watched him.

I, on the other hand, felt like crying. Not one to miss out on an opportunity for harassment, Capone moved in to give me hell.

"Lovely day for a picnic, huh Kentucky?" I replied with a half-assed nod without looking up.

"You'll get used to it."

Yeah, yeah, yeah. I thought. *You're a veteran, and I'm a rookie. I get it.*

"Here."

I looked up and he was holding out two cigarette butts.

"Put these in your nose. It'll help."

I did as he said. I crammed a butt in each nostril and a lit a cigarette for my mouth. It wasn't Mom's kitchen, but it was about as good as it could get while you're eating lunch in a cesspool. Capone sat beside me. I thanked him and we, to my surprise, shot the breeze for a few minutes. As we talked, he picked maggots off a rotting Jap corpse beside him, carefully set each one on his knee, and tried to flick them into an ammo can a few yards off. He was a decent shot, I'd give him that.

He told me he had a baby daughter, and that his wife had started seeing another man after he was deployed. She'd admitted it to him in a letter he received just before Sugar Loaf. Even Capone didn't deserve that kind of crap.

I'm not sure what had gotten into him that day, but he even assured me I'd see my girls again. It sort of warmed my heart, if you want to know the truth. I guess he finally accepted me as an equal.

The next morning Lt. Bussard ordered Hut and me to help

with a communication operation at the Naha Harbor, so we humped it east. Dodging sniper fire, we made it to the harbor where most of the 6th Division's wiremen congregated.

Our job was to set up communication from Naha to the Ono Yama island, then to the peninsula. The project was daunting, but for a brief time, it took my mind off the prospect of being killed. We used rubber boats to string the wire from the peninsula to the island where we would meet other wiremen coming from Naha. Close to halfway between the peninsula and Ono Yama, the top half of a sunken ship poked out of the water. The mast made a perfect telephone pole.

I felt a sense of pride when we landed on that island, because just days ago—it seemed like a year—Corporal Baer was killed when we were ambushed trying to get surveillance on that sonofabitch. Now it was in our hands.

Engineers had been working since sunrise. Before we arrived, they had repaired bridges between the east side of the island and Naha, while the 6th Reconnaissance Company provided them with protection.

Working beside us, they built a long bridge with inflatable rubber pontoons to connect Ono Yama and Oroku. Progress was slow because Jap machine gunners continually shot at the pontoons to deflate them. After the Marines silenced the Jap gunners, progress continued again. When they finished their work, the 6th Engineer Battalion had completed the longest bailey bridge in Marine Corps history.

From a distance, I studied the engineers, looking for my

brother in law, Earl. I never saw him. There were a lot of guys and I was pretty distracted, so I didn't really expect to see him.

We connected the wires at the assault unit switchboards and made our way back to the rest of Love Company.

Captain Haigler called us together for a briefing at the top of the hill. We could see a good bit of the peninsula in all directions. Pointing to the north, he said, "That there is Hill 53, our next objective. Dope has it that Admiral Ota and his ragtag group of navy soldiers are holed up inside. The 3/4 and 3/29 are approaching it from the west and the north, the 2/29 are coming from the east across the harbor. The south is up to us. We'll encircle those sonsofbitches and kill them all."

If any of us had any energy, we might've yelled *Hurrah*, or some such nonsense, but we hadn't any, so we didn't. The Skipper tried to encourage us, but it was akin to telling a death row inmate everything was going to be peachy.

The rest of the day we tended to the wounded and dead. Hut and I strung wire down the ridge to our previous post. After sunset, we dug in and tried to get sleep. It didn't come.

Jap artillery hammered our position off and on for hours. Sporadic firefights broke out in between shellings. Shadows moved about the hill around us. Not hearing anyone yelling out the night's password, *Lollypop*, we assumed they were Japs.

Between gunfire, we heard the haunting screams of a Marine from the hill below us. He couldn't have been more than fifty yards away. For hours, he called for his mother and cried out to

God. No one could do anything about it because getting out of your foxhole meant dying. We figured from the sound of it that he wasn't going to make it anyway and that it might not be worth risking our lives for him. Sounds callous, but that's what war does to you.

"God, I wish he would just die already," Hut said under his breath.

"Yeah, it's a damn shame to hear him suffer like that."

Hut carefully shifted his posture a bit. "Say, does his voice sound familiar?"

I cocked my head. "Could be anyone. I hope it's not familiar."

I could make out other voices closer to the Marine telling him to be quiet or he'd give away our position. The kid continued to moan and carry on. It was heart-wrenching. I wanted him to shut up for the reason the other Marines did, but I also wanted him silenced because of what it was doing to me. It was tearing me up.

Aside from artillery blasts, machine gun fire, and the boy's wails, the other tormentor that night was insects. With the rain gone, mosquitoes were everywhere, in my eyes, ears, and up my nose. I didn't want to swat them out of fear that a creeping Jap would hear or see my movements.

The damn lice made matters worse. They were ubiquitous in war, crawling into your hair, ears and nose, eyebrows, and even in the skivvies. I yearned for the powder treatment they gave new recruits at boot camp. To avoid making even the slightest sound, it took everything I had to refrain from scratching. It was maddening.

With fatigue tightening its grip, I said a quick prayer the boy on the hill would die soon, and I fell into a restless sleep.

While we did our damnedest to get some rest, Love Company scouts made contact with the 3/29 on our left, officially connecting the ring of Marines around Admiral Ota.

The next morning, mine disposal teams were hard at work in the field between us and Hill 53. We moved out to tighten the noose around the Japs.

A hand slapped me on the shoulder from behind, and I jumped.

"Hey, Kentucky!"

It was Bushrod, donning a big smile.

"What the hell are you doing back here?"

"Oh, I'm fine. I just needed a little rest."

Better man than me, I thought. "Good as hell to see you, buddy."

He clapped me on the back of my neck. "I'm sorry about Folgers. I know you guys were good chums."

I didn't say anything.

He gave my neck a little squeeze, then adjusted the strap on his rifle. "Sucks about Angier."

"What about him?"

"Got hit," he said.

"What do you mean, got hit?"

"Jap shell. Lost one of his legs and part of his arm."

"No shit?"

"No shit. Screamed half the night. No one could help him.

You probably heard him."

I didn't know what to say. I was stunned.

"Tough son of a bitch though," Bushrod continued. "Made it through the night. He's on his way to a hospital ship by now."

The news hit me hard. Sergeant Angier was my rock, the glue that held our unit together. It was disheartening to know that a guy so tough could be driven to cry for his mom and sob all night.

CHAPTER THIRTY

HILL 53

FIGHTING OUR WAY TOWARD HILL 53, Love Company climbed the south side as the other battalions approached from the other directions. We had the Japs surrounded. The intensity of the fighting increased as we confined the Japs to a smaller and smaller area. Casualties became heavier and heavier with every yard we advanced. Blood soon saturated Hill 53.

Marines fell all around me. Casualties mounted. Waves of men were taken to the rear with wounds or combat fatigue. My company was rapidly reducing in number.

A strange new sound suddenly filled the air above us. The damn Nips were launching gray canisters the size of ash cans at us. They were enormous, 320mm spigot mortars that we naturally called the "flying ash cans." They employed huge eight inch rockets too. Normally used as coast defense guns, the rail-mounted rocket launchers were redirected inland. The massive shells flew awkwardly end over end and made a demonic sound earning it the name "Screaming Mimi."

Flamethrower tanks caught up to us and unleashed their awesome death torches into tombs and caves. Their cannons spewed huge streams of jellied fire onto the hillside, igniting all vegetation and humans in its path. It was an amazing, and horrifying, sight.

A stretcher bearing Frank Salazar, our radioman, made its way past me. He looked at me and gave a thumbs up. He was missing his right hand, but the smile on his face told me he knew he was going home. His million dollar wound cost him a hand. Apparently, he'd been hit by friendly fire. While advancing around the hill toward our position, someone in the 3/29 had thought we were the Japs.

I gave him a wave goodbye. As I turned back toward the hill and saw what still lay ahead of me, I sort of envied him. It was sick, but at that moment I would have given my right hand to go home to my girls.

The 6th Marine Division continued to close in on Admiral Ota's force. As the noose tightened, their resistance became increasingly fierce. Casualty traffic became so heavy that we had a shortage of stretchers. Jim Laughridge and five other guys carried a wounded Marine on a door they'd ripped off a house. They had to transport the wounded about eight miles to the nearest first aid station.

After walking all night, Laughridge and a buddy hit the deck next to Hut and me just after dawn. Exhausted, Laughridge said, "the next son of a bitch that gets hit, if he has to be carried out, I'm gonna shoot him right here."

A supply drop intended for us missed our position by about a thousand yards. No vehicles could move, so Lieutenant Bussard told Laughridge, Hut, Capone, and me to go get it.

We encountered no problems as we crossed a large field to get the supplies. But on the way back, the Japs started laying it on us heavy. They had zeroed in on us with their damn 20-millimeter aircraft cannons. It came down on us in a torrent. We all hauled ass except for Lock. He got hit and crawled behind a small knoll.

After our own artillery barrage on the position of the 20-millimeters, we went out to check on Lock. He lay on his back as if he was enjoying his time of rest. He had been hit in the leg and needed help walking.

Remembering what he'd said that morning about shooting anyone who needed to be carried out, Capone pulled out his .45, pointed it at Laughridge and said, "Lock, you ready to go?" We all got a decent chuckle out of that.

"Get that damn gun out of my face, Capone."

"Shit, now *you're* calling me that too? Sonofabitch!"

The comedy didn't last very long. It seemed as if every Jap in the area had a machine gun. We had to get our asses moving again. We dragged Laughridge to a Jeep and returned to the bedlam.

Later in the day, Lieutenant Bussard got hit around Hill 53. A shot right in the head. It was tough to see him go. He'd seemed like a good officer. Captain Haigler picked up the bullet-pierced helmet and kept it. He must have been shaken up by Bussard's death, because an American helmet wasn't much of a souvenir.

We lost a bunch more guys that day before we secured Hill 53. I believe it was June 11. It was late afternoon before we got to rest. We strung some more wire, dug in, and attempted to sleep.

The Skipper decided to camp out next to us. He had been out doing reconnaissance and came back to camp much later than we did. Everyone but him had dug their hole and eaten. This happened quite a bit to him, but tonight he was a little extra ornery about it. Doc Wright usually carried a stretcher around with him and he often lay on it to sleep. Not this night.

The Skipper said to Doc, "I'm going to use your litter to sleep on."

"Well, I've been carrying it all day," Doc rebutted, "and now *you're* going to sleep on it?"

"Yeah, you're damn right I'm going to sleep on that litter tonight."

Some Marines weren't big fans of Captain Haigler because of incidences like that or because of his souvenir obsession. But for the most part, I thought he was a good leader. He was under a lot of pressure. There's no way I could've switched places with him and kept it together. So what if he wanted a decent night's sleep or a couple of things to sell to the Seabees or take home? He'd been on battlefields for the past year.

The night he hijacked the litter, he'd had a pretty tough day. Dope had it that he and some fellas had thrown a grenade into a cave. For good measure, the Skipper had the demolitions sergeant, Joe Rhodes, throw in a dynamite charge. Assuming all inside were dead, Skipper ran in to look for souvenirs. He found several dead bodies, but a Jap lieutenant rose to attack. The Skipper shot him point blank with his pistol. Somehow, Skipper was hit at the same time. He grabbed a samurai sword and crawled out yelling, "God, he shot me! I got shot right in the balls!"

Turns out, his bullet ricocheted off the Jap's helmet and came back at him. There was no damage done, but he felt like he took a kick to the crotch. He was fine in five minutes.

The next day brought more of the same misery.

Many Japs started giving up on the war effort. Many lay on satchel charges and blew themselves to smithereens. We found some with the rifle barrel in their mouths, a hole in the back of their heads, and their bare toes on the trigger. The most depressing part of the ghastly scene was that it hardly fazed me. I guess I had grown numb. I didn't really care anymore about the Jap savages. If they wanted to kill themselves, so be it.

The battle gradually slowed to intermittent firefights and cave cleanings. We became stretcher bearers and took on the duties of graves registration. We collected dog tags off the fallen, leaving one around their neck. It was a grisly affair.

I collapsed in a heap on top of the hill. I was relieved another battle was over and I was still alive. My fatigued body became limp. The tension in my muscles poured out of me into the rocky earth below.

Hut and I were sharing a cigarette when we heard a commotion to our east.

Hut got to his feet. "Let's go check it out."

It was a punishing endeavor to stand up. I felt like a decrepit ninety-year-old. Every part of me hurt and all of my joints vehemently opposed movement.

On Hill 53, a Marine stumbled on to an air duct protruding from the ground, which led them to an entrance. We followed some fellas into a passage that opened into an underground fortress.

The tunnels weren't like tunnels on the rest of the island. The walls were finished concrete and lights lined the rounded ceilings. Most tunnels throughout the island contained several ninety degree turns to slow the blast of explosives or flamethrowers, but these went so deep there was no need.

Reaching more than 1,500 feet, the tunnels connected dozens of rooms. We found complete kitchens, dormitories, code and radio rooms, a hospital, and a command center.

We were in Admiral Ota's Naval Command Headquarters. The headquarters was made up of several stories and reached more than one hundred feet deep and seventy-five feet from the sides of the hill. No amount of artillery could have fazed it.

All rooms were furnished and even decorated. Each had electricity and was well ventilated. The ventilation didn't keep us from nearly suffocating from the heavy fumes. You'd think I'd have been used to the smell of death, but you'd be wrong. It was too much to take. There was no fresh air to dilute it. I jammed cigarette butts in my nostrils.

We found two hundred dead Japs inside the fortress. All took their own lives. Some with grenades held to their throats or chest. The walls were scarred from grenade fragments and covered with blood spatter. Some of the Japs had put a pistol to their heads, and some apparently drank poison.

Deep inside, we found Ota's personal quarters and commanding officers' room. His body and five of his staff members lay on beds with their throats cut. Everything was organized and tidy. An aide must have cleaned up after the officers killed themselves.

On the white, concrete wall, black paint scribed Ota's death poem. Daniel Swinggate translated it: *To die for the emperor is the highest honor.* On another wall someone had written: *We will destroy all the evil Americans.* Creepy.

"Why are they like this?" I asked Swinggate. "Why don't the sonsofbitches surrender so they can live? Don't get me wrong, I don't care if they all die. But what's wrong with these bastards?" I didn't really expect an answer. Swinggate didn't say anything. He just stared at the kanji on the wall.

"Why can't they be more like the Germans?" Hut said. "My brother said the Krauts would surrender by the millions."

A Marine named Ray Pittman spoke up. "Yeah, you surround fifty thousand Germans and they surrender. You surround one Jap and he'll keep fighting."

Hut inspected a bullet hole in the wall under the writing. "My brother said that in North Africa a quarter million Krauts surrendered at one time. He said there was a fourteen mile line of Germans waiting to surrender.

"Oh and get this. He said in Anzio the Germans held their damn fire each afternoon to watch American GIs play softball. Can you imagine the Japs doing something like that?"

"Bushido Code," Swinggate finally said.

"What the hell is the Bull-shit-o Code?" Capone said.

"It was the code the Samurai followed, an honorable way to live and die as a warrior. As of late, the Japanese government corrupted it and used it to brainwash the modern Japanese warriors. They've been indoctrinated with it since they were kids. It's not really their fault. They were raised to worship emperor Hirohito and die for his ass. That's why they kill themselves rather than give up. It's an unbearable shame for them to accept defeat from us white devils."

Captain Haigler interrupted and told Hut and me to find the Japs' communications and dismantle anything that remained and see if there was anything useful to us. When we found the comm room, a guy named Fenton Grahnert was already nosing around inside.

"I wouldn't touch anything," he said. His baby face, big ears, and wide smile were incongruous in such a cruddy place. He looked far too happy. "Looks booby trapped."

"Shit," I said. "Are you sure?"

"Sure as I'm standing here."

Hut stepped out of the room. "I'll tell Haigler."

When Hut left, I shot the crap with Grahnert for a couple of minutes while we looked things over. He said everyone called him Gabby and he was from Rapid City, South Dakota. Said on account of the Great Depression, they moved to Portland, Oregon looking for a better life.

His older brother had enlisted in the Marine Corps back in 1939 and was captured at Corregidor in the Philippines and forced on the Bataan Death March. Grahnert was later drafted into the Corps and he fought with Love Company on Guam before coming to shore on Okinawa. Gabby was friends with Herman Mulligan, the Marine who was killed when his grenade blew up the side of Hill 27.

He showed me the tripwire that he thought was suspicious. The sneaky bastards had mixed it in with the other communications wires. We followed the thin wire behind the switchboard. The trip wire was tied to the fuse cord of a grenade.

"It's a model 23 grenade," Grahnert said. "I don't think we should mess with it. There's not much in here to get our panties in a wad over."

The grenade was about two inches in diameter and almost four inches long. It had two rings attached—one at the top and one at bottom. Metal wire passed through the rings anchoring the grenade to the leg of a table.

"Couldn't find him," Hut said when he stepped through the doorway. "They said he's hunting souvenirs. This place is a goddamn maze, and I'm not going to spend a whole hell of a lot of time looking for him."

"What do you want to do?" I asked.

"How bad does it look?" Hut asked Gabby.

"Typical Jap grenade with tripwire. I wouldn't mess with it."

Hut reached under his helmet to scratch his head. "Let's blow it up." He unclipped his grenade and told us to get out.

Gabby and I hurried down the corridor and Hut stood outside the doorway. He pulled the pin, made the sign of the cross, threw the grenade into the room, and ran toward us.

"Better get," Hut said as he hauled ass toward us.

We sprinted farther down the tunnel.

The explosion was surprisingly suppressed, but the pressure of the concussion stormed through the passageways like a heavy wind.

"Well, that ought to do it," Hut said.

We didn't bother going back to the communications room. We were confident there wasn't much to see. The three of us explored the labyrinth for a few more minutes. I had an uneasy feeling the whole time. I wasn't disappointed when we ran into a private who told us the Skipper wanted Love Company "out of the damn cave" to help with mop-up.

Outside, we reveled in the relatively fresh air and got straight to work, removing holdouts and accepting the surrender of a handful of Japs. We helped dozens of civilians come out of hiding and fed them. The Marines around me fed children by hand. One Marine took his shirt off to cover a naked civilian girl.

I came across a tiny Okinawan girl. She was maybe four or

five years old. About the same age as my daughter, Kay. She was wandering around without a family. She wasn't crying. That was the weird thing about these Okinawans. I didn't remember seeing anyone crying. Not even the children. Maybe they were in shock. Their faces held a constant look of fear and confusion.

Anyway, I went over to the little girl and picked her up. She didn't even make a fuss, looking me square in the face with no expression at all. I asked her where her parents were. I don't know why I expected her to understand me. I carried that sweet thing around for almost an hour looking for her parents. Holding her made me feel like I was with my girls again. It was a nice change from the carnage I'd been a part of the past couple of weeks.

Like I said, after about an hour, I was walking past a burned out building and I heard a lady screaming. What the hell she was saying, I had no idea, but it was probably something like, *My baby! That's my baby!* She ran over to me and yanked the girl from my hands. The mother offered me no "thank you," or "nifee doo," or whatever the hell they say. The little girl stared back at me blankly as they walked away.

CHAPTER THIRTY-ONE
UP CLOSE AND PERSONAL

WITH ADMIRAL OTA TAKEN CARE of, we had to contribute to the chase of General Ushijima at the bottom of the island. The 1st Marine Division was dealing with them several miles to the south.

On our way back through the village, I went toward the post where our switchboard was. I stepped over the threshold and a Jap with his back to me was bent over examining our switchboard. My heart jumped into my throat. I raised my rifle. He heard the stock of the M1 rattle and began to turn. For a split second, I thought I could take him prisoner.

Our eyes met. His widened with fear and hatred. Like a wild animal cornered. He started to raise his Arisaka rifle. For some reason, I noticed he was left handed, confirming that everything about him was sinister.

Without thinking, I blasted three rounds into his chest. He collapsed backward in a slump landing in the tangle of wires, pulling the switchboard over on his legs.

My ears rang from the concussion of my rifle, but the strange thing was, I never even heard it fire. I stepped toward him in a state of shock. His chest slowly raised and lowered. His breathing was labored and raspy. Each inhalation whistled through gaping holes in his chest. His face contorted in anguish, his lips moved as if trying to tell me something. Blood trickled from his mouth. His eyes were like those of an abused beast of burden.

An audible rattle emanated from his throat. I later learned this was the "Death Rattle." His body became still and lifeless, like a puppet without a master. My rifle shots still echoed through the valley, and the room reeked of gunpowder and the copper smell of his blood. His feral, glazed eyes stared at me with hatred. Blood spread throughout his tan blouse and dripped on to his hat that had fallen to his side. I thought about the promise the Marine Corps made that we'd be fighting Japs eye-to-eye.

He looked so foreign. For some reason, his strange shoes stood out. They were the split-toe jobs the Japs wore a lot. They looked like black stocking feet that had just been relieved of flip flops.

Killing him was akin to killing a rattlesnake. I say that because one summer, Hody and I went with some friends to the lake. While I was going to our car for luggage, I came across a rattlesnake coiled up on the steps of the cabin. Action had to be taken.

If I didn't kill that damn snake, it could hurt or kill Hody or my friends. I didn't want to do it, but letting it continue to live near that cabin wasn't an option.

I found an axe on the side porch. I was armed and the snake was posturing like it wanted to strike. The battle ensued. Fear and adrenaline surged through me. I was so alive, so present and focused.

My hands shook wildly and I had a hard time judging the distance. My first two swings missed. The worst part was I didn't know the reach the little creep had. With each miss, the bastard struck out at me. My heart raced. My grip became slippery with sweat.

On swing number three, I cut off its tail. Swings four and five caught the sides of him. Each time I approached, it would slither off a yard or two and turn back at me poised to strike again. Intimidating son of a bitch.

I decided to throw a long log on it to keep it still. At that point I was able to decapitate it. Exhausted, I sat in the dry dirt and watched its body continue to writhe.

When the adrenaline ebbed, I felt sad for the animal, but proud of my effort to protect my family and friends. I had prevailed over the venomous creature, but more importantly, my fears. As a trophy, I kept the rattle.

The way I felt about shooting the Jap wasn't all that different. I had learned to look at the Japanese race as animals. They were as wild and uncaring as snakes. Like taking the rattle, I felt justified in collecting a samurai sword trapped under the Jap's hip. I lifted his leg and wrenched the sword free. I unclipped it from his waist and let him fall back down with a thud.

Hut came in. "You okay?"

I continued to stare at the dead Jap. "Swell. Real swell."

When I shook myself out of a mental fog, I helped Hut and two others gather the wires and comm equipment.

Hut angled the switchboard out the door. "We gotta get. We're getting left behind."

Weighed down with about a million pounds of equipment, we humped it to catch up with the rest of Love Company.

The full weight of what I had done hit me when we were about a quarter mile down the road. I'd just ended the life of a young man. I knew he'd have killed me if I hadn't shot first. It was part of war.

What was really bothering me was that I'd grown so insensitive. I was calloused enough to take a trophy from a kid I'd killed. I was a murderer and a thief. The other guys didn't see it that way. They assured me I did the right thing. They were young though. They didn't have kids and a wife—the kind of things that makes a man value life more.

I didn't like who I was becoming. This God-forsaken island and its God-forsaken inhabitants were changing me. I used to worry about whether I'd make it home, but my greatest fear had become whether Hody would still love the man this fucking war was turning me into. Would my daughters see love in my eyes or would they see a new set of eyes? Those of a hardened killer?

I dropped my equipment, turned, and started a labored jog back to the post.

"Where the hell..." Hut yelled after me.

Of course I found the dead Jap just as I had left him. The body was unnaturally contorted on the rotten floorboards. I tugged on the carcass to lay it flat and straight. I laid the sword across his chest, crossed his hands on top, closed his eyes, and straightened his shirt. I tore a ragged curtain from the window and covered his body with it. I whispered that I was sorry, then hi-tailed it out of there to catch up with my unit. We continued south without mentioning my return to the Jap body.

CHAPTER THIRTY-TWO
MEZADO RIDGE

THE MARCH SOUTH WAS MORE mud, bad roads, and creepy villages. I felt like I was walking on hot coals. Around one o'clock in the morning, our line got held up, so we took a cigarette break in the dark. We were careful to cup our hands around the lighters to make sure we didn't give away our position. Most of us sat on our haunches to keep out of the mud. Ed Hoffman, a few yards to my right, sat on a log to smoke. He shot to his feet.

"Oh, shit!" he said. "Oh, son of a bitch!"

"What the hell, Hoffman?"

Shining a flashlight through his shirt, a Marine shed a dim light where Hoffman had beens sitting. He'd mistook the body of a dead Jap for a seat. An impression of Hoffman's ass was still visible in the rotting corpse.

"Ah, hell! It's wet! Goddamn juicy!" He felt his britches in horror. "God damn it! I've got dead Jap juice on my pants. It's soaking through. God damn it!"

Everyone erupted into laughter. The situation was impossibly hilarious. A ridiculous circumstance. I mean, who sits on a dead body? You couldn't help but laugh. Hoffman's reaction was priceless. He eventually joined in the laughter. We all needed a good laugh after Hill 53. Dark as hell humor, but humor nonetheless.

"God, does it stink?" Hoffman said as he pointed his ass at another Marine and shook it while backing toward him. "Someone smell my ass!"

More laughter.

"Get your lousy ass away from me!"

More laughs.

As good as the laughter felt, it jostled my stomach around too much. I had almost forgotten about my dysentery. The misery of war never let up.

At about two in the morning, we entered a town called Itoman, where Captain Haigler gave us a briefing in an alley. We were supposed to replace the 1st Marine Division on the Kunishi Ridge, then take the Mezado Ridge and Hill 69.

The 1st Marines passed through Itoman earlier, fighting a pretty tough battle. Apparently five officers were lost in seven minutes. Machine gun fire continued to spit out of the surrounding hills as we helped with mop up. The streets were sowed with mines, and caves on the outskirts needed to be secured, so we worked for a few hours, blasting and removing explosives.

Just outside Itoman, we found the body of a Marine we guessed was from the 1st Division. We were appalled. He was stripped of his clothes. Hundreds of bayonet holes riddled his bare chest and stomach. His head was cut off and sitting between his legs. The eyes were missing and maggots swam in the sockets. The poor guy's private parts had been cut off and stuffed in his mouth.

I vomited on the path and moved on. That's all you could do, really. With atrocities like that, sometimes all you could do was vomit and move on.

On the morning of June 17, we crossed a valley between Itoman and Hunishi. Only a few hundred yards in, we were under heavy fire, forcing us to turn back to our previous position. Captain Haigler decided we'd wait until dark. The valley between Hill 27 and 46 still fresh in their mind, no officers argued with the Skipper's decision.

Under the cover of darkness, we made an uneventful passage across the valley at 3:00am. By dawn, we were poised for an assault. Coffee, rations, rifle cleaning, diarrhea, shooting the breeze, and cat naps were in order until jump-off at 7:30am.

At the command post, I helped our new "Indian" repair a

SCR-300 radio. He had just joined us a day before. We called him *our* Indian—not very sensitive, I realize—but we were lousy kids. Each battalion had a Navajo code talker because, the Japs couldn't figure out that crazy language. The Skipper told the Indian to call up another Indian to get some gunfire from the Navy on the ridge in front of us.

By now, we were pretty close to the sea. Moments after the call, thunder clapped from the nearby warships. Screaming overhead, the shells flew toward the ridge. They fluttered so close I swear we could feel the wind as they cut through the air. The salvo battered the ridge and surrounding hills.

We moved toward the westward extension of Kunishi called Mezado Ridge. From there we went to Hill 69 to relieve one of the hardest hit 1st Marine Division units. The ominous rumble of battle vibrated in my head and my soul. The dread of combat felt like a ton of bricks in my stomach. A cold sweat trickled down my neck as we continued toward the fray.

The stench of the front line hit hard. Cigarette butts found their way into my nose again. We did our damnedest to steer clear of human remains and puddles filled with blood and mosquitos. Very few things in the world are more horrifying than slipping on another human's entrails. Believe me, I know.

The demeanor of the 1st Marines leaving the front painted a picture of the misery ahead. Their sunken faces looked despondent like ours. Other than the occasional "Get em, boys" most were quiet. Probably too tired to talk. We didn't waste our energy on conversation either.

***

Hill 69 was the tallest around, situated at the top of the ridge on the opposite side of Mezado's plateau. It was a crumby pile of coral crags. The ridge between was made up of the same crappy substrate. Sharp as hell. Impossible to dig in to. With King Company on our left flank, we started the ascent into hell. We didn't get a grand rallying cry like you see in the movies. No one called out "Charge." No rebel yells. Instead Capone yelled, "Keep your assholes tight, boys!" He had a way with words. A real poet, that Capone.

It wasn't long before we were forced to dive to the deck. About a thousand times, we got up, then dove onto the jagged coral. I'd gotten so used to diving into mud that the sharp pain of landing on coral came as a surprise every time I did it.

Left and right, men went down in sprays of blood. A guy in Love Company named Marion Rounds was one of the first. Not long after that, they hit Grahnert. The bullet went in near the left side of his nose and out his right ear. It was a very bloody sight. It looked like the whole side of his head was blown off.

Everyone moved on, leaving him for dead. Turned out, not only did he live, but he jumped back up, shot off a few more rounds from his rifle, grabbed a wounded friend and carried him a hundred yards back to the rest of Love Company. Tough sonofabitch!

For most of the morning, we engaged in some of the nastiest fighting yet. The entire 10th Army was in line from coast to coast, pushing the Japs toward the bottom of the island. Only a few miles from the southern tip of Okinawa, the Japs knew they were cornered and the end was near. They fought with more vigor and élan than ever before. They weren't about to dishonor Emperor Hirohito, their god.

We were forced back down the ridge because of overwhelming casualties. We needed replacements.

A guy several yards from me couldn't take it anymore and put a bullet through his own brain. I didn't know him. In fact, I didn't know very many of the guys left in Love Company. Familiar faces were disappearing at an alarming rate. We had so many replacements. Few of the men who were in Love Company when I came in were still around.

The fight for Mezado Ridge was gruesome. Not only were the Japs more savage, but the lion's share of Love Company was inexperienced. Even after growing somewhat accustomed to this bullshit, I was still shaking in my boots. Several times that morning, I might have soiled my underwear if it weren't for Capone's lyrical battle cry convincing me to tense up. I couldn't imagine the replacements having less experience than me. I understood how the guys felt when Folgers and I first came on.

The replacement's suicide was extra disheartening, because though we were catching serious hell now, we felt in our guts that the battle for Okinawa was near an end. If only he could've held on a little longer, he may've seen brighter days.

The only thing worse than getting killed in battle, was doing so near the end. With every new en bloc clip I jammed into my M1

Garand, I said a Hail Mary. I'd fire off all eight rounds, the clip would eject, I'd say another Hail Mary, then I'd resume firing.

The sound of the Garand's clip ejecting sent a chill down my spine. I only had a few precious seconds to reload before a damn Jap got me.

We were fighting at close quarters with these assholes. At this point in the war, the experienced Japs would wait until they heard the Garand's clip ping to attack, knowing they had a brief window in which at least one Marine was empty.

The hard-ass coral provided a potential solution to this problem. The idea was to keep a loaded clip in the rifle and throw an empty clip on the coral to mimic the ping. The hope was that the nearest Jap would come out of his damn spider hole and attack while we had a full clip to unload. I can't think of a time when this ever really worked in practice. But I know a few guys claimed it did.

Just before noon, I came across a shell crater. Daniel Swinggate was at the bottom of it. A corpsman pressed a pile of gauze on Swinggate's stomach, and blood drenched the dressing almost immediately. An IV bag hung from a Garand they'd stuck into the ground, bayonet-end first. Clear fluid leaked toward Swinggate's arm.

"Hey, Kentucky," he said.

"You alright?" Dumb question of course, but you had to ask.

"They got me, Kentucky. But I'll make it."

"We gotta get him out of here," the corpsman said. I started to help, but Capone yelled for me to get my "sorry ass" over to where he was.

"I'm sorry. I gotta go."

I never saw him again. I hated to see him get hit this close to the end. I liked that kid. I had a strange connection to him. Good kid.

Catching up with Capone, he told me Hut had been hit too. GOD DAMN IT! "He is a hundred yards to the west with Doc Wright."

I didn't think to ask how bad it was, I just started moving. With bullets flying all around me, I scrambled to where he said Hut was. He wasn't there.

"Not there," I said to Capone when I got back.

"Let's hope he's been evacuated and not captured," he said. I didn't have time to worry about Hut, because things heated up. More men fell. Capone and I stuck together. We covered each other as we crawled on the coral and took pot shots at the Nips. There almost wasn't time to be scared. The battle was a whirlwind of fire, screams, and whining bullets. Relief didn't come until the ridge was conquered around midday.

Before we could catch our breath, Love Company moved into the town of Mezado. We cleared the homes of any remaining Japs. Dead civilians were everywhere. Jap sons of bitches used civilians as body shields. Holding women's hair like horses' reins, the Japs walked toward us, shooting from behind.

Some of the crumby bastards held kids and babies in front of them as they attacked us. In the confusion of the melee, it was impossible for our boys to avoid civilian casualties.

Despite our pleas not to, many more civilians killed themselves before the battle finally slowed to a lull in our area. Eventually some warmed up to us. We convinced a few kids to eat our chocolate bars. One Marine offered a tiny child a cigarette. Classy move. A guy from King Company had the temerity to put the moves on a surviving Okinawan lady. Even classier move.

Mezado was a mess. If the devil had a cesspool, it would probably suit me better. There was human pulp all over the ground and walls. Charred human remains were scattered everywhere. A vulture might have gagged at the sensory assault.

We carried the wounded, bodies, and pieces of bodies for an hour or so in the Mezado paradise before we moved on. We crossed the plateau to Hill 69 unopposed. The rapid pace was hard for me. My feet almost couldn't support me anymore. They had gotten so raw and infected that with every forward thrust, it felt like more flesh was tearing off in large chunks. It felt like the only thing I had in my boots was bones and gooey mush.

After Hill 69, our platoon halted to organize an attack on yet another goddamn hill—Hill 79. We made time for a little chow and a few cigarettes, but our pace was at fever pitch—a mad dash toward the finish.

The 3/7 had all but finished off resistance on 79, so we helped with the mop up. At the top of the hill we could see the last mile or so that remained of the island, and beyond that, the blue sea. It was a wonderful sight. I'd never seen such a beautiful ocean.

The Skipper called us together for a roll call. He said our casualties for that miserable June 18 were very high. That came as no surprise. A lot of high-ranking officers were killed, including Colonel Harold Roberts, the CO of the 22nd regiment.

Also among the list was General Simon Bolívar Buckner, the commander of the 10th Army. Despite being advised to stay in the rear, General Buckner wanted to watch the progress of the Marines from an overlook. I think most of us knew about this before the Skipper told us, because we saw it happen.

"At 1315," Captain Haigler said, "a round from a dual purpose gun hit near the general's position. Chunks of coral hit Buckner in the chest. He died a few minutes later."

There was some argument about who killed Buckner. Love Company was actually in front of Buckner's position when he was hit. American artillery was shooting air bursts, or shells that exploded in midair, over our head by accident. We had to radio them and tell them to stop. Somehow no one in Love Company got hit. Maybe Buckner wasn't as lucky. General Buckner was the highest ranking member of the United States military to be killed in the whole goddamn war. It was a damn shame too. The stupid battle was almost over.

"General Geiger will be taking Buckner's place." Skipper continued, "In the morning, we'll make the final push to the bottom of the island." He started to walk away, but stopped and turned back while picking his pants out of his ass. "Tonight's code is 'Flimsy Virgin.' Get some rest."

CHAPTER THIRTY-THREE
DONE

I DIDN'T SLEEP SO HOT. No surprise there. My toes throbbed and burned. I couldn't get my boondockers off because my feet were so swollen. Doc Wright told me to keep them elevated and he'd look at them in the morning, so I lay on a mattress of hard coral with my feet propped up on a rock.

As promised, Doc found me at sunrise and used his scissors to cut the laces off my boondockers. He used a Ka-bar to cut the heel back. My socks were about as gross as they could be. He had to cut those off too, because they were stuck to me. He slowly peeled the socks off. About eighty pounds of my skin came off with them.

He was nice about it, but I could tell he was trying his damnedest not to gag at the awful smell emanating from my grotesque tootsies.

"They look like shit, Kentucky. You're done."

"I'm done? What do you mean I'm done? Do I have gangrene? Are they going to have to be amputated? Am I going to die?"

"Take it easy, my boy," he said. "You're done with fighting for a while."

I couldn't believe I was saying it, but the words puked out of my mouth without my helping it. "No, I'm okay. I can still fight." What in God's name was I saying? More than anything I wanted to be out of this hell hole. Shit, if I knew the devil's address, I'd rather go to his place and have a highball with him than remain here on this island that God apparently forgot about.

That's what happens though. You go through an impossibly horrible nightmare with your brothers at arms and you'd end up doing anything for them. You didn't want to abandon them. You wanted to stay by their side come hell or high water.

Thank God Doc ignored me. He called for a stretcher. *For me?* I thought. *I'm not even wounded. I just have booboos on my feet. Save the stretcher for a guy with a real wound.*

Two guys put me on a stretcher and two others helped them lift it. They started down the hill. I saw Capone and Bushrod sitting together cleaning their rifles. They didn't notice me leaving. Just as well. I was a little embarrassed. As I bounced down the hill on the stretcher, tears came to my eyes. I looked back at them for as long as my craned neck would allow. I missed those guys already.

They loaded me on the back of a Jeep and drove to the Army

field Hospital. Under a green canvas tent, they laid me on a cot. A doctor scrubbed my feet with soap and some kind of iodine solution. Holy hell, it hurt. But at the same time, it felt wonderful.

He lifted my left foot to inspect my sole. "Your feet look pretty bad. Both feet have fungus all over them and are infected. You have a pretty serious case of cellulitis. It has potential to get real bad if we don't do a good job treating it. It can get into your bloodstream and kill you. I'm a little worried about the low-grade fever you're running."

"Well, why the hell are you talking about it? Let's see some action."

"I just wanted you to know what we were dealing with."

"You're a class act, Doc. Thanks for putting my mind at ease."

"We'll get you fixed up. I can put you in for a Purple Heart if you want."

For some reason that irritated the hell out of me. A Purple Heart? Young men in cots around me had everything from soup to nuts wrong with them. Heads bandaged, arms missing, legs amputated above the knee. No telling how many had permanent psychological damage.

My feet would heal. I was very lucky to have made it through the last three weeks with a few cuts and bruises and bummed feet. I told the doc all this in simpler terms, "Purple Heart my ass!"

He understood. He stuck a big fat IV line in my left arm, said I needed fluids. I was dehydrated—probably from the dysentery.

My intestinal affliction seemed to be wrapping things up, though.

He gave me a cup of peaches and nothing ever tasted so sweet. When he saw that I could hold those down, they gave me a piece of rubbery chicken. Normally it probably wouldn't have been too bad, but after what I'd been through it was hard to eat. I knew it was all in my head, but the meat tasted like the smell of rotting corpses and mud. For almost a month, every meal I'd had was eaten among the muck of war. It would be a while before food tasted normal again.

The doctor gave me a handful of pills to take. I believe one was to help me sleep. Despite my concern for the guys in Love Company still out there on the front line, I drifted off into a deep sleep.

At around dusk, the doc woke me up to give me more pills. He gave me a dish with rice and an unidentifiable meat—probably more chicken. It was over-cooked, which evoked the smell of burning Jap flesh and napalm.

I tried to write Hody, but I couldn't string together one sentence. I couldn't even grip the pencil. I fell asleep again and didn't wake until noon the next day. I had more peaches and pills for lunch and promptly went back to sleep.

That was my schedule for about three days. I was like an infant. Sleep, eat, shit, repeat. The first two days I enjoyed a dreamless sleep. I was too wiped out, I guess. After that my dreams were evil ones filled with explosions, dead bodies, blood, and Folgers's face.

While eating in bed, I asked about Hut, Angier, Swinggate,

Grahnert, and Laughridge. No one knew anything about them.

On the morning of June 22, we got word that General Ushijima and his cronies had committed suicide. Good riddance, assholes! Shortly thereafter, organized resistance ended and the island was declared secure. I prayed I'd see my friends again soon.

CHAPTER THIRTY-FOUR
HODY

I SAT IN MY IN-laws' living room while Harry's mother, Carrie, prepared an apple pie in the kitchen. They had invited the girls and me for dinner to celebrate the Fourth of July.

With a full stomach, I collapsed in the armchair beside the crib. Despite the racket in the basement, Kay had fallen asleep on the floor cuddling her tattered stuffed animal. The radio by the side window quietly played *Sentimental Journey* by the Les Brown Band, featuring the entrancing voice of Doris Day.

Downstairs, Charles Sr. was banging a hammer. He wanted to get a little more work done between dinner and dessert. Seemed he'd been distracting himself with a basement renovation since his sons left for the war. It wasn't necessary from a practical standpoint, but it was necessary for him. He'd told me he had plans for a big party when all the boys came home, said he needed a suitable venue.

Carrie padded into the living room donning an apron and carrying a straw broom. She headed for the front porch, but was distracted by an out-of-place pillow on the sofa.

"Is there anything I can get you, sweetheart?" she asked me.

Yeah, a housekeeper, eight hours of sleep, our Harry back home, and a highball, I thought, *and don't forget the cigarette.* "I'm fine, thank you."

Carrie propped the front door open and swept the porch while swaying to the radio. I touched the side table. No dust. The house was spotless, but Carrie never stopped fussing, except when tending to her impressive victory garden.

Charles finally stopped hammering and moved on to some quieter task. I dazedly listened to the swish of the broom, the radio transitioning to commercials, and the breeze rustling through leaves of the Sweetgum tree in the front yard. The warm, summer air filtering in through the open door felt comforting. Carrie's movement on the front porch was hypnotic. Back and forth, she passed in front of the triple set of windows swatting at the dust and leaves with her broom. I felt my eyelids grow heavy as I watched her and listened to the sad song of a distant mourning dove.

On the window nearest to the front door, Carrie had displayed two service flags. One for each of her sons in the armed forces. Both flags had a blue star centered on a white background and framed by a red border. Charles Jr. phoned home a few days before to let everyone know he was stateside. This assured that at least one star would remain blue.

Staring at the flags, I started to work myself into a frenzy as I thought of the prospect of Carrie covering one of the blue stars with a gold replacement to indicate Harry had been killed in action.

It was now July 4, and there was still no word from Harry. He was not much of a writer, but even for him, it'd been too long. The last letter I received from him had been in mid-May. I'd sent several letters with no response.

Carrie came through the door. "Turn it up Rosemary, the news is back on."

I shook myself out of my reverie and raised the volume on the radio.

"CBS World News today is brought to you by the *Admiral Corporation*," the canned voice of the announcer started, "the world's largest manufacturer of radio phonographs with automatic record changers..."

"Get on with it." I sat up in the chair.

"...and now direct from the Pacific at CBS Guam..."

I wiped my sweaty palms on my skirt. Carrie gingerly sat on the edge of the couch cushion without taking her eyes off the speaker.

The correspondent delivered the alarming news. "The United States Marine Corps reports that the battle for Okinawa had the largest casualty toll in the Pacific to date." Involuntarily, I slumped. Carrie didn't budge, her posture perfectly erect.

"Estimates are coming in that twelve to fifteen thousand Marines lost their lives," the broadcast continued. "The Marine Corps is calling it the deadliest campaign in all of the Pacific theatre. The battle officially ended on June 22. Despite the toll, the strategic island of Okinawa is securely in the hands of the U.S. Marines"

Carrie, without saying a word, bowed her head and clasped her hands in prayer. Since her sons left for duty, Carrie's entire head of hair had turned a bright white.

I had to escape to a bench on the front porch and light a cigarette. The cigarette bounced in my trembling hand, rippling the column of smoke. The radio broadcast had gone on to other news. What would I do without my husband? Without my children's father? My foot bounced up and down on the concrete floor.

Patsy began to cry. I crushed the cigarette in the ashtray and went inside.

Tears poured over Patsy's delicate red face. Committing my baby to a home was an unthinkable horror. Finances added to the difficulty. But it would be best to put Patsy where she would be cared for properly. I needed to discuss it with Harry, though. I couldn't decide something like that on my own.

Harry's letters had assured me he would support whatever decision I made. He'd said he regretted with all his heart he wasn't there to help me. Unfortunately, that was no consolation at this point. Why hadn't he written lately?

I decided to skip dessert. I was no longer in the mood. Charles and Carrie didn't question me when I bid them good evening. They understood and shared my fear. We exchanged hugs and Charles helped situate the children in the car.

CHAPTER THIRTY-FIVE
HODY

WHEN WE ARRIVED HOME AFTER dinner with Harry's parents, the house was bare. The stillness inside should've been refreshing, but my heart jittered nervously. A partially torn cardboard box lay on the living room floor beside an empty cigarette box. The renters had moved out without warning. Of course, there was no rent check on the counter top nor any note to promise the money they owed. I held both girls in my arms listening to their breathing, their hearts beating. The silence was nice, but it wouldn't pay the bills. The girls gave little resistance to lying down for bed. I lay beside them and quickly fell asleep.

The next day, I got word that the tenants told the local homes association that their stay at 121 Colonial Drive had been unsatisfactory. My nerves were raw. The ungrateful couple claimed they were bunched in one room, only had one bathroom, and even said they weren't permitted to use the kitchen. A week later, the association forced me to repay the crooked tenants over two hundred dollars.

I hardly had a dollar to my name and became sick with angst. Fortunately, my stepfather Martin Kelley, paid the dues for me and ended the tenant nightmare.

The evening I learned my stepfather rescued me, I tucked the children in for bed and decided to celebrate. I poured myself a highball, lit a cigarette, and headed to the front porch to write Harry. He had enough to worry about, so I didn't mention the renter fiasco in my letter. It could wait a few years.

I couldn't help but cry some more as I wrote the letter, asking him why he hadn't written in so long. Telling him how much the girls and I missed him. How I was praying for his safe return. As always, I sealed the envelope with a kiss and affixed a stamp.

I shuffled to the mailbox hanging beside the front door to insert my letter, and realized there was already one inside. My heart jumped as I recognized the handwriting on the envelope. I tore at the parcel as I rushed to end of the porch and sat on the top step. My eyes welled with new tears. Tears of joy. It was from Harry. He was okay.

CHAPTER THIRTY-SIX
WHISTLING AGAIN

THE AFTERNOON USHIJIMA OFFED HIMSELF, I was finally able to write Hody. I let her know I was okay and told her a few generalities about the past five weeks—my feet and little more. No need to make her worry.

The war wasn't over, so I didn't want to tell her anything that might cause her concern. I let her know that I'd made some swell friends. I told her about the island being secure and that we'd soon be going back to Guam.

I asked her how Kay was doing and what was going on with Patsy. I hadn't received any mail from anyone in over a month and was anxious to see how everything was going. Was Patsy better than she was? Did Hody make any decisions about what to do with Patsy? How much would it cost to put her in a home?

On June 23, I got around to writing my parents. I told them

pretty much the same stuff I'd told Hody. I confessed that it had been pretty damn rough up there and that I had a few close shaves. I let them know I was getting treatment for my feet in the field hospital.

I asked Dad to tell Hody I would make another request for an early discharge when I got back to Guam. I'd forgotten to mention it to her in my letter. I told him not to let her get her hopes up because it was very unlikely anything would come of it. I wished them good health and assured them I was fine and dandy. I didn't know how efficient the mail was at the time so I hoped Hody and my parents didn't have to wait too long to find out I was okay.

I was writing a letter to my sister, Dorothy, when I felt a kick at the foot of my bed. I jumped a little.

"Stand and salute an officer, private."

It was Capone. I was glad to see him, but I didn't bother getting up. "Kiss my white ass, Capone." I gave him a smile.

He flashed his pearly whites. "That's Corporal Capone, to you boy."

Bushrod was beside him. He sat on my bed next to my thigh. "How's it going buddy?" He grabbed my hand and shook it.

They told me about everything I'd missed, including Capone being made a corporal. I felt guilty about leaving them on the hill, but neither one of them gave me any crap about leaving.

Turns out Love Company went into reserve just after I left and had been busy with clean up.

I was so glad to see them I let out a big whistle. Then I realized that was the first time I'd whistled in a month. I'd been so miserable, that I had no reason to. Before landing on Okinawa I'd never gone a day without whistling something. I promised myself I'd whistle a tune or two every day from here on out.

We were all so damn happy we were done dealing with the shit this island handed out.

CHAPTER THIRTY-SEVEN
FINDING EARL

I CONVALESCED IN THE HOSPITAL until June 26. When I was mobile again, Capone, Bushrod, and I visited the 6th Marines Cemetery to bid our fallen brothers farewell. We looked for a white cross bearing the names of our friends. Of course I looked for Folgers. We didn't have any luck. There were so many and a lot of dead soldiers hadn't made it to the cemetery yet.

I hobbled along as Love Company moved supplies and bodies for the next two weeks. I'd hoped I wouldn't come across the body of someone I knew. Particularly Earl Whalen, or Hut. I saw a few familiar faces.

One afternoon, I was walking to Captain Haigler's tent for something—oh hell, I can't remember what—when I ran into my brother in law. "Holy shit, Earl!"

"Harry, you son of a bitch, get over here!" We tried to squeeze each other's internal organs out of our mouths with a massive bear hug. Boy, were we happy to see each other. I was so glad to see he was alive. It was swell to have a part of home with me here in the Pacific.

"Can you believe this?" I said. "Half way around the world, a million people milling about, and we run into each other. That's a helluva thing."

"I was on graves registration," Earl said, "I drove a truck around loading dead Marines and carrying them to the burial site. I tell ya, every body I came upon, I said a quick prayer that it wouldn't be yours."

I just shook my head. He kept going. "I knew you were with the Striking Sixth and heard how much shit you all were taking up there. I was worried about you, Harry, I really was."

It was strange hearing my first name again. It had been a while. We were thrilled to be together. No work detail could distract us. We found some Pabst Blue Ribbon and drank it like there was no tomorrow.

Earl told me about what he had been doing on Okinawa as a Seabee. He said, other than graves registration, he poured a lot of coral on the roads, trying to make them serviceable for us grunts. He helped with a lot of mass burials of the Japs.

We figured out that he was pretty close to me at one point. When I was stringing line across the Naha Harbor, he was actually helping with that bridge. We just missed each other somehow.

He was damn proud to have been part of the bridge project.

He confirmed it was the longest bridge the Marine Corps had ever built. "They couldn't have done it without my crew's help," he said with a smile. He should have been proud. That was a helluva feat. All while under gunfire too.

We drank and shot the bull for hours that night. Neither one of us had heard from Charlie in a long while. We agreed we were worried, but figured he'd be okay. We had both heard about his new baby and we hoped Charlie was on his way home to see her.

Earl and I agreed to write a letter together and send it home. We used carbon copies so we could send one to Hody, Lucille, and my parents. We agreed we needed some Old Kentucky Bourbon. I asked Dad to send us an Old Kentucky bottled in bond. I even gave him instructions how to send it to ensure we got it. In the meantime, we sucked down the PBRs.

I introduced Earl to Capone—sorry, Corporal Capone, and Bushrod. They all got along swell. We played cards and horsed around whenever we got the chance.

On July 8, I had to say goodbye to Earl. We didn't get to have that Old Kentucky together, but it was a real treat getting to see him. It was tough saying goodbye. We spoke of the big ole party we'd have when we got home. We both knew there was more to this war and it was going to get even tougher. After a hug like we'd never see each other again. I tried to hide the tears welling in my eyes from the rest of my friends. If they noticed, they didn't say anything.

CHAPTER THIRTY-EIGHT
BACK TO GUAM

LOVE COMPANY BOARDED THE *USS Golden City*, left the miserable island of Okinawa, and headed for Guam. Boy was I glad to leave that place. We sailed for a week before reaching our base.

An enormous pile of burning sea bags greeted us. The bags belonging to dead Marines had been brought to Guam and piled up and soaked with gasoline. I watched the bags burn, black smoke racing to the heavens took with it the belongings of our dead brothers. I assumed Folgers's belongings were in there. Heat gathered behind my eyes and tears began to well. Not just because I missed my friend, but for the horrible guilt I felt for being alive while he was buried on the worst island ever created. And now his stuff was up in flames.

We didn't get much rest when we got off the boat. The camp

needed to be straightened up. When we were done, it was an okay joint. We had electric lights, wood floors, and cots with mattresses that I had every intention of employing often. They were comfortable enough, but hardly a twenty-four hour period went by that wasn't filled with nightmares. I relived Okinawa in my sleep and woke in a cold sweat.

Guam's greatest amenity was the showers. Oh, for the love of God, it felt marvelous to take a shower. It was a simple thing, but it was the most glorious experience. The water never reached a consistent temperature or pressure, but I was able to wash up. I bet I was in that damn shower for an hour and a half scrubbing every—and I mean every—nook and cranny. I'd find bits of mud here and there for weeks to come.

At first, we carried out general duties as much as the weather would allow. Believe it or not, it rained harder on Guam than it had on Okinawa. There wasn't mud like Okinawa though, because Guam's sand soaked up the rain.

Everything stayed wet and we still had to deal with jungle rot. My feet were slow to heal in that damp environment. I was made Love Company's carpenter. They kept me busy fixing desks, chairs, and cabinets. I liked working with my hands and putting things together, so the job suited me well. It gave me even more satisfaction to see my products being used.

Just as I promised Hody, I put in a request for an early discharge. I was very doubtful it would take. The war wasn't over, and we were preparing for an attack on the Japanese mainland. Plus to get a discharge, you had to earn eighty-five points in the system that was put in place. I was only at fifty-one—a long way to go.

Here's how that worked: you got one point for each month of service, another point for each month overseas. You got five points for earning an award, five points for campaign stars, and my favorite—twelve points for each child you had. So anyway, according to my math, I had to get thirty-four more points. I wasn't going to have any kids on Guam and I knew I wouldn't earn any awards, so all I could do was serve my time like a prisoner. I put the letter in anyway. No joy.

CHAPTER THIRTY-NINE
THE BOMBS

ONE MORNING, BUSHROD WOKE ME up before reveille. "I got a surprise for you. Come on, get your ass up." I tried not to move, but he spanked my ass. Grudgingly, I threw my blanket off.

He half-dragged me to a hospital tent. Outside the entrance, Bushrod held the tent flap open and urged me to enter ahead of him. He was like a goddamn usher at a wedding or something. I gave him a look of indifference and irritation.

"Don't be such a curmudgeon," he said. "Get your ass in there and take a look."

"This better be worth it," I said, "and I'm not being a curmudgeon."

I ducked my head in the tent, wondering what the hell a curmudgeon was and how the hell Bushrod knew such a big word.

I scanned the rows of cots trying to figure out what Bushrod was getting his panties in a wad about. Three cots from the entrance, Hut was sound asleep. Outside of the olive drab blanket, his bandaged right wrist lay on his stomach. A mound of padding over his right eye was secured to his shaved head with gauze. *Holy hell*, I thought, *the son of a bitch made it*. I was suddenly awake with enthusiasm.

I looked back at Bushrod. He nodded with a smile.

I bounced over to Hut's bed. He looked at peace and I almost didn't want to wake him. Almost. I couldn't wait to talk to him. I nudged him awake. He sat up with considerable effort, looked at me, and formed a huge, crooked smile.

"Old Kentucky."

"What the hell happened to you?" I said.

"Mortar round. Shrapnel here, here, and here." He pointed at his eye, arm, and ribs.

Bushrod and I sat on the bed with him and visited for a while. We were further surprised when we learned that two bunks down was old General Motors Jim Laughridge. I hadn't seen him since we helped him to the Jeep at Hill 53. He had a bandage on his left leg. A bullet the size of a quarter was still stuck in his leg. Surgeons said it was too dangerous to remove.

Fenton "Gabby" Grahnert was in the same tent too. It was like a Love Company reunion in there. Seeing Gabby was quite a surprise because we had assumed he was dead. Last time we saw him, parts of his face were flying all over Hill 69. Miraculously, he was not only alive, but he didn't even have brain damage. He had lost a bunch of his teeth and the doctors said he might not have feeling in much of his face. He still had a lot of recovering to do, but it was good he was alive. I glanced around the tent for Swinggate and Angier. Not there.

Hut, Bushrod, Capone, and I spent many nights together on Guam. Sometimes Ed Hoffman would also join us for a game of bridge or poker. We were in pretty good spirits. I whistled a lot. We did our best to pretend we weren't still preparing for the next invasion.

We began training for the invasion of the home island of Japan—Operation Downfall. It doesn't take a detective to know how we felt about it.

Training was not as demanding as it had been in the past. What made it hard, though, was knowing what lay ahead. We had experienced how the Japs fought on Okinawa, four hundred miles from the homeland, we didn't care to see how they would fight *on* the homeland.

The brass estimated there could be up to a million American casualties. The carnage on Okinawa taught the U.S. leaders that Japs were getting meaner and meaner as we moved closer. Not only would our casualties be enormous, but the loss of Jap civilians would be through the roof. The dope was the Japs had been training their kids and women to fight us if we landed on their turf.

If the populous didn't fight, Okinawa taught us that they'd kill themselves. They were batty, I tell you. The Japs were not right in their heads. Their leaders had been brain washing them for a long time. If something like 140,000 civilians died on Okinawa, that number would pale in comparison to the mainland.

What a mess. We didn't know what we were going to do or when we were going to do it. They told us November. Then December. The latest word had it as April of '46. We were waiting on the boys from Europe to get their asses to the Pacific and help.

The invasion weighed heavily on our thoughts and haunted our nightmares. We were generally on edge. The only thing that distracted us sufficiently was beer, card games, movies, and lots and lots of cigarettes and chocolate from the PX. Other distractions walked around in bright white uniforms. The Red Cross women working in the canteen were a stark contrast to the horrors we'd seen.

They were all beautiful—not Hody beautiful—don't hear what I'm not saying. They were decidedly easy on the eyes solely on the merit of being red-blooded American girls. The only women we'd seen in several weeks were battered and dirty Okinawans, dead women, and a few Guamanian girls. It didn't hurt that the Red Cross girls treated us like war heroes. It was a good boost for the old confidence. God as my witness, I did nothing more than a little friendly flirting.

On August 9, we were at the outside theatre chugging beer and watching *Meet Me in Saint Louis* starring Judy Garland. An announcement on the intercom interrupted. The guys let out a bunch of groans and complaints. You don't interrupt Judy Garland, you just don't.

It wasn't long before we changed our minds about the interruption. The voice blaring from the speaker on the pole beside the movie screen said some kind of enormous bomb was dropped on Hiroshima three days ago and on Nagasaki that morning. We had no idea what these bombs were, but we cheered anyway. We hoped it meant we wouldn't have to fight the Japs on their home island. We didn't count on it though because those Nips never quit.

As terrible as the bombs were, they produced fewer civilian casualties than Okinawa. There was a lot of controversy as to whether the United States committed a war crime by doing so. The answer, in my opinion, was yes. It was a war crime. The entire war was war crime after war crime. The Japs killed civilians by the hundreds of thousands, tortured and killed thousands of POWs, targeted our corpsmen and hospital ships. These were war crimes. Let's not forget Hitler's crazy ass. Concentration camps were the granddaddy of war crimes.

So dropping the atom bomb was a war crime in a war of many crimes. It was a horrible answer to a horrible problem. It was the only logical solution to the insanity of war. Our fire bombings of Tokyo and many cities in Europe incurred more civilian casualties than Hiroshima and Nagasaki. Unlike the atom bombs, which instantly killed everyone, the fire bomb raids caused people to burn to death.

It was certainly a tragedy that the bombs were dropped, but

for those of us who were in battle with the Japs, we approved. It saved our lives. We hailed President Truman for his decision. Dope had it that he made the decision based on the savagery of Okinawa.

We were incredulous about the news and were afraid to get our hopes up. We crossed our fingers and appealed to the good Lord above.

The night of August 15, some commotion stirred me from my cot. Someone was yelling that the Japs had surrendered. A lot of guys, like me, had been snoozing and tried to make sense of what this fella was hollering as they rubbed their eyes. Capone and I found an officer to confirm. "Yup, Japs are done."

At first we didn't believe it. The Japs wouldn't surrender. It was dishonorable. It took a while, but eventually it sunk in as a reality. Capone and I performed a leaping hug and tumbled to the deck. The war was over and the Jap bastards lost!

The news spread throughout the base and you can imagine how everyone felt about it. We were excited as hell, but still a little skeptical. Could this really be it? Regardless, I whistled a lot and had the three beers they issued to each Marine.

Almost immediately, the 4th Marine Regiment was shipped off to Tokyo Bay to accept the surrender of the Japs there. When the formal surrender happened, we could rest easy. Don't get me wrong, we were happy as clams in butter sauce. It was sort of a reserved happy though.

The night of August 22 I got happy as hell again. Hut had recovered enough to be out and about. We scored some bourbon and a few PBRs and were drinking and chewing the fat in my tent when I revealed to him it was my birthday. He didn't say a word. He just stood up and gingerly walked out of the tent. Where he was going and what he was doing, I had no idea. But before I knew it, he was back with a bunch of fellas in tow.

They had a big ole celebration for me. We drank highballs and horsed around a good part of the night. It meant a lot to me. It really did.

We celebrated VJ Day (Victory over Japan Day) on September 2. The Japs handed over their arms to General Douglas McArthur and signed the instrument of surrender.

Our Battalion did not get to celebrate much, because we had to continue training. Apparently the war wasn't over for *us* yet. We got to celebrate the next day.

CHAPTER FORTY
GOODBYE SKIPPER

ON VJ DAY WE WENT to the rifle range where old Captain Haigler got himself into trouble again with Colonel Shisler. Haigler was ordered to get Love Company re-qualified with our rifle accuracy. We were running behind and the Skipper knew it. He also knew that Shisler was on his way to the range to observe.

Usually the protocol calls for us to shoot from the prone position first, sitting next, and from the hip third. We didn't have time to get in proper prone position before Shisler got there, so Skipper told us to shoot from the hip first.

When Shisler saw us shooting from the hip, he let Captain Haigler have it. He took his hat off and got about one inch from the Skipper's face. "You don't know what the hell you're doing!" Spittle collected on Skipper's cheek. He didn't budge.

Shisler turned and smacked his hat against his thigh as he

created some space between them. "Any good officer should know that the prone position was first, not off-hip!"

"Sir, what the hell does it matter anyway?" Skipper said. "The goddamn war is over. Who gives a shit what order they shoot in?"

"I give a shit!" Shisler said. "Get off my range!"

Captain Haigler turned on his heel and left.

A gunny sergeant named Hinson took over. It was hard to focus after the officers' squabble, but I managed to score a 295 out of a possible 340 on my rifle qualification. Not the best, but not the worst either. I still qualified in the sharpshooter bracket.

We heard that Shisler wrote a letter to the higher-ups saying Haigler had no business commanding a rifle company and should be removed. We all wondered if Shisler was getting back at the Skipper for the way he handled himself in the valley between Hill 27 and 46. Haigler had had enough. He resigned from the Marine Corps. Shortly thereafter he left Guam and headed stateside. I didn't get to see him off.

Haigler seemed to understand me and that's not so easy to do. I hated that he left. Some guys didn't give two shits he was gone. I did though. He took care of me. He never asked for the .45 back.

Throughout September, we watched Marines ship out. Love Company stayed around with the rest of the 22nd Regiment. Word came down that we were going to Tsingtao, China soon. When, I didn't know. No one ever knew anything.

My regiment was assigned the occupation force and had to accept the surrender of the Japanese forces in China. They also gave us the job of repatriating the Japs there. As luck would have it, China had more to offer than just Japs. Turns out China was smack dab in the middle of a civil war as well. We were supposed to act as a deterrent for the Communists who were trying to take control of Tsingtao from the Nationalists. We had to prepare for more fighting. We had gotten used to the lazy, boring life of Guam. Now we faced the prospect of more combat.

Until shipping out, we continued with our general duties and put on parades. We marched around like we were in Times Square or something. I made it to mass every Sunday and consumed plenty of cheese, candy, and cigarettes.

In late September, we had another of Colonel Shisler's million inspections. Well, the son of a bitch found Haigler's .45 and took it. I was pretty sore about it. If he would have known it was Haigler's, he would've really gotten a kick out of swiping it. Of course I didn't tell him. I told him I found it in a dead man pile. At least I still had my Baby Garand.

CHAPTER FORTY-ONE
TSINGTAO

IN THE BEGINNING OF OCTOBER, we shipped out for China. Believe it or not, our ship got caught in a damn typhoon. You can bet your ass we were scared! The typhoon that hit us on Okinawa was terrifying, but at least we could hide in a damn tomb with a dead Jap. But out on the open sea, now that was a whole new level of petrified.

The whole boat swung back and forth like a rocking chair. Sometimes it felt like the damn thing was going to fall over on its side. We screamed like a bunch of school girls and took a beating from being tossed around. The ship did too. We spent the next day waiting on ship repairs before we could continue.

The storm beat up Okinawa too. It destroyed a load of aircraft and ships. Hard to believe, but the Navy sustained more damage from the typhoon than it did from the kamikazes. The storm didn't serve as a good omen of things to come in China. Some said that if a typhoon of that magnitude had happened a few months ago, the Japs would've had a better chance at beating us on Okinawa.

Guam Weather Central called the typhoon *Louise*. They should have called it *Butch* or *Killer*. Something more menacing. Because that's what that damn storm was—menacing.

We reached Tsingtao on October 11, still pretty green in the face and anxious to get off that boat. Way too slowly, the ship pulled up to the port on the tip of Shantung Peninsula.

We marched off the docks and squished into trucks that took us to Shantung University. Walls encircled rows of brick buildings situated around a courtyard. We passed through the main gates into the campus as the sun was setting.

The campus was refitted to accommodate us. Classrooms and dorms were now our sleeping quarters. The girls' high school was supposed to be our barracks. The only problem was that it burned down the night before. They said it was arson.

So they put us on the third floor of another building, six of us to a room. It wasn't the Waldorf Astoria, but it was better than Okinawa. Anything was better than Okinawa, so that's probably not saying much.

The toilets and showers were in the basement. The water could turn from hot to freezing cold without any warning. We had no privacy whatsoever. No shower curtains, no toilet stalls. There was no central heat which was disheartening because winter was fast approaching. Home sweet home, I guess. But, like I said, it was better than Okinawa.

Our main job in Tsingtao was to conduct marches into the mountains to remind the nationalists the formidable Americans were here. We could hear the all-too-familiar rumble of battle between the Mao and Chiang armies.

At night, we patrolled the city to make sure all remained copacetic. The remnants of Japanese military personnel had to be rounded up and it was our job to do it. On a couple of nights, Bushrod and I walked the walls around the university.

Some nights we stood guard at the gates and monitored who came and went. This job seemed fitting to me because my last name was Klapheke. Our name comes from the term given to the gatekeepers at the entrance of a church village of Bad Laer, Germany in the twelfth century.

After a week or so, they gave me the honor (if you could call it that) to guard the U.S. Embassy. I guess it was something special, because only four Marines were picked for the job.

On October 19, I received a letter from my dad telling me Earl was in Chicago waiting for discharge. I was glad for him and for Lucille. The points required for discharge had been reduced and I hoped it meant I'd be going home soon too.

Dad also informed me that Mother had a bad fall. He said the two of them were having some horse play in the garage (what that meant, I had no idea) and she grabbed the handle of the garage door to pull it down. Well, apparently it was too much for her to control and it came down fast and heavy. She slipped and fell under it before it crashed down. She hurt her back pretty bad, but he said she was recovering okay.

Dad said my little brother Charlie had come home a few weeks ago, but was sent back to California to the Amphibious Training Division. He was taking charge of an LCS boat in the South Pacific. My whole family was pretty sore about it because he had served a long time. It was unfair to send him back out. We were crossing our fingers the new points system would discharge him soon.

Sadly, my dad had to ask me to send them a letter or postcard—anything to let them know where I was and what I was up to. The mail system was pretty bad in Tsingtao, but I hadn't realized it had been so long since I last wrote them.

October 25 was a big day. We donned our dress greens, stood in formation, and marched through the streets of Tsingtao. The Chinese citizens gathered on the roadsides and watched as their band of heroes marched by. We were a sight. We marched in cadence with our slick uniforms on, our backs straight, and rifles against our shoulders.

More than 12,000 of us congregated in the Tsingtao Racecourse's oval infield and stood in company and battalion mass columns. A bunch of M4 tanks parked behind us. The U.S. Military did a good job reminding the Japanese of our might.

Bandstands full of spectators surrounded the track. Beyond,

residents sat on the rooftops of the surrounding houses. Big wigs stood motionless on a platform. Among them were Major General Eijie Nagano, the Japanese commander in Tsingtao, Lieutenant General Chen Pao-tsang, Deputy Commander of the Nationalist Eleventh War Area, and General Lemuel C. Shepard, the commander of our 6th Marine Division.

The instrument of surrender sat on a table in front of them. Bullet cartridges served as paper weights. General Nagano and General Shepard signed the Act of Surrender. Nagano and his staff laid their swords on the table as a show of their submission. The 6th Division MPs escorted the Jap commanders off the field.

There was a palpable energy amongst us troops. We wanted to jump up and down and holler. We stayed in formation, though. It gave me goose flesh to see those Japs throw in the towel, to watch them succumb to the "white devils."

I received another letter from Dad letting me know that Earl was officially discharged and home for good. Everyone else thought he looked good, but Dad thought he looked terrible. He was still rather jittery and his eyes had a distance to them. Like he was still on Okinawa. Dad hoped rest would do him some good. It killed me to think this damn war had messed up my brother-in-law. I said a quick prayer he would be his old self again soon.

In early November, scuttlebutt indicated that my unit might be going home soon. We were told we'd be on the first boat. But no joy. Then we were told we'd leave on November 15. I even wrote home telling Hody and my parents the good news. Again, no joy. That very same day, as luck would have it, the Communists started up some more trouble. They were causing problems at the airport. They were shooting at planes or some such thing. Instead of going home, we had to guard the airport.

We rotated shifts at the airport for the rest of November and most of December. Our shifts consisted of spending three nights out in the open. Let me tell you, I froze my ass off! Even with clothes on and tucked inside a GI sleeping bag, I found no comfort. That was not how I'd intended on spending Thanksgiving, but that's what happened. The United States Military provided us with dry turkey and runny cranberry sauce. They were real sweethearts, the military. They treated us like kings.

The old rumor mill had us believing we would be leaving in mid-December and we would be home for Christmas. Nope. Then the week before Christmas we were sure it was time to go home. Nope.

Christmas was depressing as hell. I was very homesick as you might imagine. I hadn't seen my girls in a year and a half and this was the second Christmas I'd had without sitting around the Christmas tree and seeing what Santa brought the girls. Over the holidays, you could say I was as low as E flat.

The university where we were billeted was about as cold as a nun's conundrum. The heating system wasn't worth a tinker's damn and the Mongolian winds ushered in some frigid temperatures. New Year's was a little better, but only because of the highballs.

Don't get me wrong, Tsingtao wasn't all bad. We were able to get out and have some fun on our liberties. Hut, Capone, Bushrod, and I had a great time going into the city. The streets were filled with rickshaw traffic and people standing on the street corners trying to get us to change money. They wanted American dollars something awful. "Change money, Joe!" they'd yell.

Also on the corners were lots of prostitutes. Mothers were pimping their daughters, girls were pimping out their little sisters. It was absurd. It was hard to blame them because many lived in a box in the alley. Some areas were very impoverished.

In the business district, I was really surprised how modern everything was. Most of the Marines found their way to that part of town because a lot of clubs, restaurants, and shops catered to the Americans. The bordellos were especially concerned about providing quality service. You couldn't even get into a bar without coming across a line of soliciting prostitutes. Marines would inspect the girls like cattle before making their choice.

One of the best parts of Tsingtao was the beer. Tsingtao beer was much better than I had guessed. There was a shortage of glass in China and the beer came in all sorts of different bottles. Some were in former Coke or milk bottles. They were capped with a wad of wax. A bottle of beer cost the same as a prostitute —25,000 Chinese dollars (about twenty-five American cents).

The local tobacco was a little iffy. It was darker than American tobacco and mixed with who knows what. It was strong and produced a black smoke. I had a bad feeling about it, so I didn't partake too often. It was easy enough to find Camel cigarettes, so that's what I bought. I had loved Lucky Strikes, but the scent and taste of them would forever be associated with Okinawa.

Back at the University, we cringed when we'd hear about an impending "short arm inspection." Our male equipment was referred to as our short arm. In the Corps, it was important to know what a rifle was and what a gun was. During boot camp, if a "boot" called his rifle a gun, he was often punished by standing outside holding his rifle with one hand and holding his crotch with the other while yelling: "This is my rifle, this is my gun. One is for killing and one is for fun!" I get it. Its a rifle.

So the short arm inspection was where they would line us up in the courtyard of the university and we would present our man parts to the corpsman. He would check us out for venereal diseases. He got awfully handsy for my taste. Of course, I was a good boy and had nothing to fear, but calling the process unpleasant would be a gross understatement.

CHAPTER FORTY-TWO
OLD KENTUCKY HOME

JANUARY 24 MARKED OUR 7TH wedding anniversary and three year anniversary of the death of our little Judith Rose. You can bet your ass I wanted to be home. Four days later, word came down that I was soon to be there. I had been in Tsingtao for almost four months. By that time it'd been seven months since I left Okinawa. I couldn't get on that boat fast enough.

We boarded the troop transport ship and sailed across the Pacific Ocean. It was a relatively uneventful voyage—boring as hell, really. Long as hell too. After a century, we arrived at San Diego. There were no crowds cheering for the return of the war heroes. The war had been over for a long time and America had moved on. Only a crumby, small brass band, lacking in enthusiasm, greeted us.

Parades, parties, and what-have-you were put on for

American soldiers who came home months ago. When my unit of gyrenes returned, hardly anyone noticed. We were herded onto a train and started the long trek east. It was good to hear the old locomotive again.

For five nights, I'd fall asleep to the clickety-clack of the wheels. My nightmares had become less frequent. On several occasions, though, the rumble of the train woke me with a start into a cold sweat thinking I was hearing the rumble of artillery. When the train shook, lurched this way and that, I felt like I was in an Okinawan tomb with artillery shells shaking the ground around us.

We made it to Camp Lejeune in North Carolina where we were discharged. Before signing my discharge papers, the officer asked me if I wanted to stay in the Corps and get another stripe. It didn't take Sherlock Holmes to deduce my answer. I gave him an emphatic, "Hell, no! I'm going home to my girls. But thank you very much." *Horse's ass,* I thought.

The Marine Corps gave me a travel allowance of $.05 per mile. A total of $177.88. They threw us on a bus to Jacksonville, NC. We had different trains to catch, so Capone, Hut, Bushrod, and I said our goodbyes. Nothing dramatic. Just handshakes and pats on the back. We cared deeply for each other. In a different world, the next one perhaps, we could handle hanging out together. We could have drinks or go out on the town. Unfortunately, the world we had been thrust into didn't work that way. None of us said it, but we knew seeing each other again would bring back horrible memories. We went our separate ways, anxious to be with our families and put this war behind us. I never saw them again. They eventually became obscure memories in an elaborate dream. Hut, Bushrod, Capone, Swinggate, Folgers, and all the others seemed like figments of my imagination.

From there, I rode the rails to Louisville. I was excited as hell. By my estimation, that train moved at a snail's pace. I was a little nervous about how the girls would receive me. Would Kay and Patsy recognize me? My body had changed a lot since I last saw them. I had grown up quite a bit. You could say my mind aged twenty years in the two that I was gone.

How would I tell them about what I had been through? Would I tell them about it at all? It was certainly not something I cared to relive. Even if I had the words to describe it, I didn't think my girls needed to hear such things. I decided to just move on. Leave the war where it was—in the past and in Okinawa.

Being alone for the first time in almost two years, I sat on that train and occupied my mind with thoughts of the future. Would I go back to the Mengel Company? What will we do with Patsy? Would we have more children? I enjoyed thinking about these things, because for a while, I'd assumed I wouldn't have a future. Now I knew I had a life ahead of me. I just wondered if I could put the war behind me.

My thoughts turned to the fellas who didn't make it home. They were the true heroes. They gave up their lives for our country. The men who were wounded and maimed and bore deep psychological scars would never be the same again.

I guess I was experiencing what they called "survivor's guilt." Questions flooded my mind. Why was I spared? Why had I been so late arriving to Okinawa? Sugar Loaf Hill surely would have killed me. Why wasn't I one of the wireman who was killed on that hill? Why didn't I have any permanent wounds? Why didn't a great guy like Folgers get to come home and fulfill his potential? Guys like Grahnert, Laughridge, Maharidge, and Haigler, who were on the front line much longer than me, would not only carry with them physical wounds, but would be burdened with heavy psychological baggage.

I thanked the good Lord above for taking care of me. I realized how lucky I was compared to millions of young American men.

When the train pulled into the Louisville station, I saw the most beautiful sight in the world. My girls were standing on the sidewalk. Patsy was sleeping in Hody's arms. Kay was wearing a yellow dress and her blond hair was blowing in the breeze. She was waving at the train. At no one in particular because she couldn't see me—I was seated on the opposite side. I about knocked three guys out and broke my own neck trying to get off that damn train.

When she saw me, Kay broke free of Hody's grip and ran full clip toward me. She jumped into my arms and I swung her around. I nearly squeezed her to death and then carried her to Hody where the four of us embraced. I held them in my arms for a good two minutes. Couldn't have been happier. The tears poured from my eyes.

I opened my eyes briefly and noticed a storm drain in a sidewalk across the parking lot. My blood turned to ice and I broke out into a cold sweat.

For an instant, I thought the drain was a damn Japanese pillbox. Then I smelled Hody's hair and felt a sense of warm calm.

I knew then it would be a long time before I could put the war completely behind me. Even while holding my girls in Louisville, Okinawa had its hold on me, trying to ruin everything.

I needed to learn to live in the present moment. Move on. That was what I promised myself I'd do. I closed my eyes again and tightened the hold on my girls.

AFTERWORD

Harry never spoke to his family about the war. War talk was reserved for basements and parlors whose only occupants were veterans. Describing the experience of fighting a fanatical enemy in such heinous conditions could never be put into words that would make a non-combatant understand. It is akin to telling someone about a nightmare experienced the night before. But no matter how articulately delivered, and how much detail is provided about the nightmare, the listener will never grasp the full extent of the horrors of the dream. It seems so unreal to them.

How much the war affected Harry, we will never know. If it haunted him, he did a good job hiding it. He never let on that loud noises set him off, never spoke of nightmares, and didn't lose his temper. If he struggled, he didn't let on.

As rough as the war years were for Harry and Hody, they never complained. They didn't hold their experience over anyone's head. There was no "Woe is me."

The 6th Marine Division received the Presidential Unit Citation for its participation in the battle of Okinawa. The citation states,

"extraordinary heroism in action against enemy Japanese forces during the assault and capture of Okinawa, April 1 to June 21, 1945. Seizing Yontan Airfield in its initial operation...smashed through organized resistance to capture Ishikawa Isthmus, the town of Nago and Heavily fortified Motobu Peninsula...withstood overwhelming artillery and mortar barrage, repulsed furious counter attacks and pushed over the rocky terrain to reduce almost impregnable defenses and captured Sugar Loaf Hill...they took the city of Naha and executed surprise shore to shore landings on Oroku peninsula, securing the area with its prized Naha Airfield and Harbor after nine days of fierce fighting...By their valor and tenacity, the officers and men of the SIXTH Marine Division, reinforced contributed materially to the conquest of Okinawa, and their gallantry in overcoming a fanatic enemy in the face of extraordinary danger and difficulty add new luster to Marine Corps history, and to the traditions of the United States Naval Service."

The 6th Marine Division, being the only division created overseas, was disbanded in Tsingtao on April 1, 1946—the anniversary of Love-Day. The division was unique in that it never set foot on American soil.

Harry's little brother, Charlie Klapheke Jr., was spared from going back to the Pacific with the Navy. After the war, he joined the active reserves where he was eventually promoted to Lieutenant Commander. He retired from the Navy in 1963 after serving his country for over twenty years.

Charlie's wife, Dorothy, delivered their first daughter while Charlie was in the Pacific on September 22, 1944. Charles III, or "Skip," was born August 29, 1946, and their third child, Martha Lynn, was born March 14, 1949.

After the war, Charlie went back to work at the Seagram's distillery in Louisville. The company moved the family to Baltimore in 1957, then to New York in 1962. When he retired from Seagrams in the late 1960s, he and Dorothy moved back to Baltimore where Dorothy died in 1992.

After Dorothy's death, Charlie moved back to Louisville to be near his siblings—Harry, Carolyn Bryant, and Dorothy Roehrig. In 2008, Charlie died, leaving behind seven grandkids, three step-grandkids, fifteen great grandkids, and two step-great grandkids.

Earl Whalen, Harry's Seabee brother-in-law, went on to open the J. Earl Whalen Refrigeration and Air Conditioning Company. Lucille served as bookkeeper for the business while also proving to be a virtuoso on the violin as well as in dance. Lucille died March 22, 1963 and Earl died September 25, 1977.

Captain Frank Haigler, aka the Skipper, received the Silver Star for his leadership on Hill 53. After he resigned from the Marine Corps, he returned home and studied pre-med at UCLA , then graduated from the University of Illinois Medical School. He became an obstetrician resident at the Mayo Clinic until he moved with his wife and daughter to Salzburg, Austria, for a year on a Fulbright Scholarship. He later took a residency in anesthesia. After Salzburg, he moved the family to Sunnyvale, California, where he opened a family practice.

Haigler's habit of collecting war souvenirs did not end when he left Okinawa. His doctor's income afforded him the ability to bolster his collection. He owned a Sherman tank, a 1918 Renault tank, an amphibious Jeep, Nazi motorcycles, and other various, big ticket items from both world wars and the Civil War. At his home, he displayed Lt. Bussard's helmet with the bullet hole in it and carried it with him to memorial services.

The Skipper outlived all of the high-ranking officers of Love Company. He died quietly at the age of ninety-two in the summer of 2011.

Ed Hoffman, who landed on Okinawa the same day as Harry, left Tsingtao in a ship guarding fifteen hundred Japanese prisoners as they were transported to Japan. While there, he observed the destruction the atom bomb caused at Nagasaki. He then returned to China where he stayed until the late spring of 1947.

In 1948, he attended college while working construction to support his new wife and son. In 1950, he found himself in the Korean War. College had to wait again. His second son was born while he was overseas. When he returned stateside in 1951, he and his wife divorced.

He remarried in 1972 and started his own construction company. He had another daughter in 1975. He moved his family from the San Fernando Valley to Minnesota. His wife, Susie, said he never talked about the war.

Jim Laughridge, the admirer of General Motors who refused to carry any more men off Hill 53, left the Marine Corps in 1947 and attended North Carolina State where he struggled. Before the war he'd been an honor student. In 1953, he married his wife, Beverly, and had two kids. Appropriately, he went to work for General Motors as a sweeper and worked his way up to foreman.

Laughridge's war would remain with him for the rest of his life. Suffering from what is now called Post Traumatic Stress Disorder, he took to the bottle. His PTSD may have been what caused him to take on six police officers who were breaking up a fight in his apartment. He nearly beat one man to death. He said he didn't know what happened. He was on auto pilot. The war had made a machine out of him.

Because he couldn't fight off the demons of war, and Beverly suffered from manic depression, the marriage was rocky. He learned to despise his job at GM. His health suffered from his dark past. In 1977, Laughridge's wife used his .45 pistol to commit suicide. He had multiple heart attacks and bypass surgeries. His son "Jimbo" also took his own life in 2004.

Jim Laughridge could never escape the ghosts of the war.

Until the day he died, he hated the Japanese. He felt the Marines did not kill enough of them. He didn't speak of the war until the final years of his life. He died November 3, 2011. He still had a bullet in his left leg and pieces of shrapnel embedded all over his body.

Fenton Grahnert, who helped discover the booby trap inside Admiral Ota's headquarters, spent a year in the hospital recovering from the head wound he received on Hill 69. Grahnert's brother, James, was a POW on the Palawan islands in the Philippines, where he died in December of 1944. It was not until 1948 that the U.S. military told the family that James and 149 other Americans were forced into a bunker where gasoline was poured on them and set on fire. It is not hard to imagine why Grahnert, like Laughridge, hated the Japanese for the rest of his life.

Grahnert married Marjorie French and lived in Vancouver, Washington, where they raised their daughter, Linda, and their sons, Jim and Wesley. He worked in a slaughterhouse until he retired in 1974. Somehow the sight of blood did not affect him. For the rest of his life, he had strong reactions to loud noises. Miraculously, the only serious effect he had from the face wound was numbness and frequent nose bleeds. He did not speak of his time with Love Company until he was in his eighties. He died December 21, 2012. He still had over forty pieces of shrapnel buried under his skin.

* * *

Steve Maharidge, who blamed himself for letting Herman Mulligan throw the grenade in the ammunition dump on Hill 27, did not receive a warm welcome home when he made it back in 1946. He was spat upon by a woman who claimed the "good ones died over there" and he shouldn't have come back. Steve became a heavy drinker to numb the pain of the war.

Shortly after his return, he witnessed his brother, Bill, hitting their sister, Helen. Flying into a fit of rage, Steve tackled Bill and put a knife to his throat and threatened his life if he ever touched her again. He didn't.

Steve lived outside of Cleveland, Ohio, where he worked at Cleveland Twist Drill, a thriving manufacturer of industrial cutting tools. He and his wife Joan had three children—Dawn, Dale, and Darryl. He was a good father to his kids, but had a side of him he attempted to hide.

He continued to have fits of rage. Sometimes he yelled at non-existent Marines. He often got into fist fights. He managed his rage enough to open his own business called D&D Tool Salvage. Just as it became successful, he was hit by a drunk driver causing injuries that kept him from performing his services properly. He lost many clients and had to shut the business down.

Later, with the help of his son Dale, they launched another business call D&D Tool Company which they ran together while Steve worked for the Postal Service. Like the rest of Love Company, Steve did not speak much of the war. Just occasional comments.

A photo of Steve and his friend Herman Mulligan hung on

the wall of his metal shop. He never got over the incident with the grenade and the ammunition dump on Hill 27.

One day, while working with Dale, he spoke of the war for the first time. The pain medication had loosened him up enough to divulge a few details. Looking at the photo, he said, "They blamed me! I came in that night with his .45. They said I killed him! But I didn't kill him! It wasn't my fault!" He gave no further detail and never spoke of it again.

In 1985 Steve and Joan followed Dale to California where they bought a house in Sacramento. Steve and his children remained close. Steve died June 30, 2000.

Dale Maharidge became a professor at the Graduate School of Journalism at Columbia University and taught at Stanford University for ten years as a visiting professor. He authored several books and won the Pulitzer Prize for nonfiction in 1990.

After the death of his father in 2000, Dale embarked on a quest to learn more about his father's time with Love Company. He soon found himself obsessed with the man in the picture that hung on the wall of the shop. Who was he? How did he die? Was his father to blame for his death? Why did his father keep that picture for so many years?

Maharidge learned the mysterious man was Herman Walter Mulligan and that, like his dad, he was in Love Company, 3rd Battalion, 22nd Regiment of the 6th Marine Division. Maharidge spent twelve years studying archives, making hundreds of phone calls, writing letters, and spending hours interviewing men from Love Company.

In his book Bringing Mulligan Home, he paints a grim picture of the trials Love Company faced. His interviews with the survivors of Okinawa brought to light several of the men featured in this book. If it weren't for Maharidge's efforts, the accounts of men like Captain Frank Haigler, Ed Hoffman, Jim Laughridge, and Fenton Grahnert would not have made it into the story.

Harry "Old Kentucky" Klapheke and his friends were late coming home from the war. Whether he realized it or not, his extra time in China may have helped him recover from his war experience. Many veterans who came home quickly after the surrender in Europe and Japan, were greeted with parades and parties, but they had no time to decompress. One week they were in the throes of combat and a few weeks later, they were back at home with people who did not understand what they had gone through. Life at home was comparatively boring.

For Harry and Love Company, they had time together without being under fire. Together they were able to assimilate slowly back into society. They had each other, with whom they could hash things out for a while before being thrown back into civilian life.

After his return, Harry and Hody spent every possible second together. Hody, no doubt, felt the war had changed her husband. He spoke only of the friends he had made, funny stories, and generalities. She in turn never complained about the hardships she endured during his absence. They both were optimistic and were ready to move on and enjoy the rest of their lives together.

There was just one thing that needed to be done first. Hody had had enough of Harry's foul mouth. She did not appreciate his "art of profanity." She understood he needed time to heal from his psychological scars, but he had to clean up his act. She sent him to a retreat at the Abbey of Our Lady of Gethsemane near Bardstown Kentucky. The monastery was home of the Trappist monks and was the oldest monastery in the United States. The retreat offered him a place of much-needed silence and reflection. After his return, Hody was not convinced the retreat had a lasting effect.

Harry went back to work at the Mengel Company. On September 14, 1948, Harry and Hody had their fourth child, Harry Jr., or "Bud." Having to care for both Kay and Bud, it became more important to commit Patsy to a home. Doctors feared Bud would emulate Patsy and it would hinder his development.

They had decided that upon reaching the age of six, Patsy would be a prime candidate for a home. Charles Sr. made great effort to expedite her admittance. He used his political sway to push the proceedings through. A judgment was issued and a jury found that Patsy was indeed "feeble minded" and required professional care. March 29, 1950, Patsy was admitted to the Kentucky Training Home in Frankfort.

On December 29 of the same year, a Christmas present was due—Harry and Hody's fifth child. But sadly, the baby was still-born. Her name was Barbara Ann.

Harry left the Mengel Company in 1952. Had he known about it, it would have been to Jim Laughridge's chagrin that Harry went to work at the Ford Motor Company Assembly plant. After six years, he left Ford to work for about a year with Earl Whalen at his refrigeration company. From there he went to work for Bill Manning Equipment Company. He was then employed for a year by the state of Kentucky and was nominated as State Representative in the 34th Legislative District. It was his goal to improve education and recreation for the youth and handicapped of Kentucky.

Never finding great satisfaction in his other ventures, he returned to Ford where he took great pride in the company and even had his hand in some small innovations. In 1969, he was awarded a new car for making a suggestion to Ford executives that proved to save the company $268,212 per year. The newspaper article stated "he suggested that the plant inventory basic diesel engines and various engine conversion parts and then modify or convert the specific engine needed."

Patsy's health rapidly declined in the spring of 1963. On April 10, she passed away to be with her sisters in heaven. Harry and Hody were crushed. They stiffened their upper lips and pressed forward.

Charles Sr. and Carrie died in 1964 and 1969, respectively. By this time, Harry and Hody had seen it all. Living through the Great Depression, the passing of three of their children, and now the death of their parents. Harry had witnessed the death of hundreds of strangers and dozens of his friends. The Klaphekes were no strangers to hard times.

It would be difficult to blame Harry and Hody for their love affair with alcohol and cigarettes. Drinking highballs was part of his family history and after seeing what he saw and going through what he went through, Harry found it difficult to quit. His favorite bourbon was Early Times. He bought it by the case. He was so loyal that Early Times sent him birthday cards.

Harry and Hody carried on with their lives and tried to have as much fun as they could and help as many people as possible. They were members of the Knights of Columbus for a number of years. He sold candy bars and raised money for the organization in a number of ways. They were even awarded the "Family of the Month" in December of 1986. He was active in the Parent Teacher Association at both Nazareth and St. Raphael School. Harry kept busy with Meals on Wheels, selling Christmas trees at St. Raphael, and always helping his elderly neighbors with chores or home repairs.

The Klaphekes belonged to the Richmond Boat Club where Harry took the seat as president. The family spent many Sunday afternoons playing softball and nights playing poker or dancing. Avid bowlers, Harry and Hody were a big part of a bowling league and could be found at Rose Bowl every Wednesday night.

In 1970, Harry and Hody became MaMa and PaPa (pronounced Maw-maw and Paw Paw) when Kay gave birth to their first granddaughter, Kristen. Two more granddaughters from

Kay and three grandsons from Harry Jr. would soon follow.

In his spare time, Harry continued his love of solving jigsaw puzzles. No size or pattern intimidated him. He glued many together and framed them. They were displayed on the walls of his basement. To this day, one is on the wall above this author's desk. On the weekends he tackled home improvement projects, worked in the yard, and tended to his above-ground pool.

His love of locomotives did not fade either. He and my father, Bud, amassed a large model train collection and built railroad cities in the basement. At the time of this writing, Bud continues to add to what would equate to an entire county in his barn. Along with his grandchildren, Bud plays with the trains when he is not tackling home improvement projects, working in the yard, or tending to his above-ground pool.

Toward the end of the 1980s, MaMa's health began to deteriorate. Throughout the 1990s, she had multiple surgeries and hospital stays. She was diagnosed with Chronic Obstructive Pulmonary Disease (COPD). Glaucoma caused her to go blind in one eye.

The COPD prevented proper circulation to her legs. A blood clot in her right leg was so severe that she suffered from gangrene. Her leg was amputated on July 26, 1994. In her usual spunky spirit, she named her missing leg "Casper." In February of 1995, she was treated for an aneurism in her left leg.

In 1998, her health took a turn for the worse. Her lungs gave her trouble again. On April 5, she suffered congestive heart failure. On Good Saturday, the doctors informed Harry that her kidneys were failing and it wouldn't be long before she passed.

Harry stayed by her side through Easter Day and night. On Monday, Harry's nephew, Bobby Bryant, came to visit. Somehow finding strength, Hody took the hands of each man. She looked into Harry's glazed eyes and said, "Honey, I'm glad I'm leaving before you are." And to Bobby she said, "Harry's a good man. Take care of him." She died soon after. It was April 13, 1998.

It goes without saying that losing Hody devastated Harry. The passing of his children and fighting the war were colossal tests of his fortitude, but saying goodbye to the love of his life was herculean. But he had been tempered for this sort of thing. He knew loss. If I've made it through so much in my life, he thought, I can make it through this. Harry had a strong support system in his children and grandchildren. He had more living to do.

PaPa did his best to continue enjoying the little things in life. He worked his puzzles, drank his Early Times, and sometimes took trips to see his family. He visited my family in Kingston Springs, Tennessee, just west of Nashville. My brothers, Matthew, Timothy, and I loved to tease him and enjoyed his salty rebuttals and wisecracks. My mom, Bernadette, wasn't so sure she approved.

PaPa then drove south to Atlanta to stay with Kay and her husband, Bob, and their three girls, Kristen, Kara, and Kelley.

He attended the weddings of his grandchildren and took

great delight in his great grandchildren. As his health declined, he required the attention of nurses at his home. As he worsened, the family checked him into Twin Brook Nursing home.

Never losing his pluck, he staged a great escape from the home with the assistance of his brother Charlie. They succeeded in driving back to Harry's house on Tremont Drive, but the doors were locked. To gain entry through the back door, Charlie attempted to climb over the railings of the back deck (there were no stairs). He fell and broke his hip. The ambulance came for Charlie while Harry was "captured" and returned to Twin Brook.

Harry's dirty language and his ogling of the nurses earned him a reputation. He was one to keep an eye on. On more than one occasion, a friend or family member smuggled Early Times into his room. Unfortunately, the employees of the home grew wise to this offense and he was expelled from the institution.

His health continued to wane. Like his True Love, he was diagnosed with COPD. He too lost circulation to his lower extremities. Doctors were forced to amputate his big toe and eventually another toe. For the most part, he was confined to a wheelchair and carted around an oxygen tank.

It became apparent he needed the care of Twin Brook again, but was denied a return because of his behavior. They said he drank too much. "To hell with those lousy bastards," he said, "I'd rather die at home anyway." He knew he was dying, but refused to do so until he saw Harry, Kay, and the grandkids again.

On a whim, I had suggested to my family that we go up to Louisville for PaPa's 88th birthday. Miraculously, we were all available to make the trip. His birthday was on August 22, but we spent the night with him the Saturday before.

We had a good visit. I remember him looking and acting relatively healthy. He felt good enough to call me a "horse's ass" if I teased him. The highlight of the trip was when everyone decided to play cards with PaPa. He, Timothy, and myself broke out PaPa's special gold, for-bourbon-only cups with the black rim. After everyone else went to bed, the three of us imbibed Early Times and shot the bull for a while. What we talked about, I don't remember. What I do remember is that it was a very special night.

At the time, I hadn't yet developed an interest in his experience in the war and I could kick myself now for waiting until he was gone to do so. There is so much I wish I would have asked him. Whether or not he would have shared it remains unknown.

I suppose not asking him about it turned out for the better. Chances are he wouldn't have shared his experience with me. But, had I heard his stories, perhaps I would not have felt compelled to immerse myself in researching his life for the past three years. If I hadn't started this quest, there is so much I never would have learned. So many characters and stories that might have been left out of a verbal exchange. I would not have connected with people like Dale Maharidge, Love Company veteran, Joe Lanciotti, or Captain Haigler's daughter, Lynn. Most importantly, I may never have known the full extent of what great people my grandparents were.

After we left PaPa on the 20th, his health rapidly declined until he was forced to go back to the hospital. PaPa waited on the front porch for the ambulance to arrive. With the oxygen tank at his side, he sat in the wheelchair and smoked a cigarette. "Well it's about goddamn time," he said as the ambulance arrived.

Kay, Kristen, Kara, and Kelley rushed from Atlanta and were with him in his final hour. Seeing the rest of his girls gathered around, he knew it was time to go. Up to the last few hours, he put on a brave face and made jokes. In true form, his last clear, spoken word was a final brushstroke in his Art of Profanity. On August 30, 2006, PaPa was reunited with Hody and their three angels.

AUTHOR'S NOTE AND ACKNOWLEDGEMENTS

Referring to his time on Okinawa, my grandfather described it as "rough as hell" and said he had "many a close shave." He left it at that, but it wasn't enough for me. My quest to learn more about that quote, and what happened between May 13 and June 23, 1945, began in my late thirties when I returned to college to finish my degree.

My concentration was military history. During my studies, I was drawn to WWII more than any other American war—particularly how combat affected its participants. As my interest grew, so too did my desire to learn what my grandfather experienced during his service in the Marine Corps. I became even more curious when I made inquiries to my dad and aunt about their father's time in the war. Neither of them knew very much about it.

My first clue came from a family reunion booklet Martha Lynn Klapheke Fazio put together. I learned my grandfather was in the Marine Corps and served in Okinawa and Tsingtao, China. From that I deduced he must have been in the 6th Marine Division, as this was the only division to have served in both locations. For a long time, this was all I knew about PaPa.

Sixthmarinedivision.com stated that the division had approximately 24,000 men. A daunting number. It was too big to learn anything specific about where he was or what he saw. I had so many questions. Did he land on Okinawa in the initial invasion? Was he a replacement? What were his duties? Did he even see action? What kind of horrors did he endure? I didn't even have the date he entered service.

On a regular basis, I attempted to jog my dad, Harry Jr.'s, memories. He said PaPa never talked about it, so everyone just quit asking. My dad was able to supply me with great stories about growing up with PaPa. With these accounts, I added some personality to his character.

I called PaPa's sister, Dorothy, to ask her what she could remember. She was in her nineties, so I didn't expect her to remember much. Though she was very sharp, she had little to offer about PaPa's war experience. She said he cussed a lot and loved his bourbon. She gave me some great anecdotal stories that I incorporated into the story.

My younger brother, Timothy, who was in the Marine Corps Reserve, picked up a few small details when he interviewed PaPa for a high school project. He had a memory of PaPa saying a friend had died in his arms and that he had a job involving his unique voice and the foul language he used so often. Other than that, the details were fuzzy.

A phone call to my Aunt Kay reaped some great stories about growing up, but she knew nothing of the war. After our conversation, she searched her closet and found a tattered envelope filled with letters. Correspondence between PaPa and his parents during the war.

Pay dirt.

In a blocky font, the letterhead said *Love Company, 3rd Battalion, 22 Regiment, 6th Marine Division.* In his letters home, PaPa was more concerned with the well-being of his family and the latest developments with their handicapped daughter, Patsy. He shared details about himself and his unit's activities, but avoided writing anything that would cause worry at home.

PaPa wasn't very consistent with his writing, but there was a larger than usual gap between May 13 and June 23. His June letter had "Okinawa" penciled in under the date in the upper right hand corner. He gave no details about what he had been doing for the previous five weeks except that his feet were infected with fungus and cellulitis. He also mentioned he was worn out and had been sleeping for three days.

PaPa's brother, Charlie, served in the Navy in the Pacific during the war. His son, Skip, was gracious enough to send me copies of Charlie's letters home during that time. This became an invaluable source of information about Charlie's experience and provided a little information about PaPa as well. At the time of the war, even Charlie knew nothing about PaPa's whereabouts or what he was doing.

My next big break again came from Aunt Kay, who found a recording PaPa had made in 1999. In it, he shared stories about his life with Hody, his beloved wife. Everyone spelled it Hodie, but in all of his letters, PaPa spelled it with a "Y," so that is why I spelled it that way.

Twenty-seven minutes into the recording, PaPa's voice became noticeably more somber. He gave a quick summary of his war experience. No details. He hinted that he doubted anyone had any interest in hearing it anyway.

The most important war information was that he had been with the Headquarters Company and functioned as the company wireman. He mentioned his foul mouth, distinct voice, and the fact he was a tough Kentucky boy had landed him the job. He briefly spoke of stringing communication wire at night and that daylight was spent fighting and moving dead and wounded. Again, he described it as "rough as hell, I tell ya."

I read dozens of memoirs from Marines in the Pacific and watched countless hours of documentaries. I consumed anything about Okinawa or the 6th Marine Division I could get my hands on. I wanted to know what a wireman did and why his voice was important for the job. From the memoirs, I learned about the experience of fighting in the battle for Okinawa. The accounts were similar in many ways. The terrain, the mud, the rain, the assault on the senses, the fear, the fanatical Japanese, the misery, and how combatants coped afterward.

Saying I understood what those soldiers went through would be like a dog owner saying they understood parenting, but I could appreciate their experiences and sympathize with them. I had an idea, anyway, of what PaPa might have gone through. But that was not enough for me. I wanted to know where he was and when.

For a year or so, the closest I could get to his actual movements came from a source on the internet. It laid out a detailed timeline of what the 3rd Battalion, 22 Regiment (the 3/22) did. The 3rd Battalion was made up of around a thousand men and was divided into several companies, so they could have been scattered throughout a wide territory. I still wasn't satisfied and was losing hope of discovering more.

A serendipitous discovery changed everything.

Perusing the WWII section of a used book store, a title stood out among the others. It was on the bottom shelf and did not match the titles around it that evoked images of blood, firepower, or hell. It was called *Bringing Mulligan Home,* written by Dale Maharidge, the son of a man who served with none other than Love Company, 3rd Battalion, 22 Regiment, 6th Marine Division. PaPa's Company! I was blown away. Suddenly I had narrowed my search down to a couple hundred men.

The book provided details about Love Company's involvement in the battle of Okinawa. I exchanged emails with Dale and learned much more about PaPa than I ever thought possible. Dale sent me muster rolls with PaPa's name on it as well as Dale's father, Steve.

Dale told me because PaPa was with the HQ Company, he was most likely with Captain Frank Haigler. Dale's interviews with Haigler allowed him to include a great deal of the captain's accounts. Dale also put me in contact with Haigler's daughter, Lynn, who added to the stories. Knowing Captain Haigler's story meant almost knowing PaPa's.

Dale also provided the accounts of eleven other men from Love Company, two of which were replacements like PaPa, and entered combat the same day. The chances of them knowing each other were pretty good.

A chapter of Dale's book was dedicated to Love Company member, Joe Lanciotti, from Wood Ridge, New Jersey. In Lanciotti's memoir *The Timid Marine,* he gave an honest and detailed account of his experience with Love Company on Okinawa and his struggle with combat fatigue. After reading his memoir, I searched for his name on Love Company's muster roll for May 1945. I found it four names below PaPa's.

Not expecting too much, I did a Google search for Lanciotti and found him to be alive and well in New Jersey. He was gracious enough to spend some time on the phone with me one Saturday afternoon. He did not recall the name Harry Klapheke. He said it was total chaos toward the end of the battle for Okinawa and he could have been beside PaPa at one point and not even had known it. I told him PaPa was a company wireman.

"He would have been going out at night while we all dug in," Lanciotti said.

I mentioned that PaPa had said he fought during the day

and strung wire at night.

"Oh, that poor fella had double duty," he said solemnly.

Mr. Lanciotti confirmed the relationship PaPa would have had with Captain Haigler and was also able to corroborate important points of my version of PaPa's story.

It was a real honor and pleasure talking to a World War II veteran, but it was especially gratifying knowing he was with Love Company and possibly beside my grandfather. Talking to Mr. Lanciotti was almost like talking to PaPa again.

It was clear PaPa shared many a colorful word, but nothing about the war. Nor did he or MaMa ever say anything about the trials she faced at home. This is partly why I started this quest. I was drawn by the amount of tragedy they dealt with, how they survived it, moved on, and never brought it up or used it as a crutch.

My grandparents and the rest of the "Greatest Generation" would shake their heads at our spoiled generation. I never heard them whine about facing the worst depression our country has been through, the most devastating war the world has ever known, and the most horrifying experience a parent could ever go through—losing their children. This book is a tribute to these people and a reminder of just how easy we have it these days.

Everyone should know about the sacrifices the men and women in our armed forces make—past and present. They should all be honored. To everyone above who assisted me in paying due tribute to the heroes of Love Company, thank you very much. And thank you to my wife Alisha for your editing work and loving support.

For photographs and source details, visit http://www.danielklapheke.wordpress.com

70364215R00196

Made in the USA
Columbia, SC
05 May 2017